Winner: Best Thriller

Independent Ebook Awards 2012

"Great action in this medical thriller!"

GABixlerReviews

This was a thrilling and compelling read for me.

Literary Litter

Hartlove delivers on the tension in *Goddess Daughter*. Fans of his first novel will be pleased to find that the narrative runs through a rampage of deceit, double-crossing and the darker side of human motivation all in the same fashion as *Goddess Chosen*.

J. Malcolm Stewart, author of *The Eyes of the Stars*

"Writing which in its depth invokes past masters like Crichton, Benchley, and Straub."

Critics Studio Magazine

"Some of the most evil 'end justifies the means' bad guys I've ever encountered in a book."

Abyss & Apex Magazine

"Hartlove is a master of spellbinding suspense, mystical mayhem, and spiritual surrender."

Library at The End of The Universe

GODDESS DAUGHTER

Book Two
of the
"Goddess Rising"
Series

JAY HARTLOVE

DEDICATION

*To my wife Denisen,
my best friend and most loyal companion*

ACKNOWLEDGEMENTS

I placed this story in June 2005, which was a very exciting time for the field of cloning. I knew I had to get the details right if I was to push the envelope to tell my story, and for that I would need some real expertise.

I would therefore like to thank my beta testers, my fact-checking posse, without whom this book would not be nearly as plausible, and therefore that much scarier: Doctor Susan Kane, Professor of Tumor Cell Biology at the City of Hope; Sherry Hamilton, Registered Critical Care Nurse at John Muir Medical Center; Steve Price, religious scholar and former Assistant Professor of English at Pacific Union College; Troy Hughes Palmer, film producer and production designer; and Laura Ferguson, Associate Professor of Music at Indiana University of Pennsylvania.

Thank you all for your diligent and honest feedback.

1

T HE FIRST THING RANDOLPH MACKLIN NOTICED was the sound of surf. It was soothing, familiar, and safe. He caught a whiff of sea air, which prompted him to take a deeper breath. It made him feel good too. Then he felt the sun on his face, and the surf took on context. He cautiously opened his bloodshot blue eyes and found himself alone in a wooden deck chair overlooking a beach. The sun was low in the sky, and the scattered clouds were still frosted with pink. The pink of dawn? The air was still crisply chilled. Everything was wet from dew. Yeah, dawn, but beaches faced sunsets, not dawns. Unless he was facing east.

He was wrapped in a blanket and slouching down in the chair like he had been there a long time. Had he slept there? He started to sit up and his aching stiff joints made him take the motion slowly. He looked around. The wooden deck was on the front of a house that looked familiar. He didn't connect why, but it was reassuring all the same. He decided he wasn't dreaming after all.

He got up and started to stretch his six-foot-three frame, but didn't want to drop the blanket. He noticed he was wearing jeans, a t-shirt and sandals. Like everything else around him, the clothes looked familiar, but he couldn't remember putting them on.

He looked up and down the beach, and found that it stretched empty in both directions as far as he could see. The house was a cottage, and behind it were more buildings with trees all around. He knew this house.

He was working to recall who owned it when a neatly groomed Korean man with salt and pepper hair, wearing a Nike jogging suit stepped out of the cottage sliding glass doors. The man gave him a big smile.

"Young Nae," Randy breathed with relief.

"Randy! You're up." He stepped up and gave him a hug around the shoulders, reaching up to cover their ten-inch height difference. "You are also looking much clearer. Are you feeling any better?"

Randy squinted and blinked, and ran a hand through his short sandy hair. "I'm still pretty disoriented. I hardly recognized this place until you walked out here. I feel wrung out, like I've been crying or something."

"Well, you have. A lot of crying. A lot of drinking."

Randy stared at him as he felt the pieces fall back into place. "Oh, God. Now I remember why I'm here. Cheri is dead, isn't she? We're at your beach house in Malaysia, because she died here in a ..." he struggled.

"Car crash," Young Nae supplied patiently. "Four months ago."

Randy blinked and shook his head. "Four months? I've been here for four months?" He shivered and pulled the blanket back around himself. "What, just moping around?"

"It's called grieving. She was the love of your life. Do you want to come in and have a cup of coffee?"

"Sure." He lingered on the deck for a moment gathering his thoughts as Young Nae went inside. "Thanks."

He followed his friend into the living room, which was looking more familiar by the moment. The yellow Philippine mahogany paneling and the dark brown leather furniture all felt right.

"Have a seat," Young Nae offered from the open kitchen.

"I feel like I've been sitting for too long already. I can't believe four months have passed. So what is it now, May?"

"June. June 2005. Cheri died in February. You and Desiree came here for the funeral."

"Right." Randolph nodded. "I remember the country was just recovering from some kind of disaster."

"Well, it wasn't this country, but Indonesia, which is right next door. It was the day after Christmas, with a 9.2 earthquake, followed by a tsunami that killed 130,000 people. Back in February it was all anyone would talk about."

"So I've been out of it for four months since then? That seems unbelievable."

"Well it's not like you've just been sitting here looking out at the ocean all that time. We've had plenty to do with Desiree's problems too."

Randy could only stare at his friend in wide-eyed confusion.

It took Young Nae a moment to look up from his pouring the coffee to notice the reaction. "What? You're drawing another blank, about your daughter's accident?"

"Accident? What kind of accident? What are you fucking telling me? My nineteen-year-old daughter has had an accident and I don't even remember it? Is she okay?"

Young Nae crossed quickly to him and put his hands on his arms. "Slow down. Don't panic. You've been in a bad way for a long time, but now you're not making any sense. You don't remember the snakebite? How we fought to keep her alive, how she slipped into a coma, and how we're waiting to see if she comes out of it?"

Randy stared into his face, shifting his focus from one eye to the other trying to retrieve any memory of what his friend was saying, but coming up blank. "Jesus Christ," he pushed through gritted teeth. "It's like I've never heard any of this before. You say she's in a coma? A goddamn coma! Snake venom is nerve toxin. If you stop breathing, the brain is damaged permanently. Is she going to live?"

"Yes, it seems so," he assured Randy calmly. "She's been stable for two months now. The doctors say we just wait on the coma."

Randy slumped onto the couch. "Now I'll sit." He shook his head for a long moment trying to make sense of it. Young Nae sat down next to him and said nothing. The sound of the surf outside seemed to keep time. "My wife is dead, my daughter is in a coma, and I don't remember hardly any of it. This isn't fucking possible. How the hell did this happen?"

"Cheri was here on one of her UN charity junkets and she got broadsided by a truck down in Kuala Lumpur. The only good news is she died instantly."

"That much I remember. I wish I didn't, but that's still pretty clear. There was a fire, or something, right?"

"Yes, the car caught fire, so we lost her body. Then you and Desiree came here for the funeral. A week later, Desiree went hiking and was bitten. We didn't find her for almost half an hour, so the anti-venom didn't do much. She fought on death's doorstep for almost a month, and then she slipped into a coma. Her body stabilized and we moved her here."

"She's here?"

"Yeah. I've got her set up in a suite in the main house with a full-time nurse. You don't remember any of this?"

"No." Frustration cracked his voice.

"You started drinking, understandably. I let you, figuring you'd come around in your own time. Here we are."

"The memory loss is just scary."

"I'm no shrink, but it's probably your brain trying to protect itself. I loved the both of them too, but I cannot imagine what you have gone through."

"Can I see Desiree?"

Young Nae slapped Randy's knee and gave it a squeeze. "Of course."

As they walked to the main house, the landscaped tropical gardens looked and smelled familiar, and gave Randy hope of piecing his memory back together.

"This is embarrassing, but I have to ask. Where is here, exactly?"

"You mean on the map? We're just outside Kuantan, on the east coast of Pahang, facing the southernmost edge of the South China Sea. Straight out about 500 miles is Sarawak, the eastern island of Malaysia."

"So we're not near Kuala Lumpur. I remember driving a long ways from the airport."

"That's right. We're on the other side of the Malay peninsula from Kuala Lumpur, about 240 kilometers away. K-L faces west toward Indonesia. Does that help?"

"Yeah, I guess."

When they stepped into Desiree's room, all recollection vanished again. Was this all just too painful to remember?

The smell of antiseptic and soap was oppressive. Randolph wondered how even a strong smell like this wasn't triggering anything. He noted out of the corner of his eye that Young Nae dismissed the nurse who was sitting across the room.

Randy stepped up to his daughter and took her hand. He was taken aback at how limp it was. She had an oxygen tube clipped to her nostrils and a clear plastic tube draped from the corner of her mouth, but was otherwise free from medical hardware. She was propped up slightly on pillows, but lay there so relaxed she seemed collapsed, much more than a sleeping person.

"Is there any higher brain activity?"

"Just baseline. We check her once a day for an hour, but we haven't seen anything."

"So what are the chances of her coming back?"

"The doctors say in cases like this it could happen at any time, or never at all. We just wait."

Randy bit down hard and shook his head slowly. "Isn't there anything else we can do? I just can't stand to see my baby like this." His voice tightened. "Are you sure we did absolutely everything we could have done for her?"

"Yes. I'm afraid so."

Sadness overwhelmed him. He felt guilty, not just because he had let this happen to her, but even more so because he couldn't remember any of it. What kind of father can't remember the near death of his child? He pulled up the chair next to the bed and sat. Taking up her hand again, he stared at her and tears trickled down his face.

"So, old friend, this is what I am left to," he said to Young Nae while still looking at his daughter's face. "We work our whole lives to give people longer, happier lives, and fate steals my family out from under me." He turned to face Young Nae who was standing by the foot of the bed. "I can't thank you enough for all you've done for us, for me."

"We've been friends for thirty years, and I wouldn't be the rich man I am without your discoveries. It was the least I could do. You're welcome."

"God, thirty years ago. UCLA. That was before you, me, and Cheri became the Three Musketeers. Now she's gone, and this poor child is all I have left of her." He looked back at her and touched her cheek. "Oh, Dez, how am I going to go on without you or your mom? What I wouldn't give to see your impish smile again." He looked up at Young Nae. "She gets the cutest little dimples at the corners of her mouth when she smiles." He looked back at her. "You've got to come around, you've just got to."

He turned back to Young Nae. "What about stimulation? Isn't talking to a coma victim supposed to help their brain wake up?"

"Yes, it does. I have the nurses read and sing to her pretty much all day."

"Good." Randy put on a brave smile and turned back to her. "We're going to pull you through this. We can do it."

2

"SO HOW LONG HAVE YOU TWO KNOWN EACH OTHER?" Sanantha Mauwad's dark brown cheeks dimpled deeply when she grinned. She made no effort to hide the sing-song lilt of her Caribbean accent. She knew she needed to keep this initial interview light and friendly to get Dr. Macklin talking.

She leaned her elbows on her burl wood desk and laced her fingers loosely together to put her patient and his friend at ease that she wasn't writing down their every word. She looked from the tall Caucasian scientist to his short Asian businessman friend as they sat facing her. Young Nae Yoon was leaning back in his chair with a casual assuredness that told her he was used to being in control. The very expensive-looking crisp white shirt he wore added to this air.

Randolph Macklin had his long legs crossed, his body twisted around in the chair, and hands clasped. His dark blond hair looked like he hadn't combed it that morning. "From the way you finish each other's sentences, I'm going to guess you met as college roommates."

Young Nae chuckled. "Very good. UCLA, Class of 1978." He pointed first to Randy, then himself. "Pre-Med and Business Administration."

"Have you been in touch ever since?"

"Well, no," Randy started. "There was a big...gap in there."

"Yeah," Young Nae picked up. "Randy went off and became a doctor, and I went into business. As luck would have it, I ended up in pharmaceuticals, and he ended up in medical research."

"So years later, in the late nineties," Randy continued, "I was working at Johns Hopkins in Baltimore, and I developed some treatments that I couldn't exploit. So I looked up Young Nae, and we went into business together."

"You said you couldn't exploit your findings," Sanantha explored. "Why not?"

"Patents," said Randy.

"And testing," added Young Nae. "This is really cutting-edge stuff, and the FDA and the American medical review process would require years of trials and a whole public vetting of the ethics of the science before the first bottle could appear on a shelf."

Sanantha didn't want to appear critical while trying to develop Randolph's trust, but this sounded unsafe. She covered her hesitation by shifting in her chair and straightening the tails of her light yellow suit jacket. "Doesn't that process save trouble down the road? I mean, isn't it better to spend money on testing up front and save yourself the lawsuits later on?"

"We did do testing. We satisfied ourselves the drugs worked, without side effects, and I figured we could collect clinical data from our customers. Other cosmetics firms do the same thing all the time, adjust their formulas as they get feedback from their customers."

"So these discoveries were for cosmetics?"

"Actually, the science was much broader," Randolph interjected.

"The practical application that we wanted to move on was in cosmetics," Young Nae added. "You've probably heard of our line, CytoSkin."

"Oh my goodness, yes! I am a big fan of your face treatments. I had no idea that was your line."

Young Nae put on his salesman smile. "They work, don't they?"

"They most certainly do," she said touching her face. "The wrinkles around my eyes completely disappeared. Most remarkable."

"I use it myself," Young Nae said proudly. "Well, CytoSkin isn't available in the U.S. It won't be until we put it through FDA trials."

Again, Sanantha had to restrain herself. She was glad they couldn't see her curled toes under her desk where she had slipped off her pumps. "So the treatments I've been using, you did your own testing before putting them on the market?"

Randolph picked up on her doubt. "Yes, we did test them extensively. We just didn't go through the FDA protocols."

"Is that," she grasped, "prohibitively expense?"

"It is expensive, but that's not the problem." He took a breath, and he and Young Nae exchanged a glance. "It's the exposure and the criticism. Can I assume that the confidentiality we enjoy with you as my doctor also applies to trade secrets we talk about?"

"Oh yes. My lips are sealed on anything we talk about." She chuckled. "Unless you tell me you've killed someone."

"Really?" Young Nae asked jokingly.

Randy continued. "CytoSkin works so well because it manipulates the genetic make-up of the skin. It literally convinces your cells they are young again."

Sanantha did her best to remain non-judgmental, but she had to ask. "Are you sure that's safe?"

"Absolutely," the scientist assured her. "There is nothing foreign introduced. It is all your own genetics. The formula rebuilds the telomeres on your DNA so as to turn back the clock, as it were."

"Okay, wait a second," Sanantha asked, as she absently smoothed a few errant gray hairs back into the bun which held her large mass of curly dark brown hair. She decided engaging Randy on his work might be a way to build trust and get him to open up. On the other hand, she was having some serious ethical issues with where this was going. She knew she would have to pedal fast to keep up. She hadn't thought about genetics in years, and he was clearly one of the world's leading genetic researchers. "I'm going back to cell biology in med school. Telomeres are the locks at the ends of the DNA strands?"

"They're more like zipper pulls than locks, but yes, you've got the right idea. After millions of DNA strand replications, the telomere starts to shorten, which causes genetic information near the ends of the chromosome to be lost over time. This is what we believe causes aging. If you rebuild the telomere, then you start getting complete genetic information and the cell functions as it did when it was young."

She made a mental note of how Randy used a clinical approach to shield himself from exposing his feelings. She would have to move carefully.

She also noticed how Young Nae seemed bored with the scientific details, since he was looking around her office at the colorful paintings of Caribbean dancers while she and Randy talked.

"You two think this will be criticized by the medical establishment?"

Young Nae jumped in. "Absolutely. Manipulating genetics in any fashion inflames the ethics nay-sayers."

"I remember reading about a couple of women who discovered the enzymes you're talking about."

"Yes, telomerase," Randy affirmed. "I worked with Carol Greider at Johns Hopkins. She and Elizabeth Blackburn first discovered it back in 1984. There's talk they will get the Nobel Prize for it at some point."

"Won't the Nobel Prize add legitimacy to your work?"

"They're doing pure research," Randolph explained further. "We've moved on to products. People get much more cautious when you put products on the shelf."

"The public is focused on genetics right now," Young Nae added. "My countryman Hwang Woo-suk very publicly criticized President Bush's stem cell policy last month, and then turned around just last week and published the rather stunning advance of creating human embryonic stem cells."

"I don't understand why this is bad for your work."

"It isn't, if Hwang's work proves to be legitimate," Randolph explained. "He claims he used somatic cell nuclear transfer. I really don't think you can get to his result via that method. If he jumped the gun, genetics is going to come under greater scrutiny and suspicion than ever before."

"Okay, so there is reason to move cautiously. Still, aren't you guys sitting on the Fountain of Youth?"

"We're hardly sitting on it," Young Nae said. "Randy's research has moved way past face creams. It'll take some time to develop products. The cosmetics are paying for the new research."

Sanantha took a breath and gathered her thoughts. "Now, you two are in business together, but Randy, you still live in the States, is that right?"

"Yes, I'm still on staff at Johns Hopkins. They've made it worth my while to stay with them. They've got fabulous facilities, and the work is very exciting."

"More cutting-edge stuff you can't talk about, I imagine," she ventured with a grin. The grin of course covered her actual dread at what ethical compromise he would share next. "Can you give me a hint?"

"Well, I will say we are a lot further along than the public knows when it comes to things like using viruses to deliver gene therapies throughout a living organism."

"You mean splicing in genetic fixes?"

"Yes."

"The popular scientific press talks about gene therapy all the time," she countered.

"Yes, but we have recently learned how to, as you put it, 'splice' in as much genetic material as we want. Enough to correct entire syndromes of mistakes like Muscular Dystrophy, hemophilia, or Tay Sachs. The trick has been getting the altered cells to pass the new complement onto the daughter cells."

"You mean, to replicate with all the changes you put in with the virus?"

"Precisely."

"This is what you're working on back in Maryland?"

"Yes."

"You've been here for the last four months. Do you still have a job back home?"

Young Nae answered. "Yes. I arranged a leave of absence for him while he was here mourning. He can get his job back whenever he returns."

"Well, that's good. That brings us to the reason you're here today." Sanantha turned specifically to Randy. "You've been in mourning for a while now. Do you feel that you've made any progress with accepting what has happened to your wife and daughter?"

Randy looked down in his lap and re-clenched his hands. "I am still very sad about my wife passing. I guess I am used to the idea. I mean, it's no longer shocking. Whenever I think about her, well … I still can't not think about her."

"You think about her a lot?"

"Pretty much every time I have to make any decision, about anything. Cheri was such a big part of my life. I just can't get used to the fact that I am alone."

"Well, that's something I can work on with you. I have a lot of experience in guiding folks through the grieving process. The point here is it is a process. It doesn't just happen all at once. You don't just get used to the idea that a loved one is gone."

Young Nae interjected, "Did you have a lot of patients after the tsunami?"

She did her best not to react to the inappropriateness of the question. "No, I'm not affiliated with the clinics that helped after the disaster."

"My wife came here in January to help out with the relief effort. She was a UNESCO director."

"Really? Did she travel a lot?"

"Yes, all the time."

"That's something I'll want to talk with you about when we get into private sessions."

She turned to Young Nae. "I appreciate what you did for Randy, letting him take as much time as he needed, and I don't mean to criticize your plan. As you can see, though, four months later, Randy isn't that much closer to being able to live his life again."

"I don't know if I want to just move on," Randy said quietly.

"I understand. I'm not talking about forgetting her. You were married to her, what, twenty-five years? She will always be a huge part of who you are. It will be okay to miss her for the rest of your life.

Missing someone isn't the same as feeling like your life has been ruined, which I venture to say is where you are now."

Randy nodded.

"So we will walk through this process, together."

She waited for a reaction, and he nodded.

"Then there is how you are handling your daughter's condition. You said you don't recall any of the details of how she came to be in the coma."

"Yeah. That's still a complete blank. Young Nae said maybe my brain is trying to defend itself from too much bad news all at once."

"That's possible. There are a lot of possibilities. We will explore those, again, together. It's not the same as grieving, but it is similar in some ways. It's more about learning to cope. There is a process for that too. We'll get to all this when we start our one-on-one sessions."

"How does that work?" Randy asked. "I mean, I've never seen a psychiatrist before."

"We should meet twice a week for an hour each time. We'll talk, and I'll give you little tasks and pointers. Then each time we get together, we'll talk about how you did with those tasks in the couple of days you've had on your own. I sense that what you're asking is how many sessions will it take before you start to see any change."

Randy nodded.

"You've been living with Cheri's death for four months, and it seems to no longer be shocking to you. I'm pretty sure we can get you seeing some improvement in your outlook. Getting you to accept what has happened to your daughter may take more time, since we have so many facts missing. How many sessions will depend on what we find as we talk about how you're handling all of this. I won't kid you. You've got a lot of ground to cover. Two major back-to-back crises are not going to be easy to straighten out. As I said, I have a fair amount of experience helping people through this process. Are you prepared to stay here in Malaysia for as long as it takes?"

Young Nae addressed Randolph. "It is a three-hour drive from my beach house in Kuantan where you've been staying, to here in Kuala Lumpur. On the other hand, I've got an apartment here in town that you can use. So, you've got a place to stay for as long as it takes."

Randy took a deep breath and let it out slowly. "We're talking about my mental health here. I guess we take as long as it takes."

Sanantha flashed him a big, warm, full-face smile. "Well then, you've taken the first step, by agreeing that it will be possible to grow strong again."

3

*C*HI TO FIST – PUNCH!
    Chi to foot – Turn!
    Chi to legs – Leap!
    Chi to fists – Triple punch – Stomach, Chest, Throat!

Lo Cheung loved the feel of his Chi coursing through his body during his Kung Fu workouts. The sound of his black canvas robes slapping against his arms and legs as he struck his imaginary opponents added a dramatic flair, and made him feel like he was moving more than just his own body. He was aware that it was illusory, but he still enjoyed the sensation that he was moving energies outside his body.

    Chi to calves – Flip!
    Chi to foot – Kick!
    Chi to arm – Deflect!
    Chi to fingers – Strike!

He had been going at this for twenty minutes, and he was starting to feel fatigue. Each time the tough robes stretched across his broad shoulders he had to push just a bit harder to complete the move. It felt good, but there was no reason to strain his sixty-year-old body. He was also aware that his assistant had been standing patiently outside the garden gate for some minutes waiting for him to get done.

He pulled himself up straight and took a series of long, slow cleansing breaths.

Chi to groin – Release.

Chi to stomach – Release.

Chi to chest – Release.

Chi to throat – Release.

Chi to brain.

He smoothed back his grey hair and stepped from the central gravel square, past the bamboo and orchid planters, and opened the gate. "Thank you for waiting."

The clean shaven young Asian man in a black business suit bowed slightly before answering. "Of course, sir. I have important news for you. Young Nae Yoon has liquidated a large block of his own stock in his company CytoLink."

Lo Cheung blinked in surprise. He stepped past his assistant and started walking down the wood paneled central hallway of his home toward his office. The young man fell in behind him. "How large?"

"Nearly fifteen percent of his personal holdings. The transaction leaves him owning less than sixty percent of the outstanding stock."

"If I remember correctly, he has used that particular subsidiary as an equity source before."

"Yes, sir. Yet he has never sold such a large block at one time."

They reached the office door, and Lo paused and raised an eyebrow for dramatic effect. "Let's take a closer look."

He stepped around, sat behind his enormous carved dark wooden desk, and opened one of three laptop computers. After pulling up some charts, he opened another of the laptops, and ran a series of searches on it. Then he opened the third laptop and pulled up a blank screen. "You gotta see this," he called with childlike enthusiasm to his assistant. "I spent a king's ransom for this software whiz to get this to work. He says it's the wave of the future, but I've got it now." He grabbed the one mouse on the desk and started clicking and dragging charts from the first two screens onto the third screen, building a multi-layered graphic. "Pretty cool, huh?"

"Yes sir," the thin, suited man said with a small bow.

Lo Cheung rolled his eyes and returned to the screens. "It does not look like he is spending any of this money on building out any of his other businesses. In fact, I don't see where he is starting any new projects, which is not his style at all." Lo propped his elbow on the edge of the desk, leaned closer to the third screen and stroked his chin with his fingers. "Mr. Young, what are you going to do with 4.1 million dollars in cash?"

•   •   •

Somewhere lost in a fevered dream, the colors of sunset played opalescently off her short, raven-black hair, which framed her face like a rainbow. Her pale skin seemed richly tanned in the warm, fading reds and oranges, but somehow the light seemed unable to taint the pure white of her lace-covered wedding dress. This incongruity didn't bother Randolph. He was simply overjoyed to see her again.

He couldn't recall having been here before, but everything seemed familiar enough that he didn't question it.

She smiled longingly at him with her dark brown eyes and reached out with open arms toward him across the rocky chasm. He reached toward her and could almost touch her hands. With no footholds available on either of their barren, windswept, gray rocky plateaus, he tried leaning out with just one hand. The wind calmed to a whisper, and the air smelled sweet and clean. Although he didn't feel any movement of the earth, the gap seemed to widen. He didn't stop to question this dream obstacle, but simply reached further. So did she, and the space between their questing fingertips shortened. He felt the stone edge under his feet crack and give. Still he stretched further and at last, they touched.

In his relief, he relaxed and rested lightly against her hand. Just then, something distracted her, as if someone had called her name. She reflexively looked back, just for the briefest moment, but it was long enough. He stumbled and fell forward, tumbling down into the dark, cold, bottomless abyss.

As he fell, he caught a glimpse past her of another woman behind her. No, not another, but the same woman, younger, with blue eyes and long brown hair, dressed all in black, as if in mourning. He looked up as he spiraled away and, just as all the times before, he saw no one at the lip above him.

More taken with the despair of having lost her again than concerned with his own fate, Randolph didn't even look down to see what awaited him. The feeling of wind rushing past him was gradually replaced with an ocean-scented breeze.

He opened his eyes and found himself on the brown leather couch of the beach house. His body was twisted around like a rag doll, clearly from flailing about in his sleep. It was mid-afternoon. He remembered lying down for what he thought would be just a few minutes. He checked his watch. Two hours. He felt cold, probably from being drenched in sweat, despite wearing cut offs and a t-shirt.

He lay there reeling from the dream imagery. The sound of the surf outside mixed with the radio playing faintly in the kitchen. A Scorpions song swept Randy up in its strident, melancholy tones. Klaus Meine sounded like he was about to cry singing about the things that killed his love, pride building walls, and whether there really was no chance to start again.

Randy felt like crying.

He blinked and shook his head free of the song. He decided he could sort out the dream images better under a shower.

The hot water felt very, very good. The water splashing hard on his forehead and the trickling rivulets that ran down his body soothed him in an almost hypnotic way. He felt at ease. He opened his mouth and let the water splash deliciously against his teeth. The worry oozed out of him and washed down the drain.

His intellect told him he was regressing to a state of fetal security. It felt good anyway.

It was no mystery why he was dreaming about Cheri and Desiree, and longing and mourning. He was sure he had dreamed this dream before, many times before, which worried him. It smelled of unfinished business. When he was awake, he couldn't remember what happened to Desiree. Yet in the dream, the recurring dream, he knew Desiree was somehow tied to his losing Cheri. Was Desiree in black to mourn him, since he was the one who falls? Did his falling mean he was somehow responsible for all the harm that had come to his family? Why did he think of his daughter Desiree in the dream as his wife Cheri, only younger? Maybe the dream wasn't so obvious after all. He hoped Sanantha could help him sort it out.

He got out of the shower and started to towel himself off when he felt a hard lump on the skin of his back. The mirror in the bathroom was all fogged up from the shower, so he went into the bedroom.

He twisted around in front of the dresser mirror and let out a yelp. All over his back, there were little brown hard spots. He slipped off the towel he had around his thin hips and found they extended all down onto the backs of his legs as well. He felt one and it was hard like a callous. He moved into better light and found they were hard skin, like scar tissue. They were all about the diameter of a pencil eraser. He estimated there were at least 30 of them.

He quickly threw on some clothes and headed for the main house. He found Young Nae up in his room packing an overnight bag.

"Hey there. You going on a trip?"

"Yeah. Just a couple of days over to Hong Kong to meet with some clients. What's up?"

"I found something I need to ask you about."

Young Nae looked up from his folding.

Randy peeled off his t-shirt and turned around. "What are these?"

"Ooh, you've got a bad case." He stepped over to Randy and touched a couple of the sores while he spoke. "Those are insect bites. We have a particularly potent strain of mosquito here in Malaysia, and some Europeans have a really bad allergic reaction to their saliva. I've seen this before, but never so many of them at one time."

"Mosquito bites? They don't itch."

"Well, not anymore. Those are the scars the bites leave after you have had the reaction. I've heard of some folks getting them removed with hydroxy acid and dermabrasion."

"Wait a minute. How could I have them all down my back like this?"

"It looks like you fell asleep at some point lying on your stomach, probably down on the beach. Just be glad they didn't get you in the face."

Randy was having a hard time believing bug bites could do this. "I would have to have been lying on the beach buck naked. They are on my butt too, where a swimsuit would have covered my ass."

Young Nae sighed and shrugged. "Like I said before, you were in a bad way for a long time."

4

"FIRST, I WANT TO CONGRATULATE YOU on taking the initiative to protect your mental health. You've been living with your grief for a long time now, and it's smart of you to realize you can't get through this kind of pain on your own with just the passage of time."

Sanantha sat facing Randy in identical low back, light blue armchairs across a small coffee table in an alcove end of her office, away from her desk. She was pleased to see him sitting more relaxed than he had in the initial interview. Although his long legs were still crossed, he had them stretched out and crossed at the ankle. Instead of clasping his hands together, he was absently stroking the textured fabric of the chair arms with his fingertips.

"You said you've never seen a psychiatrist before, so coming to me was also a step outside your comfort zone. For that, you should be proud of yourself."

The sandy-haired scientist smirked slightly and said, "Thanks for the pep talk."

She gestured in the air with her pencil while a pad lay across the lap of her long white skirt. Her tall yellow turban accentuated her head movements. "It's not just that. I want you to start these sessions with the feeling that we will be making a fresh start. I want you to have the confidence that we can do anything. Have you moved into that apartment here in town that Young Nae mentioned?"

"No, not yet. I don't mind the drive. At least I haven't tired of it yet. I want to stay in Kuantan to be with my daughter."

"Okay. Then I have to make sure you get real help to make it worth that long drive."

"Well, I know a psychiatrist helped my mom a lot when my dad died. So I've seen that this can help."

"How old were you when he passed?"

"Sixteen."

"How did his passing affect your mom?"

"Badly. She pretty much had built her world around him."

"Were you close to him? How did it affect you?"

"Yeah. It hit us both pretty hard."

"Do you have any siblings?"

"No. Just me."

"I don't mean to open up any old wounds, but I need to know how you've handled grief in the past. Did he die after an illness, or was it sudden?"

"Oh, quite sudden. He killed himself. He had a string of bad things happen and it just overwhelmed him."

Sanantha tilted her head and waited for him to continue. Her tall turban made the gesture more dramatic than she intended.

"He thought my mom was having an affair with his best friend. She wasn't, but he became convinced of it. He also lost a bunch of money on a failed business venture. I was pretty rebellious and so I gave him no comfort. He just couldn't handle it. We didn't see it coming, so it was quite a shock when he did it."

"You said your mom sought counseling and it helped her. Did you talk to anyone about it at the time, like a priest or a family friend?"

"I remember our priest wanting to help. I also remember I wasn't having any of it."

"What church did your family belong to?"

"We're Episcopalians."

"Do you still go to church?"

"No, I haven't been in years. Not since Desiree was in grade school. What does that have to do with how I'm dealing with my disasters today?"

"The faith traditions we are raised in help mold how we think about responsibility and how we process guilt. Do you still feel any guilt over your father's suicide?"

"No, I've come to peace with it. I did blame myself at the time, but that was 35 years ago." He laughed. "Remember, I'm an Episcopalian. I think it was Robin Williams who said Episcopalianism is Catholicism-lite, all the ceremony but only half the guilt."

Sanantha chuckled good-naturedly while she made a quick note on her pad: 'Suicide watch.' "How did you feel toward your father for having killed himself?"

"Angry. Eventually I came to understand what he had faced, and how he must have felt. It took a few years, but I did finally see that he wasn't trying to harm me."

"Did you forgive him?"

"Yes. I guess it was right around the time I graduated from UCLA."

"Do you think of yourself as a forgiving person? Or do you hold grudges?"

He scratched the back of his head while he worked on the question. "I hadn't thought about it in those terms. I guess I am pretty forgiving. Young Nae has given me crap about it a few times. He says I'm too tender hearted to be in business. Good thing I've got him to play hardball for us."

"So Young Nae is not as forgiving as you?"

"No, not really. I figure, we all make mistakes, and we all need a little slack. If I never let anyone slide, then no one will ever let me slide."

Sanantha made another note, 'Needs forgiveness.'

"Let's move forward to now. Do you feel any guilt over your wife's death?"

The question took him by surprise. "Guilt? No. She traveled the world as part of her job. She was a UNESCO director. We always knew there were dangers in her job. I mean, she had a couple of close calls. She would go somewhere to raise money or oversee how money was being spent, and she'd have to be evacuated by the military when some riot broke out or a coup went down. Thankfully, she wasn't in Indonesia last December when the tsunami hit. She rushed down here in January to help. Their area headquarters is in Jakarta."

"Do you feel any connection between her being halfway around the world and her being in danger?"

"No, she died in a car accident. She could just as easily have been going to our local supermarket. So no, letting her wander into dangerous places had nothing to do with her death."

"Clearly you miss her. Other than that, how do you feel about her death?"

"Isn't missing her enough?"

"Well, are you angry? Do you think more could have been done? Do you still have questions about how the accident happened? Are you suspicious or are you satisfied that you have a clear understanding?"

"No, I'm pretty clear on what happened. Young Nae checked it out at the time and he gave me a complete report. It was just an accident. A truck slammed into the driver's side of her car. The truck's engine caught fire, and both the driver's and Cheri's bodies were lost."

"Oh dear. I didn't know."

"Yeah, it was apparently quite violent. As far as we can tell, she died instantly."

"Do you feel that you had a chance to say goodbye to her? I don't mean to be insensitive, but I assume there was no casket at the memorial service?"

"No, there wasn't," he answered, but then hesitated in thought. "What do you mean by 'say goodbye'?"

"An important step in grieving is identifying that point in time when you have accepted that the person is gone — the time when you say goodbye. That's why people have caskets at funerals, even if they are closed. Since you were in the U.S. when she died, and you didn't get to see her body when you got here, I was wondering if you had noticed a moment when you realized she was gone."

He looked at the floor beside his chair for a long moment. "No, I guess not." He looked back up at her. "I mean, I didn't doubt the news when I heard it back in Maryland. I have accepted that she was gone. I remember everyone talking about all the death from the tsunami once we got here. Death and loss was kind of in the air. You're right, though. I don't think there was ever a moment when I felt like she was no longer part of my life."

"That's an important landmark to achieve. Without that, you will color all your future experiences with comparisons to her and regrets of her passing."

"I had a moment like that when I first saw Desiree lying in a coma the other day. It hit me all at once that Cheri was gone, and Dez needed my help. That I was alone to help her."

"How did that leave you feeling?"

"I remember the irony slammed me pretty hard."

"Irony?"

He looked up and met her gaze. "Yeah. Like you said the other day, I may have discovered the Fountain of Youth. I know so much about how life works, but I can't do anything for my own family."

"Do you feel more could have been done?"

"No, it's not that. I believe Young Nae and the doctors did everything they could. I just can't shake the feeling there was more I could have done, with what I know."

She made a note, 'Guilt after all.' "We will make a point of addressing this feeling as we work on how you're handling Desiree's condition. Last time, you said you were having difficulty making decisions on your own, now that Cheri is gone. Were you the kind of couple that made a lot of decisions together? I mean, if she was on the road a lot, how did that work?"

"Well it wasn't like we were co-dependent or anything, but we were in touch pretty much all the time, on cell or online." He uncrossed and recrossed his legs, this time more tightly above the knee. "I never thought about it then, but now I'm seeing just how much I counted on always being able to talk with her about things, anything. I found her work fascinating, and she loved to tell me about all the interesting people she met and places she saw. Our house is filled with trinkets she brought home from her travels."

"What about raising your daughter? Were you happy with being the parent who stayed home?"

"Oh yeah. Dez and I have always been best buddies. With Cheri on the road so much, I think we were lucky to have skipped that whole mother-daughter power struggle thing that I've seen so many other families go through."

"You are a highly successful professional person yourself. Did you ever feel strained having to juggle raising a teen with the demands of your work?"

"Sure, there was stress, but I happily stepped up to the challenge. I mean, Cheri wouldn't have been able to do the great things she did without my support on the home front."

Sanantha noted, 'Self-sacrificing love. Still hasn't let go.' She looked up and flashed her big warm smile. "New subject. You mentioned before that you have been having graphic nightmares. Are these nightmares preventing you from getting good sleep?"

"Yeah, when I have one it usually wakes me up. I'm finding myself taking a lot of naps, so I get enough rest."

"Are you napping because you're tired, or is it from boredom? Are there any particular situations that seem to bring on the urge to sleep?"

Randy frowned and thought about this for a moment. "Now that you mention it, I find myself nodding off a lot when I'm sitting with Desiree. I just assumed it was the quiet of her room."

Sanantha jotted down, 'Stress sleeping — depression.' She scratched her scalp under the corner of her turban with the eraser of her pencil while she looked at her notes. "You described the nightmares as 'graphic.' What do you mean by that word?"

"Oh, they're horrific. I remember every detail when I wake up, even if I wish I didn't. You know how you usually forget details once you wake up? Not these. The images linger in my mind for hours afterward."

"Are they violent? Are you hurt during the dream?"

"No, not that. They're just overwhelming. I feel completely out of control, tossed around by events."

"Can you recall one in detail for me now?"

"Sure, the one I had last night. I was climbing along this ridge of rocks that was sticking up out of a desert, looking for Cheri. For some reason, I thought she had come that way and I might catch up to her. The sun was blazing and I was sweating. I was barefoot and the rocks had lots of sharp edges. My feet started to slip, and I assumed it was from sweat, but I looked down and it was blood from where the rocks had cut my feet. I looked back and saw I had left a trail of bloody footprints on the rocks. Then the blood started eating away at the rocks, and water started bubbling up through the holes. I remember being kind of awestruck at this, and I stood there and watched. The water trickled down the sides of the ridge, and out onto the desert floor. Wherever the water went, plants started springing up. Even in the dream, I recognized the savior fantasy aspect, that my blood was bringing life to the desert."

Sanantha smiled and nodded for him to continue.

"Then things turned sour." He uncrossed his legs, spread his feet, leaned forward and started gesturing with his hands. "I spotted a scrap of white fabric further down the rocks. I climbed over to it and it was a scrap of the white wedding dress that Cheri is always wearing in these dreams. I looked around for her, but then I heard the water rushing behind me. The footprint trickles had become founts and the water was gushing out like rivers and spilling all out over the desert. The sun was covered over with clouds and it started to rain. By now, the desert was an ocean and big swells started lashing at the rocks I was standing on. I scrambled for better footing and that's when I heard her. Cheri's voice was calling me over the wind and the crashing waves, from somewhere up ahead. I tried to continue toward her, but a huge wave swatted me off the rocks. I remember going under right away, being tossed around by the currents, helpless to find the surface. That's when I woke up."

Sanantha kept her sober, unaffected expression as best she could. She did jot down, 'More than grief.' She looked up at him and smiled again. "Thank you."

"You aren't going to share with me what you think of that."

"I will level with you. It could mean a lot of things. It could mean very little. We are going to figure it out together, but we don't know enough to figure it out yet."

She noted the skeptical look he gave her.

"Dreams do sometimes give us a glimpse of what's going on in our heads, but interpreting them means finding the right context. We need to know a lot more about how you are processing all that has happened to you before we can start trying to explain dream images.

"Let's look at the whole sequence. You said you recall getting the news from Young Nae about Cheri's death. You recall coming to Malaysia with Desiree for the funeral. Then your memories go completely blank for almost four months until you woke up at Young Nae's house last week. During that gap is when your daughter was bitten by a poisonous snake and went into a coma."

"That's right."

"So hearing about what happened to Desiree was quite a shock to you?"

"Utterly blew me away."

"Have you gone back over the last thing you can remember, before the gap starts?"

"Yes, I remember coming back to Young Nae's house with him and Desiree after the funeral. That's it."

"So you don't remember blacking out at the funeral, or anything happening of note once you got back to the house?"

"No. We were all really sad. We were all crying and hanging on to each other. Then my recollection just ends. Do people's memories just break like that?"

"Usually something has to change. Being a doctor yourself, you've probably heard of state-dependent learning."

"Yeah, it's why you don't really learn anything from cramming. The memories of what you cram are encoded while you are stressed out and exhausted. You get some sleep before the test, and then you can't access those memories anymore because your brain chemistry is different." He paused and thought about what he had said. "So you think something happened to my brain chemistry to mask my memories?"

"It's one possibility."

Randy ventured further. "Can alcohol create a big enough change to accomplish that? I mean you can't remember where you parked your car after you've been drinking, for the same reason."

"Alcohol and stress dependent learning mask details," she explained. "You may not remember where you parked, but you don't forget that you drove a car to the bar, or what your car looks like. That kind of memory loss means something much more significant happened, like a trauma. Since we don't know if there was a chemical change, or if there was, then what that chemical change was, we can't test the theory directly. Thankfully, the brain is a very flexible organ. There are other ways to help it to find a memory. Have you ever been hypnotized?"

Randy laughed nervously. "Young Nae said you came with a reputation for being results oriented. If I can be completely honest, I have to admit that when I first met you, I wasn't sure what to think. I mean you come highly recommended and all. I have to say, though, with your accent and the turban and the paintings, it wasn't what I expected. No offense, please believe me."

"None taken. I usually don't discuss my personal details with patients, but my resume is not a secret. As you noted, I am indeed from Haiti. I received my degree and did my residency at Rush University in Chicago. I worked for a few years in Washington, D.C. before coming here to Malaysia. So yes, I have seen a lot of strange things in my life and in my practice. The good news is, all my experience is now at your disposal, to help you find what you need to find."

He nodded, a bit embarrassed. "Fair enough. Still, isn't hypnosis a bit extreme?"

"Please allow me to recap. I am very happy to find you do not seem to carry significant guilt about your wife's death. Guilt is far and away the biggest impediment to completing the grieving process. I am also very glad that your memories of your learning of Cheri's death and your memories of the funeral are still intact. That will be crucial in you coming to grips with her being gone. So I am confident we can reach a healthy result for your dealing with her death.

"On the other hand, I do not see how you are going to be able to come to a healthy grasp of what has happened to your daughter as long as you have no recollection. You said you wish there was more you could have done, especially given your special knowledge. That's going to haunt you as guilt."

"Well, I don't think I had anything to do with it." His voice tensed up. "Young Nae says she was bitten by a snake while hiking. Sure, I wish I had been there to help, but Young Nae says we didn't find her for a while, a half an hour after the bite. Does that make me responsible?"

She knew she was putting him on the defensive, but she needed him to face this. "I don't mean you are responsible. We're talking about your feelings. Since you can't remember what happened, I need to know how you feel about what happened."

"Well …" He clasped his hands together and seemed to struggle. "What kind of parent wouldn't feel like they failed their child when one day you wake up and find she's almost been killed?"

She leaned back in her chair. "Very good. That's what you need to hear yourself say. That is a feeling that will plague you until we get rid of it."

He looked away and frowned. "From what you've said, that means I have to remember exactly what happened in that four months."

She was surprised by his sudden reluctance. "Isn't that why you came to me?"

He took a shaky deep breath. "I guess so."

"Can you tell me why you wouldn't want to learn what happened?"

"Not really. It's nothing rational, it's more a feeling I can't shake. My only window on that time is my nightmares. They leave me wondering if I did something terrible during that time."

"Do you have any factual basis for such a suspicion?"

"No, the facts all point to me just being the victim of Hamlet's outrageous fortune."

She raised an eyebrow and smiled. "Hamlet had a playwright who made sure he was doomed. What he needed was a psychiatrist, which you now have. You can't put too much credence in dreams. Yes, dreams like yours mean you have unfinished business to work through. That they are scary and end badly does not mean you did anything wrong. It certainly does not mean you should fear uncovering your memories for such a large period. Especially when learning what happened will allow you to cope with the whole turn of events."

"Because if I don't know, it will just continue to plague me?"

"Most certainly. You need this. So no, hypnotism is not too extreme a tool. We need to fill in your memory gap or you will never be able to look at your daughter with a clean conscience, even though there is no evidence you are responsible for her condition."

Randy thought about her words for a long moment. His hands unclasped. "I see your point."

"To put your mind at ease, hypnosis really isn't that big a deal. It's just a way to take advantage of the brain's language-centric processing to achieve a heightened state of focus. Think of it as concentrating on something, but with me as a partner helping direct your efforts."

"Okay. How do we do this?"

"Oh, right here." She got up and went to a bookshelf. She returned with a nautilus shell that had been cut in half and stripped to expose the opalescent mother-of-pearl interior. She sat it on the coffee table between them. "I want you to stare at this shell while you listen only to my voice. Are you comfortable in that chair? People tend to slump when they're hypnotized."

"Yes, I'm fine,"

"Let's begin. You must listen to my voice as if it were the only sound in the world. Every word rings in your ears with a clarity and surety of a church bell. My words are the center of all direction in your universe. You are free of all inhibitions and fears because you know you are safe within the sound of my voice. You feel wonderful, healthy, strong, and potent. You are gifted with the ability to do anything I tell you to do. The more you hear my voice the more confident you become.

"Look at how the light reflects off the shell. How every color and every curve require your full attention. Your world is simpler now. Your total sensory experience is just seeing the shell and hearing my voice.

"Your body is completely relaxed now. Your breathing is calm. You can no longer feel your hands or your feet. Your world is simplifying and becoming more comfortable. The shell is fascinating, captivating. You cannot look away from it. My voice is soothing yet invigorating. You draw strength and confidence from my voice.

"Now close your eyes, but continue to imagine the shell. Your whole world is now only the image of the shell and the sound of my voice. You have complete control over your thoughts. Any doubts you have had about controlling your thoughts is gone now, because you can take the power from my voice.

"I want you to imagine yourself in the past. Go back to the day of your wife's funeral. Imagine yourself standing at her grave side. Look around at the people there. Smell the flowers. Hear the minister's words. Young Nae and Desiree are there with you. Are there others as well?"

"Yes, but only a couple of people I don't know. I am surprised there isn't a crowd of Cheri's friends from her work."

"What is the weather like?"

"It's a beautiful day. Sunny, but with a breeze so it's not too hot."

"Okay. Now you're getting in the car to leave. Who else gets in the car with you?"

"Just Dez and Young Nae. It's a big limo, and it seems kind of empty. I try to lighten the moment by asking Dez if she had talked to her boyfriend back at Syracuse."

"Do you go straight back to Young Nae's house?"

"Yes."

"Now you're going into the house. What do you do when you get inside?"

"We go in the main house. I go into the kitchen to get a beer. I ask Dez if she wants anything, and she says ice water."

"Where is Young Nae?"

"I don't know. I guess he went upstairs."

"So you get your beer and you take the water to your daughter?"

"Yes. She is sitting on the couch crying. I sit down next to her and put my arm around her. I start crying too."

Without any warning or sign at all, Randy stopped talking and his head fell forward onto his chest.

"Randolph?" Sanantha got up and grabbed his hand from his lap. It was limp. "Randy!" No response. He had stopped breathing. She put her head to his chest. No heartbeat. She blinked furiously thinking of what to do next. She wondered if she would be able to find the Epi-pen in her medical kit in the bathroom.

She startled and sucked in a short breath when she realized what had happened.

She got up in his face, grabbed his head with her hands, pried his eyes open with her thumbs, and yelled at him. "Randy! You are still in complete control of your mind! Roll the clock back to the funeral site! You are still standing at your wife's grave!"

Just as quickly as he had dropped off, he was back. She let go of his head and it came up straight. His breathing resumed. His eyes fell back closed, and he was still hypnotized, but he was back. She put her hand on his chest, and found his heart was beating normally.

She dropped back into her own chair and blew out a deep breath. She grabbed her mouth and squeezed her cheeks with her hand, stared at him, and slowly shook her head.

5

"I HAVE NEVER BEEN TO JAPAN, so I couldn't tell if this décor is authentic or not." Sanantha Mauwad flashed her ample white teeth playfully at her date sitting next to her on the floor cushions. Simon Carrera was in his late forties like Sanantha, but was showing his age a bit more with his receding hairline and his graying goatee beard. She still found his long Latin eyelashes hard to resist.

He smiled back. He gestured broadly at the paper room-dividing screens, the woven mats on the floor, and low dark wood furnishings. "Neither have I, but every Japanese restaurant I've ever been in has tried for the same archetype."

"Oh, now we're dredging up work jargon?"

"Hey, just because I left the couch at the office doesn't mean I had to leave my vocabulary there too."

"Or the critical thinking, I agree. The place looks lovely, and expensive. I haven't had Japanese food since I left Washington last year." She gave his hand a squeeze. "Thank you."

He turned his hand over and held hers. "Speaking of D.C., can I tell you again how happy I am you followed me here?"

"Yes, you smoothie, you can, for the hundredth time. Your get-away-from-it-all sailing trip found just the spot I needed to do my own getting-away-from-it-all. I am glad you didn't turn on the charm right away. It's taken me a few months to sort things out. Thank you for being patient with me."

"Well, while we are doing couch work, I will admit that I wasn't sure where you and I were going, if anywhere at all. I was still figuring out my divorce." He corrected himself. "I'm still figuring out my divorce. We both just seemed to need a fresh start. Thank you again for covering my practice for me while I went on that cruise."

She grinned with her big dimples and cocked an eyebrow at him. "You do know you are going to owe me for the rest of your life for handing me a patient who dragged me into Armageddon."

"I had no idea he wasn't just paranoid," he laughed. Then he grinned back. "Actually, I don't mind owing you."

She picked up a menu. "You can start by helping me interpret this. I do not speak a word of Japanese outside of the handful of things I usually order."

"How adventurous are you feeling?"

She lowered her chin, raised her eyebrows, and stared at him.

"Not a loaded question," he laughed. "Do you want to try something new or stick with your standbys?"

She went back to looking at the menu. "I'll tell you, one thing that's going to take me long time to get used to is the smell of cigarette smoke in restaurants. I am so spoiled from the States."

"Asians do smoke a lot, and everywhere," he agreed.

She zeroed in on an item on her menu. "What in the world?"

"Where?"

She pointed. "It says 'Tessa', but then in parentheses, it says 'torafugu'. *Fugu?* Isn't that puffer fish?"

"Yes. Only really high-end places can afford the specially trained chefs and to get the licenses to serve it."

"Licenses? I thought it was illegal outside of Japan."

"No. I hope not. I like this place and I wouldn't want to see it shut down."

"This is tetrodotoxin. Do you know how poisonous that stuff is? It's something like ten times as poisonous as cyanide."

Simon smiled at her sudden interest. "How is it that you know so much about obscure Japanese fish cuisine?"

"Because it isn't just from Japan." She leaned up against him and lowered her voice. "Back home in Haiti, poisonous fish livers are believed to be among the ingredients used to make zombie powder. This compound is a paralytic that shuts down nerve transmission, but it doesn't cross the blood-brain barrier, so you are fully aware of the horrors that are happening to you."

"Has the zombie connection ever been proven? I seem to remember a professor in med school saying that was anecdotal."

"It is not dismissed so easily where folks have first-hand experience."

"Have you seen a zombie first-hand?"

She bit her lip. "No. Just the idea of someone being able to do anything to you while you are wide awake and unable to do anything to stop them … it's just horrible. Yet here these people eat this stuff on purpose."

"It is a bit of thrill seeking. Asian men see it as a test of their machismo. Some say it has aphrodisiac effects. They even pay extra for chefs who rub just a little of the poison on so you get a numbness in the tongue and lips."

"No way!"

"I couldn't make this stuff up," he said raising his hands in surrender. He then pointed to the menu. "Look, it's almost $200 for a plate of sashimi made from *fugu*. Anyone who pays $200 for just a main course is getting something out of it."

She spotted a waiter and waved him over. "Excuse me. Could you tell me about your *torafugu*?"

The young Japanese man in the short blue robe and white slacks seemed unsure of himself, as if he were afraid to give the wrong answer. "What does madam want to know?" he asked in a thick accent.

"Does your chef prepare the sashimi so you get a numbness …?"

The waiter tilted his head and frowned at the word. His hair was gelled up into a single point in front and it comically exaggerated his gesture.

"I'm sorry, a tingling in the lips?"

"No, no, we not do that here." She couldn't tell with his accent, but she thought he may have taken offense at the suggestion.

"I meant no offense," she tried to assure him. "So if I order something else, like the tuna, there is no chance of any of the fugu getting on my food, right?"

The young man smiled and bowed. "Yes, ma'am. Chef specially trained. Have license. *Fugu hiki* kept away from all the other knives. Completely safe."

She bowed her head in return. "Thank you."

"Shall I get your waiter for you now?"

"Yes, thank you. That would be fine." When he had gone, Sanantha turned back to Simon, who had a wide but contained grin of bemusement on his face. She took a deep breath and rolled her eyes. "I think I'll stick to my tuna and shrimp."

6

"Y OU KNOW, I DON'T USUALLY GO OUT ON EXCURSIONS with patients. From what we've seen, I am convinced something traumatic happened to you that has cut you off from your memories of what happened to your daughter."

Randolph smiled at her careful explanation without taking his eyes off the road in front of them. "I don't mind a little field trip."

Sanantha was glad the country road was nearly empty, and Randy was able to drive and talk safely. The road was still wet from the morning rains, and the jungle came right up to the edge of the road for long stretches, which gave them no room to maneuver in an emergency. She was also glad Young Nae had lent them this Land Rover. Her tiny Fiat coupe would have been a hazard out here.

She still had to draw him out. "I'm hoping that if we fill in some of the details by going to where she was bitten, we can either jog your memory or maybe get more clues as to what trauma you experienced."

"I know we went over this before, but I've got to say how conflicted I am about filling in these details. I mean, as much as I want to come to peace with this, in a way I'm glad that I don't remember the gory details. Just seeing her in a coma is bad enough. Revisiting her actual attack may prove to be too much."

Finally, she had him talking about his feelings. Now she needed to keep his trust. "I understand, and let me say how sorry I am in advance for any pain this is going to cause you. That's why I want to go over how important this is for you. It is going to be painful and you will come away sad. You will also come away knowing. That's the key."

She glanced up and saw a car making a turn onto the road in front of them. The car had plenty of room, if Randy slowed down for him. Randy didn't. He speeded up and swerved around the car, passing it in the opposing lane. Thankfully, there was no oncoming traffic.

It was all Sanantha could do not to grab hold of the door handle and dashboard as they careened on the wet road. She managed to prevent any surprise from showing on her face as she took note of Randy's expressions. He was not upset at the other driver. He just didn't want to let the guy get in front of him.

The maneuver reminded her of the legal and ethical corners he and Young Nae cut off in their business dealings. She made a mental note to watch for more rule-breaking and risk-taking.

Randy glanced at her and continued as if nothing had happened. "You were saying I can expect some pain. I understand the theory. You want me to get to the day when I can resume my life without the emotional baggage." He sighed and shifted gears to go up a grade. "I'm just looking forward to the day when all the hurt stops."

"I know this is tough. I will be right here for you through it all. As unfair as it seems now, the ugly truth is, you can't get past the pain until you free yourself from the baggage."

He looked at her and nodded his resignation. "So it has to hurt more before it hurts less."

"I wish there was another way."

Randy nodded ahead. "We're here."

Randy pulled off onto a muddy dirt road at a sign that said 'Kampong Kuala Dong.' A few hundred yards down the road, the jungle opened up into a village. As they drove to the center of town, Sanantha noticed all the houses were identical wooden bungalows set in straight, parallel rows.

Randy parked in front of a general store and they got out. The pungent smell of wet tropical jungle warming in the morning sunshine brought back a flood of memories for Sanantha, memories from halfway around the world. While this jungle did not have the drone of insects the Caribbean had, the gentle breeze blowing through the trees created a very familiar pervasive background rustling sound.

She must have had a quizzical look on her face, because Randy started right in on an explanation. "This town, and hundreds of others like it, was built as a workers' camp in the 90's when the big chip manufacturers started building factories across Indochina. Workers would move from their farms to towns like this, and from here, they would be bussed daily to the factories. They would send their pay back home to their families in their villages. Young Nae employs most of the folks in this town in our plant ten miles down the main road. He still does the bus thing, but this town is now their actual permanent home, for their whole families."

"This is where Desiree was bitten?"

"Yeah. Young Nae says she wanted to get away from everything, just to go hiking on her own for a while. He suggested this village as a remote but safe place. He brought her out here, and he got busy talking to folks in town while she went hiking. This area is not known for snakes. I mean kids play here all the time and no one gets bitten."

Sanantha sensed a growing anxiety in Randy's voice, and moved to intercept it. "So you weren't here at the time?"

"No. I have been here before, but I was back at his beach house that day. At least that's what Young Nae tells me. I don't recall that day at all."

Sanantha looked around and noticed the town was very quiet, with only a few people on the streets. There were no children playing among the houses when they drove in. "Isn't today Monday? I thought Monday was the traditional day off in the work week. That's why I thought it would be easy to find people here to talk to today."

Randy looked around. "You're right. It looks like a regular work day, with the kids off to school and the adults off at work. Odd."

"Do you think these people speak English?"

"I don't know." He brightened a bit. "I guess we'll find out."

They walked into the general store and the first thing Sanantha noticed was the smell — an unpleasant combination of mildew, chili spices, dust, dried fish, and of course, the ever-present cigarette smoke. The shelves that lined the walls and filled the floor were sparsely stocked with bags of basic foodstuffs and boxes of building materials. She noticed the plastic and cloth bags had no labels. She stepped up to the counter and called to the proprietor in the back room. "Excuse me! Hello?"

The short, thin, middle-aged man who came out had bronze skin, and was wearing a Budweiser t-shirt and a San Francisco Giants baseball cap. He shifted his toothpick to one side with his tongue. "Can I help you?" he asked with only a moderate accent.

"Oh good, you speak English. Can you tell me, are the townspeople all off to work today, even though it's Monday?"

"Yes. Overtime day. Boss man pay more for today."

"So everyone works what, seven days a week?"

"Yah. Make good money."

Sanantha and Randy exchanged a dubious look. "Thank you. I need to speak with someone who may have witnessed an accident here in your town a few months ago. Can you please direct me to a constable or other official I can speak with?"

The man looked the two of them up and down while he spoke. "We don't have our own police here. We use the district sheriff. He's in Raub, twenty kilo south on Highway 8. What kind of accident?"

"It was a snake bite. Maybe you remember it? A young white woman with dark hair, about four months ago."

Randy cut in. "She was with Young Nae Yoon."

The man blinked and startled at the mention of Young Nae's name. "You gonna sue somebody?"

"No," Randy continued. "We're with Mr. Young. I'm his business partner, Randolph Macklin. We just need to talk to someone who witnessed what happened. Did you see anything?"

He tongued his toothpick around for a moment. "I remember a white woman getting bit. Mr. Young came and got her. Yeah, it was a big deal. Right after the New Year."

Sanantha calculated out loud. "It's early June now. Four months. Then you mean the Chinese New Year in February?"

"No. Regular calendar New Year. Five, six months ago."

Randy and Sanantha looked at each other. "Are you sure?" Randy asked.

"Wait a minute." With that the man disappeared into the back room. A moment later they heard a door slam.

"Did he leave?" Sanantha asked, incredulous.

Randy chuckled. "It seems so. He said to wait."

Sanantha idly perused the goods in the store. The huge box full of cartons of Marlboro cigarettes behind the counter didn't take long to spot. A rack of cellophane bags with dried food drew her attention. She realized she couldn't tell if she was looking at a large dried mushroom or a small dried octopus.

They heard the door creak and footsteps. The man had brought with him a woman who Sanantha couldn't help but think looked just like the man, complete with a Coors baseball cap, only female. Except instead of a toothpick in her mouth, she had a lit cigarette.

With no introduction whatsoever, she stated flatly, "January." Her accent was much stronger than her husband's. "My sister birthday."

"You saw the incident?" Sanantha asked.

"Oh yeah. Pretty lady. Mister Young really upset. Whole town stirred up."

"Who found her after she was bitten?"

"Kids. Playing in woods. She moaning when they find her. She not moving anymore when they get her into town. Real shame."

"You saw her, yourself, with Mr. Young?" Sanantha pressed for personal verification to try to give Randy closure.

"Oh yeah. Pretty lady. Dark hair, dark brown eyes. Too bad."

Randy frowned and interrupted. "Wait a minute. Brown eyes? You mean blue eyes, right? My daughter has blue eyes, like me."

The shopkeeper's wife squinted into Randy's eyes for a second, then shook her head. "No. Brown eyes like yours," she said pointing at Sanantha.

Randy looked at Sanantha. "Could this have been some other woman?"

Sanantha asked the shopkeepers, "Are there a lot of snake bites around here?"

"No," answered the man. "Maybe once a year. We have snake bite medicine," he volunteered brightly.

Sanantha shook her head. "Have there been any other times this year when a white woman was bitten by a snake?"

The shopkeeper and his wife looked at each other and then both looked at Sanantha as if she were making a bad joke. "No," said the man. "Just the one."

The woman added, "Tao only need one."

"Excuse me?" Randy cut in. "Please explain what you mean by that."

The man tried to explain. "The Tao, you know, ah, Nature. Yeah, Nature. Nature only took one life from us."

Sanantha gritted her teeth. Here she was trying to find answers for Randy and these folks were bringing up more mysteries.

Randy pressed. "Do you think the snake was doing Nature's will?"

The wife spoke up. "Snake is Tao. Tao is snake. Real shame. Sad day."

Sanantha noticed Randy frowning at the whole exchange, looking like he wasn't making sense of it.

"Thank you so much for your time. We're so glad to meet you." Sanantha held out her hand, and both the man and his wife each shook it in turn. "Have a great day," she said as she took Randolph's arm and led him out of the store.

"What was that all about?" he asked with quiet tension.

"I wouldn't read too much into it. It is natural for folks to comfort themselves in times of natural calamity by assuming the bad thing is somehow just God's will — that it was meant to be, whether we can understand it or not. Back home in Haiti, snake bites were often explained away like this."

They got into the car.

Randy still sounded worried. "There for a second, it seemed like the woman was saying Desiree got what she deserved."

"No, I'm sure that's not what she meant. Like I said, don't read too much into how the native Malay culture interprets signs in nature."

"What about the brown eyes?"

"Now that one." She shook her head. "That one has me stumped. As much as I wanted to get you independent verification, it looks like we may have to go back and ask Young Nae about that."

7

RANDOLPH HAD WAITED ON THE DOCK FOR AN HOUR for Young Nae's fishing boat to return. In that time, he had turned the situation over in his mind many times, trying to come up with a way to ask his friend about the inconsistencies in his story without offending him. As the boat finally pulled up to the dock, Randy still wasn't sure which tack to take.

"Ahoy there!" Young Nae called when he spotted Randy.

"Ahoy there, yourself. Did you have a successful trip?"

"Do you like Ahi?"

"Sure." Randy noticed there were no fishing poles in the racks around the aft fishing deck. As the crew tied up the boat, Randy hopped aboard. "Where's all the tackle?"

Young Nae laughed. "I was spear fishing." He slapped the chest of the wet suit he was wearing. "More sporting that way."

Randy didn't try to hide the concern in his voice. "These are tropical waters. Aren't there sharks out there?"

Young Nae started pulling out coolers full of his catch and scooting them across the deck to Randy. "Absolutely. Like I said, it's more sporting if you're down there yourself."

"I guess. It sounds like you were having fun." He opened one of the coolers and found it full of large, beautiful fish. "You scored big time."

Randy helped lift the coolers onto the dock. When they had finished, Young Nae peeled off his wet suit top. "Jeez, Young Nae, when did you get so buff?"

Young Nae stood up and struck a joking muscleman pose. He was in fact hugely muscled, especially for such a short man. "I work out a lot."

"Pretty amazing for forty-nine." Randy took advantage of the humorous moment and tried to sneak up on his hot topic. "Well, while you were out on your excursion, I was out on one too. Dr. Mauwad and I went out to Kampong Kuala Dong to talk to the folks there about Desiree's snake bite."

Young Nae stood up from his unloading of the fishing spears. "What did you think you would find out there?"

"We thought having me see where it happened would somehow make it easier for me to accept the outcome."

"Did you find anything?"

"Well, yes and no." Randy took a breath and stood up straight. It did not escape him that although he stood almost a foot taller than his friend, Young Nae with all of his muscles was holding three five-foot long fishing spears. "We spoke with the guy who runs the general store there, and his wife, and they told a different version of what happened."

"How so different?" A slight note of annoyance crept into Young Nae's voice.

"Odd details that made no sense. They said Desiree had brown eyes when she was bitten, and that it happened in January, not February."

"Why exactly did you go out there?"

"Like I said, Sanantha wanted to help me find closure."

"Oh, it's 'Sanantha' now?"

Now Randy's voice strained with annoyance. "Dr. Mauwad, if you like. My point is, the trip raised more questions than it answered."

"The shopkeeper and his wife got their facts mixed up? That's hardly surprising."

Randolph didn't like Young Nae's dismissive tact. "Actually, they felt they had the facts right. It's just their facts don't agree with yours."

Young Nae switched to a calmer, more patient tone. "I cannot tell you how many times I have been speaking with a Malay, who I knew spoke English, and I would get through telling them something and they would turn around and do exactly the opposite. It's not just a language barrier, it's a cultural thing. It's like they live in their own little world. Honestly, I'm not just being a bigot. Remember, I employ that whole town at the assembly plant."

Randy tried to give him the benefit of the doubt. "You think they weren't answering the questions we were actually asking?"

Young Nae raised his eyebrows and nodded. "Very likely."

Randy watched him stow the spears in his van. He caught a particularly repulsive whiff of dead fish smell blowing off the docks while he stood there turning the situation over in his mind. "I don't buy it."

Young Nae stopped and faced Randy.

"Everything I know about what happened to Dez, I have heard from you. Yet everything I have learned about the incident from any other source disagrees with what you have told me. Am I supposed to take your version for no better reason than your Malay workers sometimes don't understand your instructions? This goes beyond my psychological need to find 'closure.' We've got a basic incongruity in the sequence of events. The guy and his wife said Dez had brown eyes, and she was bitten in January. According to your timeline, Dez and I weren't even in Malaysia yet in January, because Cheri didn't die until February. In fact, I called the airlines and verified that Dez and I flew here in February."

Randy felt his heart racing as he dumped his frustrations out on Young Nae. He considered pausing and letting him respond, but decided to press his point to its conclusion. "Now I am really trying to give you the benefit of the doubt here. We've been friends for a long time, and you have obviously been taking very good care of Dez and me for the last few months we've been here.

"You've got to admit, my world is so chock full of bizarre shit. I figured I'd go get some answers. But what do I get, more questions! Sanantha says my memory could not have a gap like this just because of booze. Then there's these weird bug bites that do not look like bug bites. Not only is my wife dead, but my daughter is in a coma, even though I have no memory of it happening. I mean, how much more fucked up is this going to get before I finally start getting some resolution? Now I'm worried at what else I'm going to find out if I ask around about anything, even Cheri's car wreck. I can't help but think there is something else you haven't told me. Is there anything else you should tell me before I find it out on my own?"

Randy expected him to give some dismissive, off-hand answer.

Instead, he looked Randy in the eye, sighed, and dropped his shoulders. "Come sit with me," he said pointing to the bench on the dock. He sat on the edge with his elbows resting on his knees.

Randy joined him, and also did not lean back.

"Sometimes you have to stretch the truth to protect people you care about, even if that stretching might look self-serving. If you know you're doing it for the right reason, then you do what you've got to do." He looked Randy in the face. "I have been hiding a couple of things from you, in hopes of protecting you from a lot of hurt. For several years now I have been at war with a powerful, dangerous rival here in Malaysia, a Chinese businessman named Lo Cheung. Actually, he is a lot more than a businessman. He is, in fact, an adherent of a Malay form of martial arts called Silat Seni Gayong. It uses a person's own chi forces against them, which is why some think it borders on black magic."

"This guy is an enemy of yours?"

"Yes. He wants what I've got here, and he is forever pulling strings in the government to screw up my distribution, leases, permits, everything. In the last year, he has escalated things, and now he's started killing people."

Randy was pretty sure he saw where this was going, but stayed quiet and let Young Nae tell the story.

Young Nae raised his eyebrows and nodded. "Yes, he killed Cheri." He took a deep breath. "In fact, it's more complicated than I have told you. It was Cheri who was bitten by the snake in Kampong

Kuala Dong in January. The townspeople have their facts straight. Lo Cheung lured her there. I found out what he was up to just as he made his move, and I arrived right after she was bitten. I gave her the antidote, and she recovered completely."

Randy frowned as he tried to wrap his mind around this telling.

"Hold on. Like I said, it's complicated. She looked pretty bad at the time, but she did recover. A month later, Cheung tried to kill her again, and this time he succeeded with the truck. So yes, she was bitten in January, but she died in the wreck in February."

"And Dez?"

"She was also bitten by a snake, also sent by Lo Cheung, but this time we didn't get to her in time. She was bitten right on the grounds of my beach house."

"Why can't you have this guy arrested?"

"I don't have enough evidence. I need a really solid case against him, given how he has all the local politicians in his pocket."

"What does he want?"

"He is attacking everyone close to me to try to get me to sell out to him."

"Why didn't you tell me about this guy from the beginning? Why the elaborate story?"

"It was actually greatly simplified. I was hoping to give you a simple enough story that you would satisfy yourself that this was all done, and you would go home to Maryland, and no longer be a target for this guy. If I could get you safely out of his reach, then I could focus on continuing to build my case against him. I'm sorry I lied to you. As I said, I thought I needed to do it to protect you."

Randy shook his head and sighed. "Oh, what a tangled web we weave. I know your heart was in the right place, but you know you can level with me. Now I know to be on the alert for any attacks from this guy. I'm vested in your fight with him — he killed my wife and put my daughter in a coma." Randy put his arm around Young Nae's shoulder. "You do not need to take him on alone any longer."

8

ISHI SHIMATO UNCROSSED HIS LEGS and stretched them as best he could under the chair in front of him in the closely packed long rows of the hotel ballroom. He glanced around hoping to find a fellow bored face among the hundreds of businessmen watching the panel presentation up on stage. He found none. He satisfied himself that no one wanted to get caught by their peers looking anything but enraptured. Ishi had heard the same predictive models for export trends at every one of these conferences he had attended for years. Not that the data wasn't relevant. It just wasn't worth the hour it took to listen to it.

He was therefore quite pleased when his beeper buzzed in his pocket. The text message was from his partner, Hideo Yamaguchi: `mtg w/yny on 4 2. lbby rstrnt`

He checked his watch. 1:35. He smiled. Just enough time to hear the conclusion of this panel, which was the only part he needed to hear.

As Ishi walked into the restaurant, he spotted his partner already seated with Young Nae Yoon. The two men stood up at his approach. He shook Young Nae's hand, then exchanged a perfunctory bow with his partner before they all sat down. "Mr. Young, I'm sure Hideo has already thanked you, but I wanted to extend my thanks for coming all this way to Singapore to meet with us. I hope we can make the trip worth your while."

"Yes, we were just discussing our long-term plans," Hideo explained. "I was outlining the advantages of vertical integration."

Ishi was taken aback and smiled to cover. "Discussing business before we have ordered the meal?" He smiled at Young Nae. "Please forgive my partner for his rudeness. He is obviously very excited about your visit."

Hideo was unapologetic. "I saw no reason not to begin. It's a big plan. There is much to discuss."

Ishi smiled nervously again at Young Nae. "I was not aware you were interested in acquiring our company. We had only discussed a long-term contract for medical sodium."

"That's true. Hideo approached me about an acquisition some time ago, and now I am interested to hear more. He was telling me how profitable some of your other chemical lines are." Young Nae paused to let Hideo finish his presentation.

"Yes, and if you owned Clearwater, not only would you be able to get all the components Cyto needs at cost, but you could enjoy the profits of our higher margin lines."

Young Nae leaned forward. "Do you have numbers on that?"

Ishi couldn't sit by any longer. "Just speaking hypothetically, as something to think about." He shot his partner a quizzical, somewhat betrayed look, but Hideo was focused on their Korean client.

"We can give you numbers if you are interested."

Young Nae looked from one to the other. "How would an acquisition work? I don't have the time to run a chemical supply company."

Ishi was completely shocked, and had no answer.

Hideo did. "You would be Chairman and Ishi would stay on to run the company as President."

Young Nae raised his eyebrows and nodded. "It certainly merits additional examination."

Ishi did not like where this was going. "We can make a more formal proposal once Hideo and I have worked out more of the details. Today, shall we talk about your sodium needs? We know you use a lot of sodium in your drug refining processes. We also know you've been buying it from several sources, including us and our competitors. Now, has this been because of price point, or have you chosen multiple vendors to assure supply continuity?"

Young Nae turned to look Ishi square in the eye. He spoke calmly but with a force of tone that rattled Ishi deeply. "Why would I want to negotiate a long-term supply contract if I am considering the purchase of your company?"

Ishi was suddenly taken by a chill and felt a sweat break out all down his back. He knew how to handle tough negotiations, yet he couldn't find the words. In fact, he couldn't form any words. He just stared blinking back and forth between the two men, wondering what had happened to himself.

Young Nae turned to Hideo. "I think Ishi needs a drink, or maybe some lunch." He picked up the menu. "Ishi, you were right. We should eat, and then we will all be better prepared to discuss business."

Eating was the last thing Ishi wanted to do. In fact, the thought of food made him ill. He shot Hideo a look of fear and doubt that his partner could not have mistaken, yet Hideo ignored the look and picked up his menu.

Ishi felt his face flush. "I am sorry. I am not prepared to talk about selling Clearwater Distribution today. Hideo and I have a lot to discuss before this negotiation can go on. I am feeling suddenly quite ill, and I must excuse myself. If you two want to go ahead and have lunch, then please do." He got to his feet, and had to hold the table edge to steady himself. "If you will excuse me," he said as he headed for the Men's Room. He glanced back one last time and caught Hideo's reaction. It wasn't concern or sympathy. It was disappointment.

9

RANDOLPH'S FIRST PERCEPTION AS HE AWOKE was a cold wind blowing off the ocean. He wasn't used to that out on Young Nae's deck. He blinked and rolled over on the lowered wood slat chaise, trying to get comfortable. The wind blew again. Was a storm coming in? He couldn't recall ever feeling a cold wind in Malaysia.

He stood up and looked, bleary-eyed, out to sea, and was startled to alertness by what he saw. About a quarter mile off-shore, a white sea serpent raised its head proudly out of the choppy, white peaked sea.

Unable to accept what he saw, Randolph blinked and shook his head. He ventured a tentative look back. Not much to his surprise, and much to his relief, he saw the white shape was the tall sail of a sailboat.

He wrapped his arms around himself and was surprised at how cold his body was. "Freezing out here," he muttered to himself, and he headed inside.

He grabbed the nearest warm thing he could find, a bathrobe, and wrapped up in it. The sound of a woman's quiet sobbing caught his attention from down the hall.

He walked into the second bedroom and was stunned stiff. Cheri was lying motionless on his bed in the wedding dress from his dreams, her short, straight black hair loosely scattered over the pillow. The sun shining through the half-closed shutters illuminated her placid white face in a golden halo.

He stopped himself and noticed he felt no compulsion to rush to her side. She was dead and he was somehow already at peace with that fact.

Desiree was sitting at her bedside, dressed in the same black mourning clothes Randolph had seen in previous nightmares. He sighed, having hoped the nightmares were over. She cried quietly, occasionally brushing an annoying lock of her long brown hair from her face and drying a tear.

In her other hand, she held a piece of bread torn from a long baguette sitting on the nightstand. She hadn't yet noticed her father. Taking another bite, she continued to chew while she sobbed. He frowned at her strange, almost ritual behavior when he noticed a half-eaten piece of the same bread resting in his wife's lifeless fingers. To his additional surprise, it was furry with blue green mold. He looked closer. So was the loaf. So was the piece Desiree was eating.

He sucked in a sharp breath of revulsion and his daughter looked back at him. Her puffy blue eyes brightened immediately and she smiled at him warmly. Without getting up, she held out a hand as if beckoning. He stepped forward to console her, but she didn't mean to embrace him. She offered him the bread. He pulled back from the disgusting morsel, but her smile was unfaltering. She turned and set down her piece, picked up the whole loaf with both hands, and gave him the unbroken end in a motion of obvious but unfathomable significance. Having not the vaguest clue as to what any of this meant, he played along and took the moldy baguette in the only natural position possible.

Holding it up like a bat, he looked back at his daughter, waiting to see what would happen next. She brushed his arm aside, gave him her dimpled, impish grin, stepped up on tiptoe, and lightly kissed him on the cheek. The warmth of that gesture swept over him in a surging wave of energy, of enthusiasm, of strength, of life. Was she forgiving him? He didn't know what she was forgiving him for, but he was so glad to have her forgiveness his eyes welled up with tears and he returned her smile.

The bread felt oddly heavy in his hand, as well it should, for now it was a long shiny knife. Ever since entering this room he had been aware that he was dreaming. Looking upon this gleaming steel weapon, though, he lost all sense of detachment. The sense of power and purpose it gave him was as real as anything he had ever felt. He didn't know what he was supposed to do with it, and he didn't care.

Desiree surprised him by stepping up and kissing him again, but this time there was something wrong. She pressed her body up against his when she kissed him on the cheek, and she didn't back away when she was done. He turned to look at her and she planted a passionate lover's kiss on his lips. He startled and tried to back away, but she wrapped her arms around him and buried her face in his shoulder. She hugged him tightly, saying in a small, almost frightened voice, "Hold me Daddy. Don't let me go."

He stood there wondering if he had misinterpreted the kiss. Her emotions seemed clear enough now. At least they did until he felt her rubbing her pelvis up against his in rhythmic waves.

He grabbed her arms and pulled her away, demanding, "Desiree! What are you doing?"

"Daddy, don't you love me anymore?" she pleaded. Again, fear colored her words.

"Not like that," he stated with genuine disgust.

Even more to his horror, she grabbed his wrist and thrust her body up against his, impaling herself on the knife.

He jumped back and pulled the knife out as quickly as he could. He was so shocked at the blood gushing out of the wound, he dropped the knife, not sure what he could do. The blood splattered over him, the floor, and Cheri's body in the bed. It was hot, and so bright red, and in such copious quantity, it made him shudder.

He grabbed Desiree's shoulders in desperation. "What have you done? Why, why did you do this?"

As if to answer, she pointed at Cheri's body where her blood had splashed on it. Cheri startled and gasped, as if coming back to life. The shock hit Randolph so hard he jerked out of the dream.

His eyes shot open and immediately filled with tears. He was soaked with sweat and the bed covers were flung all around from his obvious thrashing. He grabbed them up to see if they were covered in blood. When he saw they weren't, he curled up into a ball and cried, giving in completely to his helplessness. No matter what progress he made during the day, the nightmares continued to get more horrible, more tortuous.

After a while, he realized that self-pity was only going to make him believe there was no way out. Fearful of sleep, he got up and went into the bathroom to towel off.

He started to make a wrong turn, since Young Nae's apartment in Kuala Lumpur was laid out differently from the beach house he was used to. Waking up in a new place further disoriented him, and made it that much harder to focus past the nightmare.

He stood there staring back in the bathroom mirror, a scared, hollow shell of himself. Why would his subconscious need to dig up such images if he hadn't done anything to his daughter? Nothing he had learned changed anything. His blank was still just as dark and terrifying as ever. After this, he did not want to know what happened.

When he had composed himself, he went out to the living room and flopped down on the couch. The clock on the TV channel box said 3:04 AM. There was no way he was going to attempt sleep again.

He considered what he would talk to Sanantha about at their 10 a.m. appointment. He had actually made notes on the three-hour car trip across the Malaysian peninsula yesterday. This nightmare pretty much blew that list apart. He was glad to be in town, because he was really going to need some help sorting all this out.

Distance. Distance and perspective would be good.

He noticed the large imposing painting of a mythic Korean hero on the wall across the room, resplendent in ceremonial armor. He couldn't remember the guy's name, Dang-something. He was staring down at Randy as if ashamed of the white man's pathetic behavior.

"Fuck you," Randy quietly told the picture.

He picked up the remote, turned on the television and started channel surfing. He was amused and somewhat fascinated to find the 1931 production of "Frankenstein," both colorized and dubbed into Chinese.

He had seen the film any number of times, but this was like seeing an entirely different movie. It was quite engrossing to see Colin Clive clambering around Boris Karloff's prone body and barking out commands at Dwight Frye in a language that made Randolph see it as some bizarre martial arts film.

After a few minutes of watching, his interest became obsessive. He wondered if his fascination was just from the color and language, and decided there was more to it. Something about this silly little melodrama bothered him in a way he couldn't place.

Inexplicably, fear replaced his curiosity. He started feeling the same kind of dread that gripped him in his nightmares, the sensation of knowing what was going to happen, knowing it would be very bad, and not being able to stop it, even if he realized he was dreaming. Now he was awake. Why did he feel this way now?

His first impulse was to turn off the TV. It was too late for that, though, as his curiosity demanded satisfaction. Henry Frankenstein had the table lifted up to the lightning rods on the roof and everyone was waiting for his awesome, spark spewing machine to harness the forces of nature.

Randolph suddenly flashed on Cheri lying in a hospital bed, in a coma hooked up to IVs and monitors, but with no visible injuries. Randolph blinked and the vision was gone.

Dr. Frankenstein was bringing the monster down now, waiting impatiently to see the results.

Randolph remembered himself working feverishly in a lab to develop something that would save his wife. A gene-swapping virus? He tried to focus on this image, to recall more details, but it slipped away.

Henry Frankenstein was waiting breathlessly for the first signs of life when the monster's hand suddenly twitched and grasped at the air.

Randolph twitched as well as the memory of his deed hit him full force. He made the virus from Desiree's DNA.

The muscles in his chest constricted so tightly and painfully it felt as though an iron bar was driven through his left shoulder and out his right side, pinioning his left arm and torso in a single massive frozen spasm. The pain hit him so hard, he was sure he wouldn't be able to take another breath.

He knew Young Nae was away on one of his overnight business meetings, and he had no idea if Young Nae's neighbors would respond to his screams at 3AM The phone on the other side of the room seemed a hundred yards away. He had to try. It was all he could do to stiffen his legs under him and drive himself across the room. He landed on the far arm of the couch. The phone seemed a lot closer, more possible. He managed to get a breath and grabbed for it with his still mobile right arm. There was no 911 to call, so who? His phone call log had Sanantha's cell number from their trip to the country.

•   •   •

Randolph slipped in and out of consciousness on the drive across town to the hospital. The pain in his chest would rise and spasm to cut off his breathing, then it would subside and he would relax and fade out. While he was aware, he was thankful for the Mexican fellow Sanantha had brought along. Randy knew he had heard the guy's name, but it hadn't stuck. He seemed to know what he was doing, though, keeping track of Randy's pulse and breathing while propping Randy up in the back seat of the car. By the time they arrived, the pain had dulled a bit, but getting out of the car brought it vengefully back.

He blacked out for a moment, and thought he caught a glimpse of Young Nae injecting something into his arm. It was very brief, but made no sense. A surge of pain crashed through the vision and brought him back to an agonized wakefulness.

By now, he was on a gurney being wheeled into triage. Sanantha's friend was speaking Chinese with a doctor. The doctor left, barking orders to the nurses.

Sanantha leaned over Randy and explained quietly. "They say your heart is beating erratically. They're going to try acupuncture to stabilize you."

Randolph looked around for the first time and found himself in an unremarkable pale green modern hospital corridor that led to what were clearly emergency exam rooms. He flexed his left hand and was pleased to feel the tingling numbness of the heart attack was greatly improved. He looked up at the bags hanging above him feeding the IV in his arm, but couldn't see the labels. The gurney was slightly elevated so Randolph didn't have to lift his arms much to push up his pajama sleeves.

Sanantha saw this and asked, "What are you doing?"

"Getting ready for the doctor," Randolph answered directly. "You said acupuncture. The meridians for the heart are along the insides of the forearms."

The psychiatrist cocked an eyebrow up to the edge of her black and red turban and regarded him for a moment. "You know acupuncture?"

"Can't have a closed mind when you're trying to stay on the cutting edge."

The doctor returned and noticed what Randolph had done. He was quite short, shorter than Young Nae, but built very solidly. Randolph could tell from the man's movements, even through his hospital greens and lab coat, that he was quite strong. "Ah, you have acupuncture before?" he asked in an extremely thick accent.

"Well, yes, I guess you could say that," Randolph compromised, not wanting to belabor the details.

"Then you have heart problem before?"

"Oh no," he insisted. He hadn't anticipated the doctor's conclusion. "My heart has always been very healthy."

"This first trouble?" the doctor verified.

"Yes, the first trouble."

With that assurance, the doctor pushed the American's sleeves all the way up and began briskly rubbing the skin on his forearms. The doctor's grip confirmed Randolph's suspicions about the man's strength. The doctor stopped immediately, though, when he bumped into one of the round insect wounds on the back of Randolph's elbow. He raised an eyebrow and switched to the other arm.

When he found another wound on that arm as well, he frowned deeply, stood up straight and looked his patient square in the eye. "Take off shirt."

The chilling connection visibly shocked Randolph.

"What is it?" Sanantha demanded. "Is there something you haven't told me?"

Randolph was speechless and as white as the sheets beneath him. He sat up and began unbuttoning his shirt. Slowly, he gathered his thoughts and explained. "Yeah, when I came out of my stupor last week, I found my back was covered with bug bites. Or at least Young Nae thought they were bug bites." He grimaced at the thought. "I hadn't thought to check if there was a pattern to it."

Everyone turned when the Chinese doctor sucked in a tight startled breath. He stood there a moment, clearly trying to comprehend what he was seeing. Without taking his eyes off Randolph's back, he gave the nurse an order and she took off nearly running. Not even trying to work with his limited English, the physician began demanding answers from Sanantha and her friend in Mandarin.

Randolph caught the name "Simon". Right, the guy's name was Simon.

They spoke intently for several minutes, then the doctor snatched up a clipboard and started making drawings of the wound locations.

"It is as you feared," the black woman informed him. "Every hole is on a key acupuncture point. He's called for the hospital's leading specialist."

"What could this do?" Simon asked of anyone who would answer. "I mean, what happens if you injure one of these places?"

Randolph knew, and he took this chance to distance himself from his fear by adopting a clinical attitude. "Normally nothing. Chi energy flows all through the body, injuries or no. These spots are just places where you can manipulate it, kind of like valves."

"This pattern of broken valves on your back is so complex..." Simon ventured.

It was the wrong thing to say. Randolph's clinical shield shattered, his voice got very quiet, and his eyes averted contact. "The whole flow has probably been interrupted."

Sanantha seemed to try to put this into perspective. "We've got experts on it now. We'll just have to wait and see what the real effect of these wounds is."

Randolph sighed nervously. "Probably some goddamn time bomb."

"Don't give up before we've started," the Haitian psychiatrist assured him with a flash of her compassionate smile.

"Yes, doctor," he answered sarcastically. "If you really want to help, see if you can get me out of this hallway, or get me a screen or something."

He got a puzzled look and explained impatiently, "These things are all down my legs also."

"Oh, all right." Sanantha ignored his hostility and passed this information on to Simon who then spoke to the physician in Mandarin.

Randolph muttered to himself. "I just feel so...violated."

The specialist finally arrived with an intern and two nurses in tow. He towered over the other staff, at every inch of six feet tall, and had a very bony head and build. Unlike the other doctors who were in greens, he wore slacks, shirt, and a tie under a white lab coat. Although the doctor had all his hair, and it was all still black, his advanced years could easily be seen in the pronounced wrinkles around his eyes. The first doctor handed the older man the clipboard and briefly described the situation.

The nurses started wheeling the cot down the corridor while the specialist walked alongside and spoke to Randolph. He had surprisingly little accent. "I am Dr. Ho," he introduced himself with a handshake. "I'll speak bluntly because time may not be on our side. Your health is in serious jeopardy. I understand you have no idea how you got these wounds?"

Randolph shook his head sadly. "That's correct. I'm afraid that until just a few minutes ago, I didn't even realize these holes were acupuncture related. I thought they were a bad reaction to mosquito bites. The entire incident has been blocked from my recollection. I'm seeing Dr. Mauwad, here, to try to get my memory back." Randolph had managed to regain his clinical distance and used it to proceed calmly. "Doctor, I haven't had any ill effects for the last week. How bad can it be if I haven't felt anything out of the ordinary until now?"

"Even without seeing the rest of the sites on your legs, I can tell you that whoever did this was a master of Chi-gong. These are not just randomly chosen meridian points. They all control life energy flowing to the heart and the brain. Anytime there is an interruption of Chi to these two areas, I take it very seriously, regardless of outward symptoms."

They arrived at an empty examination room, Randolph stripped, and lay face down on the room's table, and Dr. Ho started noting the locations. He wasn't drawing pictures as the first doctor had done. Rather, he was listing the names of the points affected. When he completed his list, he told Randolph to dress, and then he sat down and pored over the list.

A moment later, he blinked with a thought, frowned at the list, and asked, "You said you have a major memory loss. How long a time is missing from your memory?"

"Four months."

His eyebrows shot up at Randolph's answer. "Dr. Mauwad, have you found any physical cause for this loss, like a head trauma?"

"No. I believe it is drug and/or emotionally induced."

Dr. Ho looked back at this list, shook his head slowly and sighed. "I can't believe this is possible." Looking to Randolph, he asked, "Is it possible that your attacker wants very much for you not to remember?"

"I guess so. I didn't even know I had been attacked."

Dr. Ho kept shaking his head as he spoke. "Only a master of Silat Seni Gayong could possibly have done this."

"What is that?" Sanantha asked.

"It is a form of Malaysian martial arts, some say combined with black magic, that takes advantage of Chi energy." Checking his list again, he breathed the word, "Unbelievable." He looked up at the half dozen people all staring intently at him. "In all my years studying the Chi, I never even suspected this could be done. It's a trap. You haven't had any ill effects because you haven't remembered anything from the hidden period. Did you remember something tonight?"

"Something vaguely reminded me of something, but nothing concrete." He noticed Sanantha staring at him for details. "I'm sorry, it was just a couple of random glimpses. They didn't even make sense. If I had actually remembered anything, I'd tell you."

"I strongly suspect that if you do remember anything," Dr. Ho said, "it will trigger a massive heart attack."

The assembled group could barely contain its astonishment. Randolph simply looked down at the floor and nodded his head resignedly.

"I would go so far as to say," Dr. Ho continued, "the minor heart attack you had today is just a pale warning of what these wounds can do to you."

Sanantha asked, "Can his Chi flow be restored?"

Dr. Ho considered this for a moment before answering. "It might be possible. Since I know of no other instance where anyone has ever abused the system so badly, I wouldn't know where to begin to set it right. It may require surgery. It will undoubtedly require rebalancing the unaffected meridians. I might do more damage than good if I were to tamper further."

Randy turned to Sanantha. "You know, at first I didn't completely believe Young Nae when he blamed Cheri's and Desiree's fates on Lo Cheung."

"Yeah, you told me that. You think this could be his work too?"

"Young Nae said Cheung dabbles in black magic, and he specifically mentioned this Silat fighting technique. Young Nae lied to me to get me out of Malaysia sooner, to protect me from this guy. I guess he got to me anyway. I must have seen something during those four months that implicates him, so he blotted out my memory and put this trap on me to kill me if I did remember."

Simon spoke up. "Are you talking about Lo Cheung, the industrialist?"

"Yes," Sanantha answered. Then, half-jokingly, she asked, "Why, do you know him?"

"Actually, yes. I mean, I don't know him personally, but his son is a patient of mine."

"Then you know about the father," she concluded. Then she sighed. "You can't tell us anything because of your confidentiality."

Randolph almost pleaded. "Anything you can tell us about this guy. Seriously. He may well have killed my wife, put my daughter in a coma, and done this to me."

Simon blinked and shook his head slowly. "That really does not sound like the same man that his son talks about. You're right, San, I can't go into details, but you're talking about a murderer, a monster. All I've ever gotten was he has a flamboyant personality and is a pretty typical overbearing Asian parent."

Sanantha pressed. "Can you please go over your notes, and look for anything that could hint at the kind of criminal mind we're talking about here?"

"Oh, absolutely." He then explained to Randolph, obviously trying to put his mind at ease. "My doctor/patient confidentiality does not stop me from reporting a crime."

Randolph nodded, then spoke up with a sudden clear-headedness that made everyone turn and face him. He asked Dr. Ho, "Do these holes affect any other part of my body besides my heart? If the trap is tripped, can you tell if there would be any other repercussions?"

Dr. Ho studied his list again and answered, "No. It appears to be very specifically directed to shut down the heart muscle."

Randolph grinned, a restrained but victorious smile. He turned to Sanantha and said simply, "Pacemaker."

10

RANDY NEARLY WALKED RIGHT PAST the downtown noodle shop, until Young Nae waved him back.

"What, this hole in the wall?"

"Exactly."

Randy sized up the table and two chairs on the sidewalk, and looked around at the busy foot traffic and the noisy, smelly cars, and motor scooters just a few feet away. Randy didn't like crowds, and the level of buzz, even just from the few minutes they had walked, was starting to get to him. "Do you think we can talk out here?"

"No. Come on in."

Inside was little more than a cracked linoleum bar with four well-worn bamboo stools. Tucked in the back was a single table with two chairs. It was two o'clock and empty, and it looked like the cook behind the counter was cleaning up to close for the day. He smiled and greeted Young Nae in what Randy recognized as Malay. Young Nae responded in kind and pointed at the table. The cook nodded and waved them back.

"I guess you do come here as often as you said."

"Been coming here for years."

The place smelled strongly of spices, but the combination of citrus and peppers and ginger didn't smell like any cuisine Randy knew. He picked up a menu and none of it was in English.

"Sorry about that," Young Nae reacted. "Let me order for you. Do you like noodles?"

"Japanese *udon* is one of my favorites."

"Well, they won't have *udon* here, but I'll get you something good." Young Nae waved his hand to get the cook's attention, then called out an order in Malay.

He turned back to Randy. "You want something to drink?"

"Tsing Tao, if they've got it."

Young Nae called out again to the cook, then turned back. "What's new?"

"Just got out of the hospital," he announced cheerfully. "I had a heart attack night before last. Had a pacemaker put in to control things."

Young Nae's eyebrows shot up and he paused for a long moment. "You're shitting me, right?"

"No, honest to God."

"Were you here in K-L?"

"Yeah. I came over to have a session with Sanantha. I ended up calling her at 3AM."

"Why didn't you call me?"

"I didn't know you were in town. All I knew was you were at a conference. I mean, you weren't at your apartment. That's where I was when I had the heart attack."

"Holy crap, Randy."

The cook brought over two opened bottles.

"It gets even more bizarre. Remember those bug bites all over my back? It turns out Lo Cheung kidnapped me at some point and injected some kind of poison into all those spots. Those spots are all Chi Gong meridians points. The whole pattern forms a trap that links my brain and my heart. If I remember the wrong thing, my heart stops."

"What the fuck? Are you sure you're not punking me with this?"

"I agree, it's unbelievable. You should have seen the doctor's face when he figured it out. It took him right to the edge of his scientific understanding."

"Well, you kind of live on that edge."

"No, I push the envelope to see what's possible. This guy was staring down something that shouldn't be possible. It was really scary. It was all I could do not to freak out."

"You've disarmed the trap now, with the pacemaker?"

"Yeah. At least it shouldn't be able to kill me anymore."

"So what, this thing is triggered by memories? Did you remember something from your missing period that tripped this thing?"

"Only flashes. Nothing I can make sense of. The doctor said if I ever fully remember, it will shut down my heart for good."

Young Nae was clearly having a hard time wrapping his mind around all of this.

"It looks like Lo Cheung kidnapped me sometime in the last three months, injected me, and returned me without you ever knowing. Is that possible?"

"I'm afraid so. You were at the beach house pretty much the whole time. I spend at least half my time here in K-L or on the road. I'm afraid I wasn't around to keep close tabs on you. I never thought he would come right onto my property and kidnap you. So I didn't put a guard on you. I'm really sorry I underestimated him. If he is pulling bold shit like this, then you really need to reconsider leaving Malaysia. He didn't let up on Cheri until he killed her. I'm afraid the same is going to happen to you."

"Isn't it bold shit like this that is going to get him caught? If I leave, then he goes back into hiding."

Young Nae sighed. "I won't disagree that you make excellent bait, but that is way riskier than I'm comfortable with."

Randy took a drink of his bottle of beer. "Now I don't buy that. You live on risk, you're an entrepreneur."

"That's not how it works. Entrepreneurs are actually risk averse. We love the thrill of the big rewards attached to risk, but we check out every option first, since it is our own money on the table. Then we make well-informed decisions. Good ones are nimble, but that just means we are well informed, not crazy."

"I stand corrected. What I cannot figure out is, why Lo Cheung would go to all this trouble to mess up my memory and then build this weird trap to kill me, but only if I remember. I mean, why not kill me while he had the chance?"

"That's a rather chilling thing to ask."

"Am I wrong?" Randy countered.

Young Nae thought about it for a moment. "Sounds like karma."

"You mean, what comes around goes around?"

"Not really. That phrase always annoyed me. Karma is the baggage you carry for past sins. If you harm more than you have to, you pick up more karmic baggage, and that can weigh down your soul. For a magician like Lo Cheung, that can mean the difference between success and failure. He has to match the damage he does to his actual need — or he ends up harming himself."

"Sounds like pretty subtle stuff for a thug who mows down innocent women with trucks," Randy sneered.

"That's all I've got. I have no idea how this guy's mind works. All I know is he is ruthless."

"According to this formula you gave, he won't kill me unless I become a big enough threat that killing me becomes necessary. What did I see, that if I remember it, I become worth killing?"

"Beats me. Does he know that you know of him? Have you learned anything sensitive about him?"

"What do you know of his motives? You said you can't go to the police until you have him dead to rights. I imagine you've got private investigators working on the case."

"Oh yes. I even have a couple of people working inside his organization trying to get dirt on him."

Randolph brightened at this. "Well, there you go. Is there anything I can do to help any of these people?"

"Oh, no. I couldn't afford the chance of accidentally blowing someone's cover. No, they have to stay well below the radar."

"How can I help? Think of something."

"First of all, I will put you under closer surveillance. If Cheung makes a move, we'll see him coming. I mean, if you want to play bait, then we don't have to set much of a trap. He knows you're here, and he will soon know that you've foiled his heart stopping Chi thing."

"That's true." Randolph thought for a moment. "He must know I'm working with Sanantha to uncover my memories, which is exactly what he wants to stop."

The cook brought over their food. Randy's was a bowl of cellophane rice noodles with vegetables and meat floating in broth, while Young Nae's was a plate of dumplings and lumpia.

"Then we're on the right track." Young Nae nodded as he picked up a piece. "Please let me know whatever you remember. It could be huge in our case against Lo Cheung. I'll put someone on your tail starting right away. You won't know they're there, so just go about your daily routines."

"They're that invisible?"

"That's why I pay them as much as I do."

"That's good." Randolph scooped up some of the noodles with chopsticks and tried a bite. "Spicy," he commented. "Lots of garlic."

"You like it?"

"Yeah, it's good. Not what I expected. Thanks." He paused to collect his thoughts. "Look, I've got to ask you something. I've been having a hard time trying to think of how to bring this up, so I'm just going to spit it out. I'm still having the nightmares. In fact, they're getting worse. Sanantha says not to read too much into them, but I can't shake the feeling that these nightmares are telling me I'm somehow responsible for Desiree's condition."

Young Nae leaned forward. "How? What do you think you did?"

"Well, that's what I'm asking you. I was drunk off my nut for four months. You may not have been around all the time, but you had your wits about you. Did I do anything during that time that would leave me feeling guilty about Desiree's coma?"

Young shook his head slowly side to side. "No. Nothing. I don't see how you could be held be to blame for anything."

"Really?"

"Yeah. I think you've got to go with your shrink's advice on this one. Dreams are just dreams."

Randolph shifted uncomfortably in his cheap diner chair. "Really? That doesn't sound right coming from you."

"How do you mean?"

"On the one hand I'm relieved to hear you say I didn't do anything to cause Desiree harm, but I thought you put big stake in dream images. You've told me you have religious visions. Some of those led to our success with Cyto."

Young Nae smiled and nodded. "True enough, but my visions from Haneulnim don't come as nightmares about people in my life. They only come after a lot of meditation and making myself ready to receive them. By the way, I haven't had a vision in years."

"Well I'm glad you had them when you did. We had some real luck following those connections, and I don't just mean getting a cool company logo."

"I was proud to adapt the Cheondogyo flag."

"It doesn't hurt that it looks like hands cupped around a cell. Do you still practice the Heavenly Way?"

"It has always been a great comfort to me, knowing that God lives inside of us. I admit I haven't been to temple in a long time. I'm just too busy."

"I haven't been to church in years, not since Dez was in grade school. I have to tell you, though, I've been thinking a lot about prayer since this all went down."

Young Nae frowned. "It kills me to see you suffer like this. I sure hope Dr. Mauwad can help."

"That's what I'm in town for."

"Speaking of in town, I want you to know where I am. I'm going to be out of touch for a couple more days. I've got this conference I'm presenting at, and I'm just staying at the hotel. You can reach me on the cell. Please do if you need me this time."

"Yes, I will. Hopefully I won't need to." In between bites, he commented off-hand. "A couple of days, eh? You sure put in the hours."

"It's what I do. You put in hours in the lab. I put in hours in meetings."

"Do you have a social life? I mean, in the last week, I haven't seen you meet with or even talk to any friends. Let alone a girlfriend."

"No, at this point in my life I don't really have time for any of that. I sure as hell don't have time for a girlfriend."

"Yeah, multimillion-dollar company, and all. You've got to have people under you that you can trust to run things once in a while?" he ventured.

"I've got a few lieutenants, but nobody that I would trust with anything strategic."

"That's got to be a lot of pressure on you. We've been spending all this time focused on my problems. How are you holding up? I don't think I've seen you take a drink or smoke a cigarette. What is that you're drinking, tea? How do you blow off steam?"

"Oh no, I don't put anything like that in my body. I need my health to be able to stay focused. Living pure is a religious conviction for me. It's all I can do to not drink too much coffee. And this tea?" he said holding up the bottle. "I know the guy that bottles it. Ginseng green tea, full of antioxidants. You should try some."

"What do you do for scheduled down time?"

Young Nae leaned back in his creaking chair and thought for a moment. "What do I do to blow off steam? I work out a lot. You see, I don't see my work as stress. I love what I do."

"Tell you what. When you get back from this conference, let's you and me go do something for an afternoon just to take a break and catch up. What about a round of golf? I'm sure they've got golf here in Malaysia. We used to love playing golf, back in the day."

"We did. My current passion is spear fishing. I could take you out on my boat."

"That's like hunting, just underwater?" He nodded to himself. "I could get into that. I don't know how to use scuba gear."

"I can teach you. I've got all the gear you'll need." Young Nae laughed. "On the other hand, we will have to rent a giant wet suit for those long legs of yours."

11

S ANANTHA TOOK A COUPLE OF DEEP BREATHS to calm herself as she walked from the parking garage to her apartment building. Traffic in downtown Kuala Lumpur had been even crazier this afternoon than usual, and she was still rattled from the collision she barely escaped. She couldn't help but replay the accident in her mind.

Malaysian drivers love to crowd together in traffic. It moves everyone faster and actually cuts down on the time across town. It also makes for a lot more accidents, usually fender benders as cars bounce off one another in the high-speed jostling.

A truck had moved right into her and she jumped lanes to escape. The driver on the other side of her saw her move and thought he would jump ahead by taking what he thought was her vacated spot. The collision was literally an arm's length away, with the sound of crunching, scraping metal deafening as she veered away. She couldn't look back for fear of the ever-present motor scooters that must have been swept up in the crash.

This wasn't even rush hour. Clearly she needed to start using her horn more, a practice she felt was just rude, however commonplace.

In the midst of her ruminations, she only barely noticed the man walking up behind her. When he was a half-dozen steps behind her, she slipped her hand into her purse and found the can of mace, then turned her head just to be sure he wasn't following her. He was a non-descript Asian man in his twenties, and he was looking right at her. More to her surprise, he called her by name.

"Doctor Sanantha Mauwad?"

She stopped and let him catch up. "Yes?"

He held up an envelope right in front of her and held it there. She looked at it and then back at him.

"You might as well take it. You've been served."

"Served?" she asked incredulously. "As in a Summons?" She took the envelope. "By whom and for what?"

The man turned and walked briskly away from her. "Have a nice day, ma'am."

She glared at his retreating back and muttered, "Hardly." She opened the envelope and took out the papers.

Malaysia
Ministry of Customs and Immigration
Notice of Investigation

Dear Dr. Mauwad:

This letter is to inform you that your Foreign Employment Permit No. R48756 has been suspended pending investigation. You are hereby ordered to respond in person to Hearing Room A at the main office of the Ministry of Customs and Immigration on Tuesday, July 13, at 8:00am. Be advised to bring whatever documentation to the hearing to support your position. Until the date of this hearing, you may continue your employment, but pending the outcome of this hearing, you are forbidden from leaving Malaysia.

The address and directions to the Ministry offices are as
follows …

"What the hell?" She read it again, in case she had skipped over
the reason for the investigation. No, it didn't say. Should she call an
attorney? How was she supposed to know what supporting
documentation to bring if she didn't know why her visa was being
suspended? "*Merde!*" she blurted with a stomp of her foot.

She checked her watch: 3:35. She could just make it to their
offices. She turned around and walked briskly back to her car.

Twenty minutes to drive across town, ten minutes to find a
parking place, thirty minutes waiting in line, and finally she got to the
intake window.

"Hi. I am Sanantha Mauwad, and I was just served with this notice
that my work visa is being suspended pending an investigation." She
handed the letter to the large Samoan young man sitting behind the
counter. His creased light green uniform reminded her uncomfortably
of how marshal law, with all its unforgiving rules, was the law of the land.
She noted how his wide face was made to look even bigger by his very
short hair and the tiny, thin moustache he sported. "You have to appear
on the date on the letter," he said in a hearty baritone.

"I understand, and I will come to the hearing. Can you tell me
why my visa is being reviewed?"

"It doesn't say. You have to come in."

Sanantha smiled as politely as she could muster. "I know it
doesn't say. I was hoping you might have some record of why my visa
was pulled."

"We don't have case files here."

"Well then, can you tell me what I should bring? The letter says I
need to bring all my supporting documentation. I don't know what it
is I am arguing against."

"You have no idea why you got this notice?"

"It was a complete surprise to me."

"How long have you been working in Malaysia?"

"About eight months. I'm not up to renew it until one year. Is that
right?"

"They're usually good for a year."

"Do you see a lot of these? Is there a typical reason for hearings like this?"

"Could be anything," the clerk deadpanned.

Sanantha looked at him for a moment, searching for any sign that he knew anything or could be of any help, but saw nothing in his small, dark eyes. "What's this about my not being allowed to leave the country?"

"That's what it says." He handed the letter back to her.

"Is that typical of these investigations?"

He shrugged his massive shoulders.

"Should I hire a lawyer? If the government thinks I am a flight risk for whatever they are investigating, then does that mean I am in some kind of trouble?"

"You should come to the hearing."

"The hearing is two weeks away," she said with gravity. She got no reaction from the clerk.

"Do people usually bring lawyers to these hearings?"

"Sometimes."

"Can you tell who will be conducting the hearing?"

"Probably one of the Deputy Inspector Generals."

"Charges can be brought at these hearings?"

"If you've broken the law."

Sanantha shook her head as she spoke. "But … you can't tell me if they think I've broken a law."

The young man shook his head in unison with her. "No ma'am, I cannot."

She pursed her ample lips and raised her eyebrows. "All right then. Thanks a lot. You've been a big help." She turned to go.

"You're welcome. Glad to be of service."

She hesitated without turning back to face him. She took a breath, then continued out of the office.

After fifty rupia for an hour of parking, and forty-five minutes of rush hour traffic later, she arrived back at her parking garage. All she could think about was how good a cold glass of white wine would taste.

Three steps inside her front door, she dropped her large, black, bucket-like Coach purse by the couch and headed for the kitchen. She caught a flash of green out of the corner of her eye which propelled her into adrenaline focus. A thin green snake with brown markings had struck out from under the couch and sunk its fangs into the leather of her purse. She leapt back and sucked in a terrified gulp of air. The snake immediately pulled back under the couch. It moved alarmingly fast. Unfortunately, Sanantha was now in the dining area and couldn't see around the couch to tell if the snake had stayed under or moved out into the living room.

She knew from childhood experience in Haiti not to underestimate the speed of poisonous snakes. She also remembered to fight the panic, keep her cool, and use whatever resources she had at hand. She had a hard time getting past her pounding heart and shaking hands to pull herself together.

She considered just leaving and calling an exterminator. The government was already investigating her. Could she afford being drawn into a criminal investigation now that someone was clearly trying to kill her? She didn't have much time to decide between the unknown quantity of the police or the known quantity of the snake.

She ran into the kitchen and pulled a sponge mop and a broom out of the small broom closet. She then approached the back of the couch sweeping the broom enticingly along the edge where the snake had struck. As she prepared to bring the sponge mop down to pin its neck, the snake flashed around the end of the couch and came straight at her.

"*Mon dieu!*"

She leapt up over the back of the couch and stood on the cushions looking down over the back. The three-and-a-half-foot long snake reared up in pursuit but wavered, unable to make the vertical climb. Sanantha swung the sponge mop head round and swatted the snake as hard as she could into the dining room. "You're not putting me on the defensive," she said through clenched teeth.

She chased the snake around the corner, her two long weapons ready out in front of her. The snake wasn't in the dining room. There was nothing for it to hide under, so it had either gone into the kitchen or down the hall into the bedroom. She really hoped it hadn't gone down the hall, because that meant way too many hiding places. She advanced on the kitchen. As soon as she peaked around the counter, the snake hurled itself at her. She jumped back out of the way, and it raced past her and down the hall.

"*Merde.*"

She didn't want to give it time to find a good hiding place, so she chased after it. Thankfully it had gone into the small office and not her bedroom — fewer things to hide under.

She considered closing the door and giving it a few minutes to calm down. She knew snakes like this one could go from calm to killer in an instant. She respected the snake and wanted to do right by it. After all, her Voodou gods often appeared as snakes. On the other hand, no amount of respect was going to dissuade its interest in killing her.

The space under the standing bookshelf was too low for such a muscular creature. That left the computer desk. It was long enough that she could guess wrong on which end it was under. She poked at the carpet in front of the desk with the broom while holding the sponge mop up in her fist at the ready. She waited and prodded and waited what seemed too long.

Finally, she heard a loud, cat-like hiss under the far end of the desk. She dragged the broom slowly and noisily against the carpet in front of where the sound had come. It struck! She slammed the mop head down across its neck and held it to the floor. It hissed furiously and its thin, muscular body squirmed with all its might. Sanantha dropped the broom and leaned her weight onto the mop handle, determined not to let it wriggle free. The mop sponge was about five inches behind its head, so it still had room to twist around and try to bite the block of sponge that pinned it.

Sanantha stepped down on the exposed neck space, clamping its head to the floor with her shoe. She dropped the mop and bent down to grab its flailing body with one hand. She could feel its sinewy muscles squirming under its beaded skin. She slipped her other hand down next to her shoe and wrapped her fingers around its throat, right up against the snake's head. When she thought she had a good firm grip, she lifted her foot and picked the creature up. It fought mightily, lashing at her with its tail, but she had it.

She got her first good look at it. It was quite beautiful, and camouflaged perfectly for a leafy jungle floor, with oval brown and green spots on a light green background.

She spoke calmly to it as she walked to her bedroom. "I am really sorry you got dragged into this situation, Monsieur Serpent. I wish there was another way you and I could end this conflict. Whoever brought you here has forced me to consider ending your life. It is your nature to want to kill me now, and I just can't have that."

The dark wooden cabinet looked like a tall freestanding jewelry case. She reached down with the tail-end hand and flipped open the latch. The front doors swung open to reveal a collection of stone figurines at the bottom of the black-painted interior, surrounding a central wooden pole that ran its full height. The pole was painted with two intertwining snakes, one black and one white. The base of the pole was mounted in a hole in a stone block at the bottom of the case. The figurines were arranged on this altar stone. Standing among the figurines was a bundle of fragrant white incense and a bottle of rum.

Sanantha knelt down in front of the altar and held the snake aloft. She lowered her head and prayed. "Madame Erzulie, Grand Lady of Mercy, I apologize for not lighting any incense or pouring you any drink. As you can see, my hands are rather busy. If the earnestness of my voice can convince you to hear my entreaty, please grant me my prayer. Grand Matrisse, I cannot tell anyone this snake was left here for me. It is one of your servants, so I come to you for guidance. If there is any way to save this unfortunate creature, please inspire me. If there is no other way, then please forgive me."

She remained still for a moment, holding the snake as securely as she could, waiting for a sign. It wrapped its muscular tail tighter around her arm and jerked with all its might, hissing angrily, fangs extended. She held on, letting her soul open piously to any message that would give her a better option.

None came.

"Then, in Your holy name," she declared sadly, "I will hold whoever brought this innocent here accountable for its life."

She was thankful that she had remembered to put her cleaver back in the knife block on the kitchen counter where it was within easy reach.

12

"WHY DIDN'T YOU JUST LEAVE THE HOUSE?" Simon was horrified after Sanantha told him what had happened. He held both her hands in his as they sat facing each other on his couch. She had come over without first telling him what had just happened. "You could always call somebody to come capture the snake. It's not like you have pets or children that needed defending."

She smiled warmly at his concern. "I know how to deal with snakes. Remember, I grew up in a jungle full of snakes."

"And you killed it?"

"Believe me, I didn't want to. I couldn't think of any other way to dispose of it. I even asked Madame Erzulie for inspiration, but she didn't give me any."

Simon gave her a puzzled look.

"It's the same as you Catholics asking the Virgin Mary for strength. I couldn't call the police or anyone else without starting an investigation into my attempted murder. I had just found out the government is investigating me for deportation. I can't afford to draw any more government attention onto myself."

"Deportation?"

Yeah, my work visa is being reviewed. I've got a hearing in two weeks. I went down there this afternoon and they couldn't tell me anything. Just more stress to my day."

"You're not going to tell the police that someone tried to kill you?"

"No, and neither are you. Especially when I have a really good idea who it was, and that person is apparently above the law."

"Really? Oh, you mean Lo Cheung?"

"Absolutely. Remember, this guy has been out to ruin Young Nae for years. We think he killed Randolph's wife and put his daughter in a coma, with a poisonous snake."

"I remember what Dr. Macklin said at the hospital. Why would he come after you?"

"Randolph is still too confused to make any real connections that could implicate Lo. I have been poking around asking questions, so I am a threat."

Simon thought for a moment what this all meant. "Well, if this guy is so powerful, what can you do about it?"

"I want to meet him."

He looked at her with one gray eyebrow raised, hoping to see that she was joking. She wasn't. "You do realize that however brave you are, such a meeting could lead to your death and disappearance."

"Only if he is responsible. Besides, I have you to tell the police if I disappear. I imagine the police would love to have real evidence against such a notorious figure."

"This is your patient's mess. Is it worth your life?"

"No, it isn't. The truth is, if someone is out to kill me, I don't want to die in my sleep one night not knowing who did it. The Russell's Viper in my apartment means I don't get to just stay on the sidelines anymore."

Simon took a deep breath and let it out slowly. "I guess not."

"So," she said matter of factly. "Can you get me an introduction?"

His eyebrow shot back up again. "Because his son is my patient?"

"Do you think that violates some ethical concern?"

"Ethics be damned," he laughed nervously. "I'm just wondering if my connection is strong enough to get you in."

Her face broke into her broadest, most dimpled grin and she threw her arms around his neck.

•   •   •

Sanantha sat on the park bench in the noontime sun and wished she had agreed to a shadier spot. She was certainly familiar with heat and humidity from her life in the Caribbean. The tropical sun could be brutal on any continent. *Gotta love the tropics*, she thought. Even in the rainy season, the moment the clouds break the sun comes roaring down. She was glad she had thought to put her hair up in a white turban. Her loose white cotton dress helped too.

She pushed down her oversized dark sunglasses and checked her watch: **11:58**. She had been pondering all morning how she would start this conversation. How do you ask a man if he is trying to kill you while not accusing him if he is not? She pushed her glasses back up. She wished she could remember more from the Criminal Mind class she had taken twenty years ago in Med School.

In that moment of quiet anticipation, she realized she had gotten herself into another tangled web of men jockeying for power and hiding secrets. She came to Malaysia to recover from Charles, Joseph, and Silas. Now she was back in it again up to her elbows with Randolph, Young Nae, and Lo Cheung. What was it with these men? What was it with her?

She returned to watching the road that wound through the park. She didn't know that many quiet and public places. Most public places in the K-L metro area were far from quiet. Even this spot wasn't actually quiet. The buzz of traffic and honking horns blanketed the city. The stench of exhaust was also inescapable. She had picked this spot hoping easy access would appeal to the busy businessman. It was also visible from many tall buildings around the park.

She was surprised when the group of three Asian men who were jogging on the park path slowed and walked up to her. The man in front had graying hair and shoulders that seemed a bit too broad for his five-foot three height. The two men behind him were much younger and taller, and clearly there to protect the older man. They were all dressed in expensive looking jogging suits with the distinctive YSL logo on the breast. The short leader was wearing ridiculous gold-framed sunglasses with big square yellow lenses.

Yellow sunglasses. She put the creepy coincidence out of her mind. She stood up, but let Lo Cheung speak first.

"Doctor Mauwad, I presume," he said extending his hand.

She shook it perfunctorily. "You must be Mr. Lo. Thank you for agreeing to meet me on such short notice."

He bowed his head slightly. "Not at all. I welcome the opportunity to clear up what I think has become quite the misunderstanding between us."

She blinked involuntarily behind her own large, dark sunglasses.

"May we walk while we talk? I've got my heart rate up and I want to bring it down slowly."

Sanantha looked around to see if there were others in the park who would see them walking, and there were. "Sure. I brought comfortable shoes. You think you know why I wanted to see you?"

He smiled boyishly. "I have spies everywhere. That is what you would expect from a shady character such as myself, yes?"

She tried to play along, but wasn't sure what he was driving at. "I didn't say that."

"I know I have a reputation. I also know you have been treating a good friend of Young Nae Yoon. I am quite sure Mr. Young has told you some colorful things about me."

As she walked along beside him, she stayed aware of whether there were witnesses. She hoped her big glasses hid her looking around. She also gauged how close his bodyguards were and which way she should jump if they tried to grab her. "Well, Mr. Young is not my client, so I do not have a duty to him of confidentiality. Aside from what he may have told me, I need to ask you something a bit more directly."

She waited until he met her gaze. She did not like being confronted with those gaudy, gold-rimmed yellow sunglasses.

"Did you try to kill me last night by setting a poisonous snake loose in my apartment?"

He stopped walking, blinked involuntarily, and locked his face in a blank stare. Then the corner of his mouth creased into a tiny grin. "My goodness! You are direct, aren't you?" He took a deep breath and chuckled. Then he took another breath and blew it out noisily. He looked her straight in the eye and said flatly, "No. Not my style." Then he cocked an eyebrow at her, and added, "That was very brave of you, especially if you had thought I did it."

All the while, Sanantha did her best to show no emotion on her face. Again, she was glad to hide her eyes behind her big, dark glasses. "I will admit, it would make me a lot less nervous if I believed you. You mentioned the 'colorful' things Mr. Young has said about you. He says this is exactly your style. He says you have killed with snakes before, recently."

Lo Cheung shook his head slowly and started to walk again. "You are, of course, talking about Mrs. Macklin and her daughter. When Young Nae originally accused me of those crimes, I not only cooperated with the police, but I assisted with their investigation. You see, I have an extensive information gathering organization. I trade commodities, and I need to know whom I am dealing with at all times. The police had a hard time finding any personal records on several suspects, and I supplied them with what they needed. Unfortunately, we eliminated all the suspects and were left with no one to arrest. Whoever killed Cheri Macklin did it without leaving a single shred of evidence. Then, as if to rub our noses in our failure, he did it again to Desiree."

"Doesn't that strike you as implausible? The case isn't closed, I hope."

"I believe the police have stopped investigating. Any new evidence would of course reopen it. Maybe you are the new set of eyes we need to see what everyone else missed."

She raised an eyebrow and looked over the tops of her sunglasses at him.

"I'm not trying to flatter you, Doctor. I appreciate you still have no reason to trust me. I agree with you. We must have missed something."

"I'm not a criminologist, but I like to think I understand why people do what they do. Snakes are used in cultures all over the world to invoke the power of nature, either for faith healing or to instill fear in people. Has Young Nae made enemies with anyone who would call on the supernatural?"

"Malaysia has a long history of folk magic. Indeed, snakes are a big part of it. The police found no evidence of sorcery either."

"We do have evidence of Silat Seni Gayong being used on Randolph Macklin."

"Let me guess. Young Nae has told you I dabble in Silat black magic?" He pursed his lips and shook his head as if he had tasted something bad. "My love is Kung Fu. That *dim mak* sorcery is not remotely similar. My interests are a matter of public record. I have been sponsoring Kung Fu schools here and elsewhere in Asia for twenty-five years."

Lo was clearly eccentric. More than that, though, something about his demeanor just wasn't sitting right with her. "Kung Fu? Are you Falon Gong?"

He looked down and shook his head. "Li Hongzhi's followers are political. I wish them luck fighting the communists, but I'm old school Shoalin."

"If what you say is true, and you are this upstanding member of the community, then why has Young Nae singled you out as such a villain? You don't deny you are his business rival."

"That is true. I am his rival, on many fronts. He is in fact far more ruthless than I, especially in business. I don't know why he blames me for his misfortunes. Maybe he thinks I am an easy target. Doing so wastes a lot of time he could spend pursuing the actual criminals who have caused him harm. I have wondered about this myself, and the only guess I can venture is he needs someone to blame since he doesn't have a family to build him spiritually."

"Spiritually?"

"Now I'm having a translation problem. Of the soul. Of the feelings."

"You mean emotional support? I thought Asians held family connections very closely, especially Koreans."

"You have done your homework," Cheung commented wryly with a point of his finger. "Normally Koreans are very close to their families. Not Young Nae. He is the lone wolf. He was severed from his family when he refused to cancel a business meeting to attend his grandfather's funeral. That was fourteen years ago. He's had a lot of time to grow strong on his own."

She couldn't pin down what was bugging her about him. "You speak of him almost as if you admire him."

"Only the way you would admire one of these poisonous snakes. He has achieved things that I wonder at. He has become adept at getting the Malaysian government to let him violate zoning and pollution laws and the rights of his factory workers in the name of economic development. If there was any motive for it, I wouldn't be surprised if it was Young Nae who got your work Visa pulled."

Now it was Sanantha's turn to blink involuntarily. She hoped her sunglasses hid her reaction.

Lo Cheung paused at her silence. "I did my homework too. My point is, he seems to have come to believe he has the right to seize whatever he can. I'm not sure my amazement at his ruthlessness counts as admiration."

"Well, you've certainly given me a lot to think about." Why did he irritate her so?

"You are not convinced I'm not the bad guy in this whole affair. You spoke of motives. Other than my business competition with Mr. Young, he means nothing to me. Neither do any of his family or associates, including you. What possible motive would I have for harming you? Or Dr. Macklin's wife, or daughter, or Dr. Macklin himself? If I wanted to destroy Young Nae Yoon, I would do it on the field of commerce. Look to your learning of people's beliefs, Doctor. Would a devout Buddhist practitioner of Kung Fu be so dishonorable as to assassinate the close associates of a rival when so much more could be gained by conquest on the open battlefield?"

By now, they had walked around the park path and had returned to the bench where they had started.

It was those glasses. Those gaudy, flashy, gold rimmed glasses. "Then my question to you, Mister Lo, is if I don't matter to you, why did you meet me today, and why spend your time trying to convince me that you are not, as you said, the bad guy?"

Cheung smiled at her. "If I might be so bold as to quote the Buddha, 'Your work is to discover your world and then with all your heart give yourself to it.' I met with you because I wasn't joking when I said you might be the one to solve these murders. If you do, that will clear my name once and for all."

Sanantha stopped walking. "You're going to think I'm a nut, but can I ask you a personal question?"

"Sure, you can ask."

"Would you please take off those glasses for me?"

He grinned. "I will if you will."

She caught herself. "Oh, of course."

They did, and she was relieved to see that he had normal dark brown Asian eyes. "Thank you. Just a personal foible of mine."

"That's all right. If looking me in the eye can convince you, then I am happy to oblige."

"Like I said, you've given me a lot to think about." She extended her hand and shook his. "Thank you."

13

"MY GOODNESS," SANANTHA SIGHED as she and Randolph settled into the facing armchairs in her office. "So much has happened since we had a regular session. I feel like we're here to compare notes as much as check in with how you are doing emotionally."

"You have become my detective as much as my psychiatrist."

He was right, and she wasn't happy about that. "I don't want to lose sight of how your emotional health really remains my primary concern. How do you think you're handling all of what has happened?"

Randy thought about it for a moment. "Remarkably well, considering. Finding out my family and I are swept up in a war between Young Nae and his enemy was depressing. Finding out my body has been booby-trapped was just terrifying. Don't get me wrong, I do not feel like quitting. I'm pretty mad about it. I feel like fighting. I guess that's a good sign."

She jotted down, 'fighting' on the notepad in her lap. "It is. That's a healthy reaction, and I am pleased to hear it. You're still facing a lot of unknowns and a lot of things that are out of your control. It's really important that you let me know if it all becomes too much to handle."

"So far, so good. Of course, I might just be too busy to let any of this hit me. I tend to do that."

"Do you think you get busy as a way of not having to think about your feelings?"

"Well, yes. I've been told that I get very clinical and objective about things, and I don't let myself get involved emotionally. I've had people tell me I can be cold that way."

'Cold', she wrote. "Does that bother you?"

"I don't think of myself as cold. I mean, I've got feelings like anyone else. Saying I'm cold says that I don't have feelings, and that's not true. Do you think I'm cold?"

"It's not unusual for busy people to lose track of how they appear to others. If you are concerned that people see you as emotionally uninvested, then you can always share your feelings more with them."

"Isn't the 'sharing' talk reserved for couples therapy?"

"No. You can share with anyone you feel like sharing with. Did you and Cheri have couples therapy?"

He took a deep breath, which Sanantha took to mean he was disappointed for having let that out. "Yes, we did. It was probably five years ago. Dez was a teenager, and Cheri was traveling a lot, and things kind of spun out of control."

"Did the sessions help?"

"They did. We both got some tools to work with, and we did talk more effectively after that." He paused. "And yes, I was told to share my feelings more."

"I'm glad the work did some good. To answer your question, no, I don't see you as a cold person." She laughed. "Of course, with what we've been through these last few days, I think I've seen more of your emotions than a normal life situation would present."

"What, you don't have lots of patients who have graphic nightmares and memory flashes that trigger heart attacks in the middle of the night?"

Sanantha didn't let herself reflect on the answer she could give that question. She smiled to cover and put down her pencil. "You mentioned at the hospital that you had remembered some images. You said they were fleeting and didn't make sense."

"That's right. That's why it wasn't a surprise when Doctor Ho found that the heart attack trap was linked to my memory."

"Have you been able to make sense of those memories, or recall any more details?" She caught herself. "Of course, this is assuming thinking about it won't set off another heart attack."

"No, I've thought about it a lot and thinking about it doesn't seem to trip anything further. It's two disconnected images. One is Cheri lying on a hospital bed. Now, how can I remember seeing her on a hospital bed? She had already died in a flaming car crash by the time I came to Malaysia. So I don't know what that means.

"The other image is me making some kind of recombinant library out of the DNA in Desiree's blood."

"Excuse me. What's that?"

"Sorry. That's what I call the patches I make from a set of DNA, usually to fix a flaw in other DNA. Each virus can only carry so much genetic patch material. To work a big change, you need several viruses working in unison, a library. Again, it makes no sense. Who would I have been trying to cure using Desiree's DNA as a master version? All I can figure is the images are somehow spun off the dream I had just before I got the flashes."

"You had another of the nightmares, before you recovered the memories?"

"Oh, yeah. Really disturbing. It also makes no sense. Cheri is dead, and Desiree is there eating moldy bread. She hands me the bread and it turns into a knife, and she impales herself on it. The blood splatters on Cheri's body and she revives."

As she had before, Sanantha employed her best clinical unaffected face upon hearing the details of Randy's dream.

"I've seen that look before," Randy observed. "Yeah. More of my sick mind's explorations."

"Explorations is the right term," she explained. "The content of dreams rarely means anything. Dreams do tell us if the mind is trying to work out unsettled business."

"Well, I thought about this dream a lot. It really shook me up. The bread mold bothered me more than it should have. Then I remembered that we get penicillin from bread mold. Cheri was deathly allergic to penicillin, and Desiree was not. It seems my mind just threw in some odd medical knowledge on top of everything else."

"Let me ask you something, and I want you to think about it for a minute before you answer. Do you normally dream about things and people in your life? Or are your dreams populated with people and situations that you know in the dream, but that are not actually in your real life?"

Randy brightened at the question. "I actually have thought about this. Cheri and I used to talk about it. I tend to dream about things that have nothing to do with my real life. Like you said, I know all these people in the dream, but not when I wake up. Cheri used to have these elaborate dreams about exactly the people and places in her actual life. I used to think that was really strange. She used to think my dreams were really strange."

"These nightmares are about your wife and daughter. Are there folks in these nightmares that you don't know in real life?"

He thought about it. "No. The situations are outrageous, but the people are Cheri and Dez, and I'm me — which is also new. In my normal dreams, I am usually somebody else. What does that mean?"

"I don't know. Not yet, at least. That's something we'll work on. Have you had any other glimpses of memory?"

"Yeah, now that I think about it, while I was fading in and out after the heart attack, I caught a flash of Young Nae injecting something into my arm. Unfortunately, it was just a flash, with no context. I don't know when it happened, or why he was doing it, or even if it happened at all."

"All right. We'll just add it to the total mix of information we have."

She chewed on her bottom lip trying to decide how best to broach the next subject. She saw him pick up on this. "I'm glad you're handling all of this as well as you are, because the situation has gotten even more complicated. You were joking that I have become your detective. Well, I've actually been drawn into the whole affair myself. Three days ago, someone put a Russell's Viper in my apartment. I caught it and killed it. Someone was clearly trying to kill me."

Randy sat up in his chair and his mouth dropped open. "Lo Cheung?"

"That's what I thought too. Therefore I arranged to meet him."

"Wow," he laughed nervously. "You're just full of surprises! How did that go?"

"It was very interesting. He completely denies having anything to do with Cheri's death, Desiree's coma, your missing memories, or my snake attack. In fact, he says he has helped the police in their investigations all along. He said he sees Young Nae as ruthless and dangerous. There's no love lost between the two of them. Most interestingly, he said he hopes I will be the outsider who can finally solve the whole mystery. I'm usually a pretty good judge of character. He is certainly a colorful character, but I'm not sure he's the evil mastermind Young Nae has described."

"Lo Cheung says someone else is to blame, a third party? Who could that be?"

"I don't know. He doesn't know. They would have to be utterly evil and completely invisible. Which is why I don't believe him."

14

ISHI SHIMATO HAD ARRIVED HALF AN HOUR EARLY to give himself time to go over the numbers his accountants had emailed him that morning. Sitting alone in the drab gray and tan hotel business center conference room, he had lost track of time. The sound of rain outside and the smell of damp added to the timelessness of the room. He had expected his partner Hideo Yamaguchi also to arrive before their scheduled appointment. In fact, he was counting on Hideo's arrival as his cue to look up from the spreadsheets on his laptop.

Ishi was quite surprised to have his concentration interrupted by the cheery voice of Young Nae Yoon. "Mr. Shimato! Thank you for coming all the way to my turf here in K-L." Young Nae walked into the room and reached over the table to shake his hand.

Ishi got up to meet his gesture, and then felt compelled to follow the shake with a small bow. "Mr. Young. It was the least we could do, especially after our last meeting ended so poorly. I apologize again for leaving prematurely. I still don't know what came over me."

He glanced down at his open laptop screen and took note that it was 2:05. "I also apologize for Hideo being late today."

Young Nae took one of the eight seats around the table, the one at the head, and leaned back into it. "Well," he started with a chuckle, "if you are done apologizing, we can talk business. When we met in Singapore, I did not know that Hideo had not completely briefed you on our discussion of a merger. I assume you two have talked it over since then?"

"Yes, we have. I have all the numbers here."

"I'm sure you do. What matters now is whether you want to do this. Hideo has made it clear that he does."

"Are you interested, in principle, with moving ahead?"

"In principle. If you are going to stay on as President for me, I need to know your heart is in it."

Ishi glanced again at the clock on his open laptop. Where was Hideo? He wasn't prepared to discuss this on his own. He certainly wasn't ready to talk about how he personally felt about it. "Well, Hideo and I built Clearwater Distribution up from seed capital, so I very much want to do what will make the company prosper."

Young Nae sat up and leaned forward, putting an elbow on the light brown wood table. "I know that your wife's uncle gave you half the money to start this business. You've paid Lo Cheung back a dozen fold over the years. This company is yours, with Hideo. This way you get to still run it, and you get a windfall of cash for your half of the ownership, which you can invest as you please. What's the downside? Hideo sees the logic."

"Hideo has his own reasons for wanting the liquidity. My situation is different. He isn't trying to preserve a legacy."

"A legacy? Don't you think your family will be better off liquid?"

"Forgive me for being so blunt, but you have forced the issue. I feel I must make my position very clear. I am part of a larger family. At the risk of jeopardizing our business together going forward, and you are one of our biggest customers, I have to say, I don't think I can sell one of my family's businesses under these circumstances."

Young Nae got up and started pacing around the room. "Do you think I want this company because it was started with Lo Cheung's seed money? That was ten years ago — ancient history. You and I are talking access to wealth today."

"I just don't think of it as mine to sell."

Young Nae continued pacing as he walked. "Let's think about this from the numbers. I always feel tough decisions can be made easier with more data. Yours has been a slow growth business. You are diversified enough that fluctuations in the commodity markets have never dragged your business down too far, nor let you spike very high." By now, he was walking all the way around the room. "It is safe to say it is very unlikely you will ever see this company overpriced enough to give you an exit window. Your salary is all you're ever going to see. Your ownership equity is just going to sit, bottled up in the balance sheet."

Ishi turned his swivel chair around unconsciously to track Young Nae's pacing. "That's not the issue."

At this point, Young Nae was right next to Ishi's chair. He leaned over and put his hand on Ishi's shoulder for emphasis. "It should be. This family legacy stuff is blocking you from seeing any benefit from all your hard work."

As Young Nae let his hand fall from his shoulder, he happened to touch Ishi a couple of times on his right arm, once above the elbow, and once above the wrist, before he continued his pacing.

"Sometimes it can be worth self-sacrifice to build something bigger than oneself," Ishi insisted.

"This is a matter of principle? We are getting philosophical?"

Ishi felt a wave of anger that surprised him. "I will not be mocked." He put his hand on his chest, fighting a growing feeling of excitement. "You have quite upset me. I never lose my temper." His breathing became deeper and labored. "I am having a hard time controlling myself. I think we need to end this meeting. We have come to an impasse."

Young Nae took a seat across from Ishi. "You think so?" he asked calmly.

Ishi realized he had mistaken the tightness in his chest for anger. He really was having a hard time breathing. "I am not feeling well. Is there any water in here?"

Young Nae leaned back, relaxed. "I didn't order any."

The pressure in his chest was now undeniable. "I think I am in trouble here. Can you help me?"

Young Nae didn't answer.

Ishi eyes went wide as he suddenly realized this was no coincidence. He remembered getting sick at their last meeting when Young Nae had scolded him. "What have you …" He clutched his chest with both hands as he felt a spasm. "What have you done to me?"

Young Nae calmly looked him square in the eye. "I have secured your family's financial future. Clearwater is registered as a Japanese partnership. Under Japanese partnership law, if one partner is deemed incompetent by two independent doctors, the remaining partners can buy him out as long as they do so for a fair price. Since you and Hideo are equal partners, and I will be paying him just over four million dollars for your company, your family will get a two-million-dollar windfall."

Ishi managed to gasp out the words, "*Kyusho jitsu.*"

"If that's the name you want to use for it," Young Nae toyed with him.

Hideo knocked on the door and stuck his head in as if unsure of himself before entering. "I'm so sorry I am late. I got lost here in the hotel. I had the devil of a time finding someone to help me." He saw Ishi gasping and holding his chest, and Young Nae taking out his cell phone. "What the hell? Ishi, are you all right?"

"Hello. This is Young Nae Yoon in Conference Room 11a. We need an ambulance and a medical team up here right away. Someone is having a heart attack."

Hideo ran to Ishi's side. Ishi was clawing his shirt collar open, trying to catch his breath. Hideo helped him and turned to Young Nae, nearly yelling in his panic. "How long will they be?"

"They said it could be 10 to 15 minutes."

Even as the pain threatened to choke off his thinking, Ishi still noticed how calm Young Nae was. He tried to say something to Hideo, but it only came out as a gasp. Frustration piled on top of fear and he panicked.

"Do you know CPR?" Hideo asked Young Nae.

"No, I don't."

"Shit, neither do I! Hang in there, Ishi."

Ishi grabbed him by the arms and shook him, trying franticly to speak, his eyes bulging out wildly.

"You're freaking out, man. Try to relax. Try to breathe. Shit, I don't know what I'm doing! Do we lay him down, do we keep him upright?"

"I think you're supposed to elevate his feet," Young Nae commented without emotion and without getting up.

Hideo pushed Ishi's chair back from the table, picked up his legs, and swung his feet up onto the table. "Is that any better?" he asked the distressed man.

Ishi was barely holding onto consciousness. His body convulsed as shockwaves of pain ripped through his torso. The last clear image he saw, the last thought he could grasp, before slipping into an unconsciousness from which he would never recover, was the horrifyingly calm expression on Young Nae Yoon's face.

15

RANDOLPH CAME INTO DESIREE'S BEDROOM at the Kuantan beach house, stepped up to the foot of his daughter's bed, and was taken by her color. "Vera," he called the nurse over. "Do you think she is yellow?"

Vera left the plasticware she was washing in the bathroom sink and stepped alongside him. "I guess, yes. Just a little. I'm sorry I hadn't noticed the change."

"Oh, you've got to be more careful with the details. She's counting on us for everything." He stepped up to comatose woman's head. "Being here all the time, you didn't see the subtle change the way I did just walking in here." He opened an eye to reveal a pale but distinct yellow tinge to the white of her blue eye.

Vera looked on from across the bed. "I'm very sorry, Doctor. Shall I have Dr. Kwon come over?"

Randy considered this for the briefest of moments. "I like Dr. Kwon. He knows his stuff. We can take care of this ourselves. At least on the front end. Let's take a urine sample and a thirty-milliliter blood draw. Then call the lab for a bilirubin level in the urine, and a blood count, a liver function panel, and a check for hepatitis in the blood."

"Yes, doctor." As she set up the syringe, she asked him, "How low would her liver function have to be to show jaundice like this?"

"If this has been building up for a couple of days, then not that bad. If this is sudden, then it could be quite severe. It could be any of a number of benign causes. It could be an infection, a drug reaction, even a gallstone forming. I should have anticipated a bilirubin buildup in a comatose bedridden patient."

He considered what Sanantha had just told him about an alternate cause of the coma. He would have to add jaundice to the list of symptoms in a differential.

He continued giving his orders to the nurse. "Even before the tests come back, I want to induce diarrhea to flush out any toxins her liver has dumped into her intestines. Give her thirty milliliters of lactulose through her feeding tube, three times a day until her stool runs clear. Also, in case this is unconjugated bilirubin, let's get some ultraviolet sun lamps in here to shine on her skin."

Vera smiled. "You mean like a jaundiced baby?"

Randolph smiled back. "Yes, exactly."

"I didn't know that worked on adults," she said unsure of herself.

"Adult jaundice is usually a different kind of toxin that doesn't respond to sunlight. Since we don't know what this is, and I don't want to take any chances, let's get them set up."

Vera smiled again as she worked.

Randolph noticed. "What?"

"She is so lucky to have such a knowledgeable and loving father by her side."

"Thank you." He thought about that for a moment. "I'm glad I'm here for her too."

•　　　•　　　•

When he was satisfied he had done all he could until the test results came back, Randy returned to the beach house. As he walked back through the garden, he recalled his conversation with Sanantha about saying goodbye to Cheri. He remembered what a turning point it had been when he first saw Desiree in the coma. For all of his grieving, it only finally hit him that Cheri was gone when he saw he was alone to take care of Desiree. Working on Desiree's new condition had left him missing Cheri all the more.

Randy walked across the living room to the desk on the far wall, sat down, and opened the laptop. He pulled up the website of his favorite American oldies rock and roll station from back home in D.C., WBIG 100.3. He couldn't understand any of the singers on local radio. Besides, the music was all far too young for his taste. Nothing beat the classics. He was pleased to find them playing Steve Perry singing to and about his once girlfriend Sherrie, reveling in how their love holds on, holds on.

He had to think for a moment to remember his Photobucket login information, and was happy to get it right the first time.

He flipped through folders of pictures collected over the years. Most of the folders were just grouped by date with no real order or preference. He chuckled at the disorganization. Who has time for that?

He found a couple of holiday and vacation sets that brought back the memories he wanted to relive. Many pictures made him smile broadly.

Then he thought how Cheri was gone, and how much he missed her, and the pictures lost their luster. Even the ones that brought him back the most just weren't getting to the itch he felt. He kept looking and looking, but never feeling like he was getting to where he needed to be.

He noticed this and stopped to wonder what he was looking for. He remembered everything in the pictures. He loved thinking about those moments. They were all known. It was as if he needed to find something new.

He exited Photobucket and Googled "Cheri Macklin". He wasn't surprised to find many entries chronicling her long career with the United Nations Educational, Scientific and Cultural Organization. Then, pages down in the listings, he found something he had never seen before.

Someone had YouTubed a video clip of a speech Cheri had given at a UNESCO event. It was in some stereotypical hotel ballroom in Philadelphia some four years before. She was congratulating some committee for raising some large sum of money, and detailing how the money was going to be spent building new infrastructure for some village somewhere.

The film kept halting to download further. As annoying as it was, the wait was definitely worth it.

It wasn't the topic that captured Randy's attention. It was her enthusiasm for the material. The more she talked, the clearer it became how much she loved her work.

He watched in rapt fascination as her eyebrows danced and her head tossed, and her short black hair swung and her hands gestured in the air, and her voice rose and fell with her announcements. He thought back and couldn't recall ever seeing her so wrapped up in something. Happily wrapped up in something. Passionate.

He replayed the clip.

He had gone with her on a few trips abroad for her work, but when they arrived, he had never accompanied her on her work. He had always been very proud of her aptitude and accomplishments, and she had always been happy to share her stories with him. Still, he wasn't a part of her work life. That had never bothered him. Now that he saw a glimpse of what he had been missing, he felt he needed to know more about this other life of hers. What he would give to just sit and chat with someone who knew her day to day.

He wondered if this was therapeutically a good idea. Was digging around in her past going to bring him closer to accepting her being gone? Might this do just the opposite? Wasn't this just another way to obsess about her?

He considered calling Sanantha to discuss it, but decided not to. Doing this research felt right. It felt like he was filling a gap that had been bugging him deep down for a while. If Sanantha told him not to pursue it, that it was bad for his recovery, then he would find himself considering disobeying her. He decided to not make the call. Better to seek forgiveness after the fact than to be turned down asking permission ahead of time.

Sanantha's little field trip into rural Malaysia was supposed to have given him closure for what had happened to Desiree. Of course, it had only raised more questions. This time he would follow his instincts.

He browsed the Internet for UNESCO in Southeast Asia. He knew she came to Malaysia at least once a year, but he didn't know much more. He found the UNESCO headquarters for the whole Pacific basin was in Jakarta, Indonesia, 600 miles south on the island of Java. He read about the mission of the office, for educational, cultural, and natural resources development, and for the advancement of sciences. He found their web pages and dug around until he found the department she worked for: Creating Learning Communities for Children. Randy found the names of the officials who ran the department, but none of them rang any bells. The website didn't have a lot of details about the actual work they did. He felt compelled to see what her life with these people had been like.

He pulled out his cell phone and started calling numbers from the website.

After calling three different numbers, and being transferred four times, Randy started to feel the same kind of frustration he often dealt with back home at Johns Hopkins. Big government bureaucracies and their phone systems. Finally, he got through to the right office.

"You've reached CLCC," came the cheery young woman's voice with a slight singsong Asian accent. "How may I help you?"

"Ah, very good. I am Dr. Randolph Macklin. I understand my wife, Cheri Macklin, used to work there on occasion before she passed away earlier this year."

"Dr. Macklin? Yes, I recall Mrs. Macklin. I am so sorry for your loss."

"That's very kind of you. I was hoping I could speak to someone there who worked with her."

"Is there a problem?"

"No, there's nothing the matter. I just have a few questions I need cleared up, of a personal nature. Is there someone there who knew her well?"

"Please, let me see if the Director is in. Please hold."

Randy laughed to himself. After being shuttled around, he should have expected to be put on hold.

The receptionist came back sooner than he expected. "The Director is away from her desk at the moment. Can I have her return your call?"

He checked back on the website as he spoke. "Would that be Ms. Bodiyami?"

"Yes, Alissa Bodiyami, the National Programme Officer."

"Actually, I am on the Malay peninsula and I was considering a trip over to Jakarta. Could I make an appointment to see her? Say, sometime tomorrow?"

"I know this is a very busy time for her, but I can check her schedule. Please hold."

At least he was getting somewhere.

"She does have a small window open tomorrow afternoon at 2. It is only for half an hour. Are you sure you still want to come all this way?"

"Not a problem. I just need to sit down face to face with someone who worked with her. Even if only for a half an hour."

"I will schedule the meeting. Now, do you know how to get to our office?"

"No, but I've got maps and taxi drivers to help me. I generally don't get lost. Thank you for your help. I didn't catch your name."

"Kalpala."

"Kalpala? Well, thank you very much for your help. I will see you tomorrow afternoon."

"Good-bye, Doctor."

Randy hung up and dialed up Dr. Kwon's office. Desiree's results would be back tomorrow, and he needed to bring her doctor up to speed on what Randy had done so far.

16

R ANDY WISHED HE HAD LET KALPALA give him more precise
directions. The UNESCO headquarters was a campus of several
buildings stretching across two city blocks in downtown Jakarta. It
took Randy most of an hour going from one office to another to
fathom out which office Cheri used to work in. From what he could
see of Jakarta as he walked around, it was older and more run down
than Kuala Lumpur, but also more colorful and varied. He told himself
he would take time to explore once he had accomplished his mission.
It felt like a mission. By the time he found the right office, he knew
more about UNESCO activities than he ever wanted to.

He was also quite stressed. He knew he would not enjoy being in
such a crowded, noisy place, but he was resolved to press on. He took
a moment for some deep breaths to compose himself. He made an
effort to put aside his frustration and anxiety. He wanted to put
forward a friendly face, as he was going to be asking personal
questions.

His composure faltered, though, when he found no one at the reception desk. "Hello?" he called down an open hallway. "Hello?"

The smartly dressed Asian woman who walked briskly back to the desk looked to Randolph to be no more than eighteen. Then again, he had always thought Asian women, Southeast Asian women in particular, looked timelessly young. Her bouncy black bob haircut added to her youthfulness.

"May I help you?"

"Yes, I am Dr. Randolph Macklin. I called yesterday and made an appointment to see Director Bodiyami."

The woman perked up and held out her hand. "Yes! I am Kalpala. Did you have any difficulty finding us?"

As he reached forward to shake her hand, he had to ignore her strong, flowery perfume. "No, not really."

Let me see if Ms. Bodiyami is ready for you." She went back down the hall, and Randolph heard people conversing in what sounded to him like Chinese.

A moment later, Kalpala returned with a middle-aged woman who had much darker skin and a more angular face. "Hello, Dr. Macklin," she greeted him with a lilting Indian accent and an extended hand. "I am Alissa Bodiyami, the National Programme Officer here. I worked very closely with Cheri whenever she was in town."

Her handshake was the kind of firm that comes from meeting a lot of people. Up close, he could see her conservative suit was actually really expensive.

"It is very nice to meet you. I was hoping you might have a few minutes to answer some questions I have about Cheri's work.

Alissa looked at her watch. "I have a meeting in twenty minutes, but we can chat until then. Please come back to my office.

"You're a very busy person."

"I apologize for being so hard to catch. We're behind schedule with our mid-year reports. I have been literally running around to various offices collecting data. When I heard you had called, I had my secretary go through our files to see if Cheri had left anything here that might be of interest to you." She led him into her office, which was not small, but was made crowded by several large flower arrangements on file cabinets around the room. "Please have a seat. I'm glad you called when you did, because we were about to throw these files away." She handed a thick folder of loose papers across the desk to him.

He looked through the papers as she continued.

"This was from two quarters ago, so all the transactions have long since cleared our books. There are some personal receipts in there that might help you piece together how she spent her time here."

He looked up at her. "This is great. Thank you very much. This will be a nice window, like you said."

He noted how when she nodded her head, which she did often, her upswept hairdo did not bounce.

"I had hoped so," she said with a smile.

"She told me stories about the work you folks do, but it was always some funny anecdote or some bit of frustration that she needed to talk through. At her level, fairly high up in the organization, did she ever go out in the field and visit the schools UNESCO has built?"

"Oh yes. Cheri loved to visit the kids in the schools, or meet with the doctors in our sponsored hospitals. It wasn't part of her official responsibilities, but she loved to see the end results of our work. Would you like to see pictures from some of those visits?"

"Oh my goodness, yes. That's really what I was hoping for."

"Well, we've got a bunch of them up in the hall out here." She got up and led Randy down the narrow hallway by her office and around a corner to a larger more public hallway. There on the walls were dozens of pictures of folks in suits and dresses grinning alongside uniformed doctors or policemen or construction workers or surrounded by school children.

Alissa walked Randy down the wall. "Here she is at the opening of a school in rural New Guinea. Here she is at the ground-breaking for a hospital here in Malaysia. Here she is again in Malaysia, this time at a ribbon cutting for some kind of business, I don't recall where that was exactly."

He felt such pride in seeing Cheri this way. Her photo-op grin always struck him as just goofy enough to make him grin too.

Then he noticed the dates on the pictures. "These are all from just this last year?"

"Oh, yes. We rotate them off after a couple of years. We are involved in so many projects. These pictures come in almost every week. We've told our field staff to discourage our officials from sending them in here, but everyone wants their visits commemorated."

"Cheri was here, what, three, four times in the last year?"

"That sounds about right. Does that strike you as odd?"

"I just had no idea. She used to travel a lot. Every month her job would put her on a plane. Usually it was just to New York or one of your European offices. I kind of lost track of how many of her trips were work in the actual field. When was the last time she came in here? Do you know?"

"I remember her being here last fall, around the time of the American Thanksgiving. I remember her joking with the staff about turkey masala. She was not here when the tsunami hit on December 26. I believe she was busy with other duties."

"Really? I thought she came here in January to help with the disaster recovery."

"No, I was very much aware of what resources we had at that time, and Cheri was not available."

"Well, I know she was here in Malaysia from January until her death in February. Do you think the office would have some record of what she was working on in January?"

Alissa suddenly looked uncomfortable, like she wasn't sure what to say. Even from what little Randy had seen of her, this indecision looked out of character. "I can look up what she was working on last, sure. My recollection was she wasn't here on UNESCO business in January. We were all very busy with relief work all through January, and she wasn't part of that effort."

Alissa paused, took a breath and frowned. "Moreover, we have her as deceased in January."

Randy smiled and waved his hand. "She was bitten by the snake in January, but she recovered from that. She didn't die until February in the car accident."

Alissa's unsure look intensified. "I didn't know about a car accident. We surely did not know she had recovered from the snake bite. The whole office went into mourning when we heard. I think someone should have told us if she had recovered."

Randy was as shocked as Alissa. "Are you kidding? No one told you? Well, that's just, awful. I can't imagine how that didn't get communicated to you. I'm so sorry."

"You say she actually died in a car accident in February?"

"Yes. In fact, I didn't even know about the snake bite until after she died in the car crash. My business partner Young Nae brought me here for her funeral."

Alissa's eyebrow twitched involuntarily at the mention of Young Nae's name. Randy didn't understand why she should have such a reaction, so he didn't let on that he had seen it.

He continued. "I guess he would have been the one to disseminate news. Maybe he got confused about what he told to whom. I mean, she did actually die just a month later."

Her frown didn't go away. "This is all very irregular. I am going to have to make some inquiries."

"That's fine with me. I'm glad I had a chance to set the record straight." He brightened with a thought. "Maybe the stuff in that folder you gave me back in your office can shine some light on how this all went down."

"Maybe." She led him back. "Let's take a look."

As they walked, he decided he couldn't wait for a better time to follow up on her odd reaction. "Forgive me for prying, but do you know Young Nae Yoon?"

She kept her eyes forward and away from him, so he couldn't see how she took the question. "Yes. Cheri had mentioned seeing him on occasion when she was here. I assumed you were all friends."

"Oh, certainly."

"I have never met him, if that's what you mean. Here we are." She opened the folder across her desk.

Randy started flipping through the contents. "We're looking for anything after January. Oh, here's a printout of an internal email from someone to you, dated January 25th. It says Young Nae Yoon called to say Cheri died of a snakebite she suffered on January 18th."

"I remember that day all too well," Alissa said with a sad shake of her head.

"That's really strange. It goes on to say that Young Nae asked for any personal effects of hers to be sent to his house in Kuantan." Randy stared at the page for several seconds. "I have no explanation. All I can do is guess how this must have been some kind of confused timing problem. It would have taken a few days for her to recover from the bite. If she was bit on the 18th, then by the 25th he would have known whether she was going to make it or not." He looked up at Alissa. "It makes no sense."

He read it again, and frowned anew. "It says '… to his house in Kuantan.' There is no address given. That assumes someone took note of the address separately?"

She turned around and opened a filing cabinet drawer, and pulled out a hanging file folder. Holding it open with one arm, she leafed through it and found a page. "It's here. We've got a Kuantan address as an alternate address for her while she is in Malaysia."

"You mean like an emergency contact?"

"No. You are her emergency contact. In Bethesda, Maryland."

"Yeah. Can I see that?"

She handed the personal data record to him.

"Alternate address," he read out loud. "This is under a section called, 'Residence.' This contact number is Young Nae's. You said she came to Malaysia three or four times a year. She must have given this info as a backup, since it wouldn't change, whereas her hotel would be different every time she came."

"Actually, we have a residence contract with the hotels down the block. We have a lot of visiting officials, so we have a place for them to stay."

His mind reeled with the contradictions. He took a breath, then handed the sheet back to Alissa. "Thanks."

He gathered up the papers on her desk and put them back in the folder. "I'll tell you what. I'll take these, and go through them. I will talk to Young Nae about what he told you folks and when. If I can piece together any kind of explanation, I will call you."

I would certainly appreciate that," she said, handing him her card. "That's got my direct line."

"Oh, good. Thanks."

Alissa took a breath and straightened her shoulders. "I will call you if I find out any more of what she was doing in Malaysia in January."

It was the wrong thing to say. Randy felt like a floorboard beneath his feet cracked. He blinked several times and his face sank before he caught his reaction. He purposely pushed through and put back on the polite smile. "I want to thank you for your time today. I appreciate how busy you are."

She shook his hand. "I hope I was able to fill in some gaps for you."

"Yes. I think you did."

17

L O Cheung had just closed the refrigerator door when the house intercom sounded. "Lo here."

"Sir, three police cars just turned onto the drive and are headed to the house."

"Do they have their lights and sirens on or off?"

"Off, Sir. Shall I detain them before they get to the house?"

"To what end, so I can escape?" he laughed. "Let them come on up. I'm curious what is worth a trip at 10 o'clock at night."

He straightened his embroidered gold silk robe and tightened the sash belt as he walked through the house to the front door. He stepped out onto the front porch landing to watch the squad cars pull up. He was not in the least bit surprised to see leading the cadre of officers was none other than Inspector Najib Runnak. "Inspector Najib, what brings you all the way out here on such a beautiful night?"

The Inspector, a slight yet square-shouldered man in his thirties, stepped up but couldn't face Cheung because he was blocking the top step. He looked up at him with a face that Cheung has always thought was far too stern for such a young man. "Lo Cheung, you are under arrest for bribing a government official and obstructing the progress of a police investigation."

Cheung folded his arms over his chest. "Really? Can you tell me who I am accused of bribing?"

"You know full well it was the entire night shift of our North Sector precinct."

"A supporter can't show his appreciation of the work our fine police force does without being accused of bribery?"

"The nineteen bottles of 10-year-old scotch have all been confiscated. We also know exactly which files you were given copies of. Though what you are doing stealing the file of a routine heart attack report, I do not understand. All your hubris has bought you this time is a criminal charge."

"You took the booze? I have always thought you were a bit too tightly wound, Najib, but I never took you for a killjoy. You need to go a little easier on the starch in that white shirt collar."

"Half the officers there are Muslim and can't drink."

"Is that my fault?" Cheung deadpanned.

The Inspector raised an impatient eyebrow. "Nevertheless, you are under arrest and you are coming with us."

Cheung looked down at his nightclothes. "May I have a moment to change into something more appropriate?"

Runnak gestured to the policeman on either side of him for them to escort Cheung back into the house.

"Thank you. I won't be long." He paused as he turned to go into the house. "That is, I won't be long changing." He smiled and added, "I also won't be long in your lock up, but you know that."

The most annoying part of being arrested on his own front porch came when he stepped back out. Someone had tipped the press, and a camera crew was waiting for him, lights and microphones thrusting wildly. At least he knew he would look good on camera in his Ralph Lauren suit.

Cheung turned to the Runnak and sighed. "Was this really necessary?"

The other policemen held back the reporters as the Inspector escorted him into the back seat of a police car, then climbed in the front. "I had nothing to do with the press being called. Your own fame brings them out of the night."

"Yes, I'm sure you have no interest in showing the world how you brought down the infamous Mr. Lo."

Runnak turned around in his seat to face him through the cage bars as the car pulled away. "I admit I jumped at the chance to finally arrest you for something solid. You skate around the system long enough and eventually you're going to trip."

"Did it ever occur to you that you haven't been able to arrest me for any of my supposed crimes because I am not actually a criminal?"

"How can you be so close to so many crimes and yet not be responsible for any of them?"

"I am an attractive target. Real criminals are much more circumspect."

"Ah, yes, the real criminals, who vanish into nothing when the lights come on."

"Actually, that depends on who is holding the light."

"What's that supposed to mean?"

"It means I have brought in a new investigator to work on your favorite of my alleged crimes, the Cheri Macklin murder."

Runnak didn't try to hide the roll of his eyes.

"Mock me while you can. My new PI is uniquely qualified, and she is cracking that case as we speak. My name will be cleared, finally and completely."

18

T HE TALL, BEAUTIFUL BLACK WOMAN slowed her long strides and turned around to wave Sanantha on.

Sanantha was moving as fast as she could, picking her way past the shoppers in the crowded open-air market, dodging wandering children and animals, and sidestepping the vendors' carts and booths that seemed scattered in her path. The smells were all too intense to enjoy, from the spicy foods to the lush flowers to the acrid animal urine. The sound of all those people talking and the pots clanging and the children crying, was all just too much. It all looked familiar, yet she knew she had no idea where this place was.

She hadn't lost her tall guide, given the woman's extreme height and her bright orange robes and high turban. Still, no matter how fast she walked, Sanantha couldn't seem to shorten the gap between them.

She was so busy with the pursuit that it did not occur to her to wonder how she came to be following this woman, or for that matter, who the woman was. She did know it was desperately important to follow her.

She finally came to the end of the marketplace and her path opened up into a plaza. She looked around and realized the plaza was a park square surrounded by side streets that were crowded with merchants. She looked back, and again her tall guide had stopped and was beckoning impatiently.

Now that she got a full view of the woman, Sanantha was taken by her extraordinary looks. She must have been nearly seven feet tall, despite being in sandals and even before the turban, which added another foot. She was buxom, yet even through the robes she could see the woman was very muscular. Her neck seemed unusually long, and her broad lips smiled from under even broader cheekbones.

The woman grinned at her, and Sanantha realized she had been caught staring. The woman held out a hand and waited for Sanantha to catch up. Sanantha hesitated as she reached for the woman's long graceful fingers. The woman took her hand warmly and led her on.

In the middle of the square stood a huge pavilion tent made of wide striped black and white fabric, festooned with flags on each tent pole. They were nearly upon it when Sanantha realized this very royal looking tent was their objective. Her surprise must have been evident, because the woman gave her hand a reassuring squeeze before they walked up between the hugely muscled shirtless black guards who stood at attention. As they walked past, Sanantha couldn't help but notice the gleaming five-foot-long swords the guards held in front of them, point down with their hands resting on the handles.

The woman pulled aside the curtain over the entrance and Sanantha's head was filled with a whole new set of sounds and smells, these all very pleasing in stark contrast to those of the market outside. Musicians played gentle rhythms and sweet strains, while incense billowed up from censers and the aromas washed away all of Sanantha's apprehensions.

That is, until she stepped in and saw who they had come to see. Seated on a gold throne cast to look like it was made of skulls and bones was a full-grown African lion.

Sanantha dropped to her knees and let out a gasp. "Papa Legba."

The godhead looked over at her and cocked its head, as if waiting for something.

124

Sanantha looked up at her guide, and in a flash of embarrassing clarity recognized her as Erzulie. She felt suddenly exposed and unprepared and frightened. She looked up at Erzulie, hoping to get a sign of what she was supposed to do next. The goddess held her hands palm up, as if carrying something, and gestured toward the throne. Sanantha was supposed to give something to Legba.

Sanantha had nothing to give. She looked down at her own clothes for the first time and saw she was wearing a simple white homespun dress that didn't even have pockets. She looked back up at Erzulie and frowned, and shrugged with her hands open.

This was apparently the wrong thing to do. All of the people behind and around Sanantha, whom up until then she hadn't really noticed, inhaled sharply and stepped back away from her. She looked around at them, and they all averted their eyes, not in shame of her, but as if they were guilty. She stood up and asked the fellow closest to her, a short, fat white man in a green suit, "Do you know what I was supposed to bring?"

He didn't answer, but instead began searching his own pockets. Then everyone near him started doing the same thing. This spread until everyone in the pavilion, except for Erzulie and Legba, were looking on their persons and under couch cushions and under rugs. In this sudden pandemonium, Sanantha looked over at Erzulie, who smiled sweetly and nodded at her as if giving her permission to do something.

Sanantha began sweeping the tent with her gaze, waiting for inspiration to guide her. Then she saw it. Sitting on an end table next to a rifled couch, in plain view and standing two feet high, was a brightly painted carved wooden doll of a woman. She walked over and picked it up. It was heavy, as if made of solid wood. She hefted it and felt something move inside. She examined it and found a seam around the middle. She gave it a twist and it separated into halves, with another doll inside. This one was similarly gaily painted, but of a girl. She thought this was an appropriate metaphor for a mother giving birth to a child. When she hefted the girl doll, she again felt something loose inside. She opened this doll and found a white carved wooden snake. This jarred her and she stood looking at it in confusion.

Then she noticed everyone who had been tearing the place apart had stopped, and they were all looking at her with great curiosity.

Sanantha held the snake up for Erzulie to see, and the goddess smiled and nodded. She then gestured toward the throne.

Sanantha was more than a little cowed at the prospect of walking up to her Christ godhead. She felt very small under the lion's gaze. If Erzulie had not been grinning so proudly at her, she would not have the courage to make the seven steps. She bowed deeply and lowered her gaze as she approached, then got down on all fours in front of Legba. She held up the snake sculpture without looking, and the lion took it.

Then he gently set his massive paw on her shoulder. It was heavy and rough and warm, and filled her with a joy like she had never felt before. She felt vindicated, forgiven, accepted, understood, appreciated, exalted, vital, and loved all the way to her core. The emotions were too much too fast, and she broke down sobbing. She dared a look up into those shining golden eyes, and was met with a nod before he withdrew his paw.

She backed away before getting up. She was shaking all over, with ecstatic tears streaming down her face. She turned to go and was met by Erzulie who held open her arms for a welcoming embrace. Sanantha was so overwhelmed, she wasn't sure how much more of this she could handle. On the other hand, she wasn't about to refuse an embrace from the Mistress of Forgiveness herself.

She reached around the goddess' waist and woke up with her arms around her pillow. She was still shaking, still elated, still breathing hard, covered in sweat. She rolled off the pillow and thought she felt a gentle spasm in her groin. She sat up and checked. Indeed, the experience had moved her to orgasm.

She sat there stunned, shaking her head. She noted the dawn's light just coming through her curtains and checked her bedside clock: 6:20. She recalled that sun-up was 6 o'clock sharp, year-round near the Equator.

She tried to replay the dream, hoping to remember as many details as she could before it faded under wakefulness. She fell back onto her pillow and let her breathing slow. It had all been so vivid, she hadn't even realized she was dreaming. So many images. What could they possibly mean?

126

Then she made the chilling realization that she had never had a vision like this before. Even when she had been in the presence of demons and was fighting against Armageddon, her gods had never actually visited her. She must really be in danger if they felt they needed to contact her so directly.

She rolled out of bed and knelt down in front of her altar cabinet. She opened the doors, and lifted the bottle of rum out from the collection of amulets and carved stone figurines that filled the bottom of the tall wooden box. She found the shot glass, but had to steady her shaking hands before she could pour. Once she got the glass full, she set it on the stone block at the base of the central carved wooden pole. She then picked up the bundle of sticks and the pack of matches. Her hands were still shaking a little when she lit the end of the incense and then blew it out. She drew the shape of a heart in the air with the smoke before she set the bundle on the stone altar on the other side from the rum. The aromatic smoke curled around inside the cabinet and spilled upward into the room.

"Grand Matrisse, Heart of Forgiveness, Madame Erzulie, I send this prayer of my greatest gratitude heavenward to you. Holy Savior, Lion of Judah, Papa Legba, I send this prayer of my greatest gratitude heavenward to you. Thank you both for sharing with me your divine guidance. I will do my best to make good of the vision you have so generously given me. It may take my feeble mortal mind some time to fathom your divine message, but I promise I will act to bring your will into the world as you desire. In your Holy Names. Amen."

She snuffed the incense out on the stone block and set it back down. She watched the remaining smoke float up out of the box, carrying her message with it.

She was halfway through her second cup of coffee, sitting at the kitchen table, before she recovered from the excitement of the dream. She decided not to fret about the danger such a vision implied, and to focus on the message her gods had given her.

A snake within a girl, and the girl within a woman. Even while dreaming she had thought the girl inside the woman meant mother and daughter. Why would that be a revelation? The snake inside the daughter would certainly apply to poor Desiree, who had been bitten by a snake. This relationship was so obvious, she wondered why it would be worth a divine intervention.

Then again, Cheri, the mother, had also been bitten by a snake, but survived, only to be killed in a car crash.

The coffee was helping to clear her head, but not to make any more sense of the dream. In a whole tent full of people, the gods had trusted her to be the one who could find the missing item. No pressure there.

It wasn't the mother or the daughter dolls that Legba wanted her to find and give to him, it was the snake. Was there something about the snake that she needed to learn? Maybe Desiree wasn't just suffering from a snakebite.

She checked the clock on the stove display: 7:25. Was that too early to call? She picked up the remote and turned on the small TV she had on the counter facing the dining table. The morning news was her usual background noise, so maybe it would help her sort things out.

She picked up the phone and dialed. "Randolph? This is Sanantha Mauwad. Sorry to be calling so early. Hi, how are you? Oh, really? Jakarta? Is everything all right? Oh, I see. Are you okay? Is it anything you want to talk about now? Back this afternoon, then?

"Look, I've made what I think could be a breakthrough connection. We haven't been able to connect Desiree's snakebite on any criminal activity. I have to wonder if snake bite is really what she is suffering from. Yeah, I know it is kind of a leap, but I have my reasons for wondering. Is there any way of checking to be sure it was snake venom that put her into the coma? True, it has been months. Well, I'll tell you what. You're going to laugh at me for this. I actually have a way to test my hypothesis. It is not a strictly medical test. I need to be with her to do this. I can explain better in person.

"Wait a minute. I just heard Lo Cheung's name mentioned on the news." She watched in earnest and saw a clip of Lo Cheung being taken into custody at his home the previous night. "They say Cheung was arrested last night on suspicion of government corruption. I guess he's not as squeaky clean as he told me. You're right, that doesn't prove anything, although it does add credence to our suspicions.

"May I come out there and talk to you about this? I guess it's just as well you won't be back until later today. I've got a couple of appointments this afternoon that I really can't get out of. It takes, what, three hours to get there? If I leave right after my 4 o'clock is over at 5, then I can be there around 8. Does that work for you? Great. Thank you for indulging me. I promise to make more sense in person. All right then. I'll see you around 8. Yes, go ahead and have dinner first. I'll eat something on the way. I'll call you if I'm going to be much later. Thanks. Goodbye."

19

T HE PLANE RIDE BACK, THE AIRPORT, the drive to the house — it
was all a blur. It was as if his hands and feet just knew what they
were supposed to do. Good thing, since Randolph's mind was busy —
busy doubting and twisting and seething.

Was any of what he saw in Jakarta conclusive? How could he have
missed such an affair? How long had they been seeing each other
behind his back? How could Young Nae lie to him so boldly, even after
her death? He had no answers. He didn't want answers. Answers
weren't going to fix the rip in his heart.

It was only when he stopped the car in the driveway that he realized
he was back. He sat there and blinked. He noticed for the first time that
the radio was on. He must have lucked onto an oldies station without
even noticing. Mick Jagger added his commentary to the jumble of
thoughts and emotions that stormed in Randolph's mind.

But the song brought all the wrong images. Not being able to
foresee this thing happening to you, seeing his heart had turned black,

painting his red door black, wanting to fade away and not face the facts. The song cast everything he had learned in the worst possible light.

Randy switched it off. The clouds, which had been threatening all morning, finally let loose a light rain. In the quiet stillness of the car, it all came crashing in on him. He closed his eyes and lowered his head. Cheri's death. Desiree's coma. The powerlessness of knowing so much about life and not being able to do anything for his family. His blackout. Young Nae's cloak and dagger half-truths. Each had shaken him. Now the affair. So many bad things had pierced him in such a short time, he felt like there was no part of him left unwounded.

He buried his face in his arms on the steering wheel and cried. Hope bled out of him. The love of his life was gone. His daughter was probably never going to wake up. He could no longer trust his best friend. With that friendship went the future of his business. He had nothing left.

He thought about how Sanantha was going to come that evening and try to talk him into believing there was still something worth living for. He wasn't going to believe her. He took out his cell phone and pulled up her number. Maybe he could call her and tell her not to come. He sighed and closed the phone. Let her come. She was probably the only resource he still had.

She said she had made some kind of breakthrough on the snakebite. Pursuing justice against Lo Cheung seemed so implausible and so irrelevant, he just couldn't make himself care.

There was something he still cared about. He needed to know what Dr. Kwon had found wrong with Dez. He wiped his tears with his sleeves, took a deep breath, and got out of the car.

He took many more deep breaths to compose himself as he walked to the upstairs back bedroom.

"Ah, Doctor Macklin," Vera greeted him as he walked in. "Welcome home."

He smiled weakly, but only grunted in response and did not make eye contact. He walked straight to his daughter's bedside. "Was Doctor Kwon able to diagnose her?"

The nurse blinked at the snub. "Yes, it's a viral infection of Hepatitis C. He has her on a course of antiviral drugs starting with Interferon-alpha."

"That's a good broad spectrum start. How bad does he think it is?"

"He said it's too soon to tell. He said we should see some improvement by the end of the week. He's coming by every day after hours."

"I see the lights are gone."

She smiled sheepishly. "Yes, Doctor Kwon was rather amused by them. Indeed, they do nothing for this type of adult jaundice."

He stepped up to Desiree's face and opened a yellow tinted eye. His tone was non-committal, distant. "Fine."

The nurse continued, more cheerfully. "He agreed with your use of the lactulose. He said it was exactly the right thing for the bile buildup in her intestines."

"After all these years in the lab, it's nice to see I haven't completely lost my clinician's touch." He wasn't talking to Vera. He hardly noticed her. He also did not notice her annoyance at his aloofness.

He stroked his daughter's cheek with his fingertips as he quietly spoke to her. "Dez, it's down to just you and me ... and you're not all here. If I ever wanted a miracle, it would be that you could get up from there, and we could just go away and start a new life. Everything I've ever tried to build has crumbled to dust. If you die, I really will have nothing left. Stay with me. Please. Wake up and give your old man a reason to live again."

He looked absently away, unable to focus on much of anything. He looked up and noticed Vera for the first time, looking very prim in her pink uniform. She was avoiding his gaze and seemed somehow annoyed. "Vera?"

She looked up from her clipboard. "Yes?"

"Thank you."

She smiled and nodded. "You're welcome."

He wandered out of the room and back into his distracted haze. His feet went back on autopilot and he made his way down to the beach house.

He wondered how long this limbo would last. What could he do to change anything? Should he call Young Nae and confront him? To what end? Would an apology make any difference? It wouldn't restore their friendship. He couldn't stay in business with him. He could never trust him again. No doubt he would have to confront him at some point. He just didn't have the energy to face a scene like that now.

He flopped down on the couch and stared up at the acoustic ceiling tiles. He looked at his watch. Sanantha would be arriving in a couple of hours. She would help him choose what he could do next. She would give him perspective.

Perspective. Now that he had seen more than he ever wanted to, where could he possibly stand to see a broader, more hopeful view?

He knew he had to start by not letting himself fall into despair. Feeling sorry for himself was just going to paint himself into a corner. He didn't want to paint all his doors black.

He needed to do something to reset his frame of mind. Alcohol? Jesus no. Alcohol wiped out his memory for four months. Travel? Hardly. He was already halfway around the world from home in one of the most exotic locales on the planet. He fleetingly wished he knew more about electro-shock therapy.

No, he needed to just calm down and let himself have time to sort it all out. He just needed to do something pleasant and relaxed, and removed from everything that was stressing him out.

His stomach, which had been grumbling for an hour, reminded him that he had skipped lunch and drove straight home from the airport in K-L. His stomach gave him his lead.

The aromas of soy sauce, steamed rice, and chili spices filled Randolph's head as he opened the door to the Japanese restaurant. He loved Japanese food, and the whole serene, ceremonious way it was served. He hadn't had it in months, that he could remember, not since before Young Nae had summoned him here. He was very hungry by the time he arrived, and he was taken by how strongly everything smelled when charged with hunger and anticipation.

"Party of one?" asked the tiny, very young-looking Japanese hostess.

"Yes, it's just me tonight," he said as he folded his umbrella and shook the rain from his coat. "I called ahead. The name's Macklin."

"Ah, we have a table open right now."

As she led him to a table toward the back of the restaurant, he thought her bright yellow blouse was a nice change from the grey weather outside.

Looking over the menu, he felt a chill and looked around to see if he was under an air vent. Though he couldn't see one, the A/C was definitely up too high for the cool, damp, winter June day outside. He smiled at himself. Was he actually chilly? Clearly, his blood had thinned in the months he had been here. He was lamenting a sixty-five-degree winter day, when back in Maryland he would have welcomed a winter day that got as high as thirty-five.

The chill reminded him of the warmth of the Bili-lights he had erroneously set up over Desiree. How could he have missed that protocol so badly? He must have looked like a fool to Dr. Kwon. Great. Stress was affecting his memory too.

He didn't have to peruse the menu for long, since he knew what he wanted: Yellowtail sashimi and a big bowl of *udon* noodles with shrimp.

•　　　•　　　•

Sanantha's cell phone rang just as she was leaving the Pantai Timur Highway to enter Kuantan.

The young woman's voice was frantic through her Japanese accent. "Doctor Mauwad, Doctor Sam ... Sam—atha Mauwad?"

"Yes, it's me. Who is this?"

"This is Akuda Restaurant calling. Do you have a patient named Mr. Macklin?"

"Yes. Why do you ask?"

"Mr. Macklin is having medical emergency. We have called ambulance, but we found your card in his wallet, and we were hoping you are his doctor."

"He is under my care. What kind of emergency is he having?"

"He's all frozen up. He can't move."

"You mean he's paralyzed?"

"Yes."

"Where are you located?"

"On the north side of Kuantan. Your card says you are in K-L."

"I happen to be in Kuantan right now. Please give me directions to your restaurant and I'll drive there straight away."

•　　　•　　　•

The young Japanese hostess at the front counter already looked quite rattled even before she looked up and was startled by the black woman in a tall white turban. Sanantha had seen the ambulance parked out front, and she could see around the entrance partition that the red-uniformed paramedics were putting Randolph up onto a gurney. "I'm Doctor Sanantha Mauwad."

The hostess began to fluster, then waved her right in.

As she approached the two med techs, Sanantha asked, "Do either of you speak English?"

"Yes, we both do," the tall, thin Indian young man answered, while his shorter Malay partner checked the monitor leads.

A fat Japanese man in a black suit who was standing by stepped up. "So do I. I am the Manager."

"Good. I am his psychiatrist." She turned to the med techs. "I have him on Ambien, but that's all. What is his condition?"

Randy moaned and twitched.

Sanantha stepped up to him. "Are you in any pain?"

"He has whole body paralysis," the med tech explained. "His heart rate has slowed to 40, his blood pressure has dropped to 100 over 70, but is stable. His body temperature is also low, at 88 degrees Fahrenheit. We've seen this before, but this is an extreme case."

"I've seen it too. It's fugu poisoning, isn't it?"

"Yes, but the extraordinary thing is, he didn't have fugu."

Sanantha stepped to Randy's table and saw scraps of sashimi raw fish on the plate. "What's this?"

The manager answered. "It's Hamachi. Yellowtail."

Sanantha stepped over to Randy's head. "Randy, you're having a bad reaction to the fish you ate. We know what this is, and it is treatable. I know you can't move, and I know you are completely aware, and I know how scary this is. Try not to panic." She tried to appeal to his scientific side. She had seen him calm himself by taking a clinical view. "The poison can't get into your brain. It can't cross the blood-brain barrier. It interrupts the firing of nerves in the peripheral nervous system. Your body is paralyzed, but only until we can filter the poison out of your bloodstream. We'll keep your vitals up. We've got this under control. You're going to be all right."

The tall med tech touched her on the shoulder and gave her a raised eyebrow expression of doubt.

She turned to the manager. "Did this come on gradually, or all of a sudden?"

"Very suddenly."

"That's not the way this usually comes on, is it?" she asked the tall paramedic.

"No, it usually takes a while and the symptoms come up gradually."

"That's what I thought. Is he stable?"

"Yes, for the moment."

Sanantha took command. "His vitals might continue to drop, so be ready to hit him with stimulants. Also, watch his blinking. It could get so bad that he stops. If it does, then we need to hydrate his eyes and close them. I want you to hold him here for just a moment. There is a key piece of information we are going to need before we start treating him."

She turned to the manager. "I need to see your kitchen."

"There is nothing wrong in our kitchen."

"I didn't say there is." She picked up Randy's plate. "I need to see where and how this was prepared before I prescribe how we're going to treat him. I can't afford to make any assumptions, or I could give him the wrong treatment and it could kill him. Now please show me your kitchen."

He thought about it for a second and looked over at the paramedics. They both nodded. "All right. This way."

He led her to the cutting counter, which was in its own crowded alcove lined with coolers. Two older Japanese men in white jackets and headbands backed away from their work area with obvious worry on their faces. "Here is where the sashimi is prepared."

Sanantha noted the distinct smell of disinfectant in the air. "Now there is supposed to be a special knife reserved for cutting fugu. It's got a name. Is it the *'hiki'*?"

The manager waved to the chefs. One of them bowed curtly and stepped up. He reached up and pulled down a long thin knife from its own special block. "*Fugu hiki,*" he said, showing it to Sanantha.

"This knife is only used on *fugu*, and nothing else?"

The old man nodded. "Hi."

"What about this cutting board? Is it cleaned off thoroughly after each time fugu is cut here?"

"Yes," supplied the manager.

"The same cutting board is used for all the fish, right?"

"Well, yes, but there is no poison contaminated between preparations. We don't sell *fugu* offal, which is where all the poison resides. The health inspectors come in here regularly and they have never complained about our cleanliness."

"No, again, I am not saying you did anything wrong. I just need to know what happened. Can you show me what the *fugu* fish looks like?"

The other chef reached behind Sanantha in the cramped working area and opened a cooler with filets wrapped in wax paper. He opened the paper to reveal a white, shiny, almost translucent flesh.

She held Randy's plate up alongside it, and the difference was obvious.

"That's Yellowtail," confirmed the manager.

"The most my patient would have been exposed to was a trace amount of puffer fish blood left on the cutting board that got onto his Yellowtail." She continued to think out loud. "The blood has almost none of the toxin to begin with."

She handed the plate to the manager. "Please wrap that up. We will need to test it to make sure I'm right. I don't think you did anything wrong. I think it was my patient having a freak reaction."

"Like an allergic reaction?" ventured the manager.

"Something like that, yes."

She returned to the paramedics who were ready to move Randy. "Here's the fish he ate," she said handing the package to one of them. "Let's go. We'll talk on the way."

The manager followed them out. Sanantha turned and shook his hand. "Thank you for your help."

"I hope he makes a full and speedy recovery."

"Do you mind if I ride along?" she asked as the med techs loaded the gurney up into the ambulance.

"Sure. Watch your step."

While they strapped the gurney into place and got underway, Sanantha buckled herself into a jump seat. The Malay fellow took the wheel while the Indian fellow strapped himself in next to Randy.

"It appears he was only exposed to the slightest trace of the tetrodotoxin," she explained. "That sample will verify it, but I don't think this is a classic case of *fugu* poisoning."

She leaned over and spoke to Randy. "I know you can hear what we are saying, even if you can't move to respond."

He blinked his understanding.

"Please try to remain calm as we talk about your condition in cold, clinical terms. The good news is: I have heard of this sort of thing before."

"Really?" the Indian med tech asked.

She continued, to both him and Randy. "The bad news is, the syndrome is shrouded in mystery and doubt. As you can tell from my accent, I am from Haiti. Although I grew up in a small rural village, I never saw for myself the kind of Black Magic people expect to be commonplace in Haiti. That having been said, I think what you are experiencing is a classic case of Voodou zombification."

The Indian fellow blinked and raised his eyebrows. "In Malaysia?"

"The Zombie of Haitian tradition is someone who has been forced, by means of pharmaceutical torture, to act against their own will as a slave. It takes a deeply evil person to treat another person with such indignation. Since the formulae for making someone into a Zombie are very closely guarded, only someone who has dedicated their life to evil would know how to do it."

"How do you think it was done to Mr. Macklin here?"

"I suspect he was exposed to the tetrodotoxin poison over a long period of time, long enough that his body developed a complete chemistry of how to survive with this poison. Being exposed to even the slightest trace of this poison tonight set off a reaction where his body ..." She leaned over and gave Randy's arm a squeeze. "I'm sorry, *your* body went back into behaving like it was saturated again."

"How could he be exposed to this poison as you suggest, without showing any symptoms?"

"Oh, I didn't mean to say he didn't show symptoms. He looked like he was on a four-month alcoholic bender after his wife died. His best friend, not knowing any better, just let him drink himself into a stupor. Now we know it wasn't just alcohol. Someone systematically poisoned you, Randy. This also explains, finally, your memory loss. Mere alcohol, even massive amounts of it, doesn't explain how your memory is a total blank for that period. Now I see that your body chemistry was forced into a completely different set of norms. This poison also saps your willpower, turns you into a complacent puppet, and drastically lowers your vital signs. When you seemed to drop dead when I made you walk into that blank space under hypnosis, your body was going back into Zombie mode."

The frown on the Indian tech's face just kept getting deeper and deeper.

She nodded and chuckled. "I know this all sounds insane. Doctor Macklin and I have been through quite a bit over the last few weeks."

She turned back to Randy. "The good news is, with only a trace amount of the poison in your system, a day or so on a charcoal filter will clean out your blood stream and you should come right back to normal."

She turned her hypothesis over in her mind, and it still didn't fit all the facts.

The tech apparently saw this on her face. "Excuse me, but you don't look as convinced as you sound."

She shot him her dimpled grin. "You're right."

She turned to Randy and laid her hand on his arm again. "You're probably thinking the same thing I am. My theory still doesn't explain how Lo Cheung did this to you. We assumed the chi system injections could have been inflicted in a single day kidnapping without Young Nae knowing what had been done to you. On the other hand, for you to have been zombified like this, your diet, maybe the booze, must have been laced with the puffer fish poison for the entire four-month period. Someone on Young Nae's staff must have been doing this right under everyone's nose."

She frowned again. "That makes no sense. He tried to kill Cheri with the snakebite, and when that failed, he used a car crash. Then he used a snake again on Desiree. He also tried to use a snake on me. All direct and to the point. So why the protracted torture for you? And carefully, purposely not lethal. Why would he want to just incapacitate you? More to the point, why would he want to distance you chemically from your memories of that time? We're back to the original question. What did you see that makes Lo Cheung so nervous?"

20

T HE LITHE NINETEEN-YEAR-OLD WOMAN walked along the garden path and breathed deep the musky smells of the jungle after the morning rain. She shook her short black hair away from her face as she pulled down a banana tree leaf and drank the water that poured off it. It was colder than she expected, and she blinked her brown eyes in surprise.

She had walked this path countless times, as it led off the estate and hooked up with the seemingly endless mountain hiking trails she loved so much. Yet, something about the walk seemed different this morning. She knew every rock and turn, the twitter of birds and the buzz of insects in the trees, and the way the sun glinted off the wet leaves. At the same time, it all looked new again. She shook her head and grinned. Maybe it was the weird dreams she had been having lately. Maybe she was a bit hung over from the sake she had drunk to help her sleep last night. Whatever it was, she found it amusing to see one of her favorite hangouts as if it were new to her.

When she reached the trail head, she opted to go up the mountain behind the estate, figuring the exertion would clear her head. A few minutes into the climb, she hit her stride. The sound of her breathing and the feel of her heart pounding created beats that measured her footsteps. She loved feeling this symphony of rhythms inside her body. It focused her mind and made her feel like she was where she belonged.

As she hiked, she revisited the dream she had last night. It wasn't unpleasant, just confusing. She was going ice-skating at a large, sunny outdoor rink. There were lots of families with kids, and the place was filled with the happy chaos of getting kids ready, on and off the ice. Randolph, her ex-husband was with her. He was very kind to her, which made no sense. What made even less sense was he was helping her with her skate laces because she was somehow unable to get them to work right. He got them laced up, and they had a fine time skating. She couldn't remember anything else from the dream. When she awoke, she was sure she had missed something. Now that she was replaying the dream, she was again convinced there was something else going on that she had overlooked.

Frustrated at still not being able to crack it, she put the dream out of her mind and refocused on the trail ahead. She thought about the sensations in her body, her ribcage breathing, her leg muscles straining, the sweat seeping from her skin despite her thin top and hiking shorts. She recalled this same feeling from pumping a bicycle up a long low grade. She blinked and the memory started to fade. She wanted it back. She took a deep breath and calmed herself. "Just get back the rhythm," she told herself.

A moment later, the vision came back. She was a child, on a bike that was a bit too big for her. She was riding home from school through a suburban neighborhood. Home was at the top of the hill. Yes, now she remembered. Home was at the top of a grade that must have been six blocks long.

She kept hiking, looking down at where she was walking while her attention was turned inward, intent on retrieving the memory. She had no concrete memories of her childhood, and she really wanted to piece this one together.

She remembered finally reaching the top of the hill and turning into the driveway. She steered her bike up the sidewalk path to the front porch, and laid it down on the grass. The front door was open, and she went inside.

She smiled broadly at finally remembering so much detail. Her enthusiasm completely blotted out the exertion of the hike.

She recalled walking through the living room into the dining area. She heard her mom in the kitchen rattling pans. She felt really happy to hear that her mom was home. This confused her. It was as if it was a big deal for her mom to be home.

She called out, "Hi Mom! I'm home!"

She stopped hiking so suddenly she almost stumbled. A chill ran up her spine and tears came to her eyes. She blinked furiously as if that would make what she saw go away. She felt like she wanted to wake up from a nightmare, but she was already awake.

The woman who stepped out from around the kitchen counter to greet her in the memory was herself. All grown up. The same face she knew as her own. Cheri Macklin.

She bent over, and leaned on her knees and panted. The vision faded, but the fright still had a firm grip on her. How could a memory be so screwed up? Obviously, her trauma hadn't just knocked her memories out, but scrambled them as well.

Her fear turned to frustration. So few memories, and when one finally comes back, it's jumbled up and ruined. She picked up a rock and threw it as hard as she could out into the jungle canopy. "Shit."

She resumed her hike. Now she really needed it to clear her head.

Upon her return an hour later, she was glad to have not triggered any more memories. She had really pushed herself, beating out her frustration, and she had the sweat to show for it. As the broad verandas of the two-story wooden house came into view through the foliage, her only wish was to get upstairs and into the shower.

She stepped into the bathroom and glanced in the mirror. She blinked at just how sweaty and disheveled she looked. "Impressive." She stripped off her clothes and tossed the lot of them into the hamper basket. She gave her tanned, fit body one last assessment in the mirror before moving to the shower, when something caught her eye. Rather something in her eye caught her attention.

She leaned in close and held her lid open with her fingers. Was it a random flash of light? No, it was a spot of color. There at the edge of her dark brown iris was the tiniest speck of blue. She checked the other eye and it wasn't there. She knew irises were usually a mix of colors in the muscles, but hers were all shades of brown. Except for this spot. She blinked and touched it with her fingertip to see if it was something stuck to the surface of her eye. It was actual color in her iris. How had she never seen it before? Maybe she hadn't ever looked so carefully. It didn't hurt and it didn't seem to be doing any harm. She shrugged and moved to the shower.

A few minutes later, she heard the bathroom door open and the cheery voice of Young Nae Yoon. "Hey, sweets! How are you?"

"Young Nae!" she called out over the roar of the shower. "I didn't know you were coming up today. Weren't you at some conference down in K-L?"

"I was." He slid open the shower door. "I got done and decided I wanted to see you."

She put her hands on her hips. "Well, you certainly see me now."

He made no pretense as he looked her naked body up and down. "My, you certainly have gotten tanned. Even in winter, and all over too."

"It was sunny all last month before the rains came. Now if you're done with the peepshow, would you please close the door? You're letting all the cold air in."

"If you keep sunbathing au natural, you're going to give my gardening staff ideas."

She pulled the door shut. "I'm discreet. They all know I'm yours alone."

"You got that right."

She saw through the lightly frosted glass that he was starting to take his white shirt and dark slacks off. This time she opened the shower door. "Sweetheart. I had a really bad morning. I'm not sure I'm up for that right now."

"You do realize I drove over 300 kilometers to get here from K-L."

She nodded. "I appreciate that. Let me finish in here. I'll pull myself together. Just give me a few minutes, all right?"

He shrugged. "Tell you what. I'll get us some lunch. Food always hits a good reset. Then we'll have the whole afternoon."

"That sounds great. Thanks." She smiled and leaned out of the shower to kiss him.

He stepped up and gave her more of a kiss than she was asking for. When he fondled one of her wet breasts, she pulled back and laughed at him. "You are so naughty!"

He smiled broadly. "See you downstairs."

●　　　●　　　●

"No, I've got it," Young Nae told the chef as he carried the chafing dish to the table. "I know, presentation matters." The white jacketed Asian man followed him into the dining room holding a tray of dishes, each with a different meat, sauce, or vegetable. As Young Nae put the plates out, the chef wordlessly lit the burner under the chafing dish and poured a pot of broth into it. Young Nae nodded at the spread. "I think that's it. Thank you." The chef bowed and left just as Cheri was coming down the stairs.

"Oh my! That's some fancy lunch." She stopped at the bottom of the open staircase, and looked down at her t-shirt and sarong skirt. "Maybe I should go change into something nicer."

"Nonsense. Come sit down."

"Whatcha cookin'?"

"The broth needs to heat up to a boil, so it'll be a minute. Now you said you had a rough morning?"

"Well, yeah. I've been having strange dreams. I don't put much stock in dreams. This morning I was out hiking, and I thought I had a memory from my childhood. Unfortunately, it was all screwed up, and it gave me quite a fright. It was like I was having a nightmare, even though I was wide awake."

"That sounds disturbing. From your childhood? That would be great. I thought all your memories from before your trauma were gone."

"Me too, which is why it got my hopes up. Then it turned out to all be a mixed-up jumble. Really dreamlike. I met my mom, and she was me."

"Freaky."

"I agree. I practically ran the rest of the way up and down the mountain, trying to get the image out of my head."

"You know, I've had semi-hallucinations when I've been working out really hard. When I'm really in the zone with my fighting practice, when I'm really feeling the power move through my body, I sometimes feel like I'm part of something bigger than myself. It feels like I can affect things beyond my touch. It's really quite dreamlike."

"That's your … savat?"

Young Nae laughed. "No, no. Savate is French kickboxing, which is a sport. I do Silat, which is Indonesian, and is an actual combat fighting style."

"Oh, like Kung Fu?"

"Well, no. Kung Fu teaches you how to move chi energy around in your own body to focus your strength. Silat teaches you how to manipulate your opponent's chi energy." He leaned forward. "I'm thinking you might have run yourself into a form of self-hypnosis."

"No, I know what the 'zone' feels like. This was definitely built from a memory."

"You also said you've been having nightmares. Have they been the same kind of mixed up images?"

"Yes, but you kind of expect things to not line up right in a dream."

"Are you otherwise healthy?"

"What, you think this could be because I've got the flu or something?"

"I dunno. Low-grade fevers can cause disorientation. Any change in body chemistry, actually."

She frowned at him playfully. "Change in body chemistry? Is that your thinly veiled way of asking if I'm pregnant? No, I'm not pregnant. As much as we screw, it would certainly be a possibility, but I've been very careful."

He put his hands up to match her playfulness. "Okay, I'm just saying." He used the big gesture to cover his real concern about how she could have accessed memories that were supposed no longer to be available to her transformed brain. Could her nerves have found a way to unlock pathways that were originally encoded with her old genetics? He would have to keep an eye on this.

"The worst part of having these nightmares, or 'daymares', is the frustration. I am desperate to remember something of my past. Anything at all. Then I get teased like this."

"Well, you were clinically dead for a couple of minutes before the paramedics revived you. You don't survive being beaten nearly to death and expect to come out of it without some lasting effects."

"Yes, I know," she said, frustration still coloring her voice. "I don't even remember the attack."

"Oh, that's your brain protecting you. You don't want to remember what Randolph did to you."

"I guess," she sighed. "Hey, that's starting to smell good."

He lifted the lid on the chafing dish. "Just about ready."

"Do you have any word on where Randy is?"

"No, not yet. I spoke with the police last week, and they said they have some good leads. They think he's trying to gather what he can of his old life back in Maryland. They promised to keep me up to date."

She put her hand on his. "You know, we always talk about what he did to me, but not about you."

"How do you mean?"

"He was my husband, but he was your best friend. That must have had a huge impact on you, finding out your closest friend, your lifelong friend and business partner, is actually a violent lunatic."

He took a deep breath. "Yeah, it hurt. It made me doubt my ability to judge character. I'd like to say I saw it coming, but it was a complete shock to me when it happened. I mean, I had no idea he had so much hate in him."

Cheri squeezed his hand.

"I've come to grips with it now. Water under the bridge." He pulled his hand out and put it on top of hers. "We'll bring him to justice."

She smiled warmly into his eyes. "You take such good care of me." Then she grinned and glanced at the lunch spread. "What is all this?"

149

He stood up and pointed as he explained. "This is called *Chiri*." He laughed at the coincidence. "*Chiri* for my Cheri. It's little slices of raw fish that you skewer with these long fondue forks and dip it in the boiling broth to cook it, for just a minute." He prepared one for her as he spoke. "Then you dip it in one of the sauces here, before you pop it into your mouth. You eat it with these steamed vegetables. All subtle flavors."

She took the fork and tasted the fish. "Hmm. Really tender. The fish has a really light taste." She snagged a raw slice and tasted it. Then she smiled knowingly at him. "This is puffer fish, isn't it?"

He sat down and smiled back. "Yes, this is one of the traditional ways to prepare it. It's just such an elaborate production that you don't see it done very often."

"Why Mr. Young," she teased. "I do believe you are trying to trick me into the mood." She slid off her chair and onto her knees in front of him, and wrapped her hands around the backs of his thighs. "You know I do not need any ancient aphrodisiac fish to get me interested. You are hot enough for me, all by yourself."

21

R ANDY WASN'T ENTIRELY SURE HE HAD WOKEN UP. He couldn't feel his body, yet he knew he was in bed. He opened his eyes and looked around the hospital room. He felt his ribs creaking as they rose and fell with his breath. His arms and legs were giving him no sensation whatsoever.

He wondered why he wasn't panicked by what should have been terrifying. He was glad not to be. That would have made things a lot worse. He remembered being scared in the restaurant. He remembered the whole episode, and every word Sanantha and the paramedics had exchanged in the ambulance.

He also remembered feeling numb like this before, but he couldn't place where. He felt like this numbness should be accompanied by a lightheaded mental disconnect as well. Yeah, drunkenness. Maybe this was how he spent the four months of his missing memory. Drunk on Young Nae's booze and unknowingly poisoned by Lo Cheung.

Being fully aware and numb like this was surreal. He felt like a brain in a jar. Completely alert yet unable to interact with the world. The only good part was he knew this wasn't going to kill him, that he had been in this weird space before, and he was going to recover.

He saw Sanantha sleeping in a chair in the corner of the room. Obviously, she had stayed the night. That was really nice. How many shrinks would do that?

He couldn't turn his head. His neck wasn't stuck. It just didn't respond. He could see the call button cord snaked down by his arm. He couldn't feel his arm or hand. Good thing he didn't need to use the buzzer.

He saw the two IVs, one in each forearm. He thought he heard an electric motor going somewhere in the room. That's right, they were filtering his blood over charcoal to extract the poison.

He saw a TV mounted up on the wall and wished it was on. He would have used the buzzer to get a nurse to turn it on, if he could move his hand.

Morning light was just starting to peek through the drawn blinds, and he heard faint footfalls and voices out in the hall as the hospital floor awoke to the new day. The nurse would probably be in soon to check on him. He could somehow tell her to turn on the TV when she came.

He waited. No nurse. He waited. This was going to be a long day.

His thoughts wandered back to the blackness he felt before heading off to his fateful Japanese dinner. The anger and hurt of the affair gripped him again, despite his every conscious effort not to wallow in despair. It was just too new, too raw to set aside. The betrayal was so unexpected and had caught him so unprepared, he felt inundated, crushed. He looked over at Sanantha sleeping. Surely, she would help him out of this hole, when she woke up, and when he could move again to tell her about it.

He had plenty of other things to sort out, plenty of distractions to keep him away from that precipice. His life since he woke up had become more tangled every day. He added long term poisoning to the list of his trials. Did this change anything? Not really. Now they knew the mechanism used to wipe out his memory. The chi energy trap was still loaded to kill him if he did remember whatever dark secret was the trigger. He still had the pacemaker to catch him, he hoped, if he did spring the trap.

The one clear vision he had just before the heart attack struck, and probably the cause of the heart attack, was Cheri lying unconscious on a hospital bed, not mangled from a car wreck. It was also the one piece that did not fit any of the rest of the puzzle. Forbidden and unfitting — just the combination to fire up his scientific principles. One good piece of evidence that doesn't fit the theory is all you need to go back and question the theory itself.

Cheri's coworkers at UNESCO hadn't heard of the car wreck either. They only knew about the snakebite.

If Cheri didn't die in a car wreck, then why would Young Nae go to the trouble of making up such an elaborate story? Why indeed. Young Nae had lied about the snakebite in the worker's village. Was that also part of his covering up his affair with Cheri?

Even accepting Young Nae as a liar up to no good didn't explain all the facts.

Randy needed more facts. How to trigger more of the hidden memories? He stopped and considered that, pacemaker or not, that path was playing with fire.

Frustrated by the dead end, he took a labored breath to clear his head. He caught a strain of a song playing way off in the back of his mind and tried to identify it. He played the bar over a few times until he recognized it as Queen's "Bohemian Rhapsody." He wasn't sure he knew all the lyrics.

He did know the round about letting him go, and how Beelzebub had put aside a devil for him.

Persecution? Was he feeling persecuted? Not really.

Still, he marveled at how much sound the three band members generated in this song. He decided to let himself revel in it. Then the song shifted, from passive to aggressive. Great, now he was conjuring up revenge and escape fantasies. Why not?

"So you think you can leave me and spit in my eye?"

This didn't feel right. He felt betrayed, and angry at Cheri and Young Nae. He was still sad for her death, and still confused by Young Nae's cloak and dagger. The anger and hurt were again blotting out everything else. He knew he could not see clearly with so much blood in his eye. He could be staring straight at the answer and not see it. No, he could not afford to indulge his anger.

Sanantha could help talk him down. He wondered if just calming down would help. Lying there paralyzed, he wasn't charged up with adrenaline. His thoughts were just crowded out. He had sought comfort in the Japanese food. That trip accidentally uncovered a big piece of the crime. Comfort still eluded him.

He recalled the Old Testament Psalm 23: *"Yea, though I walk through the valley of the shadow of death, I will fear no evil: for thou art with me; thy rod and thy staff, they comfort me."*

Could he trust God to lead him to the answers? Could he trust God to lead him to comfort? He thought through the litanies he grew up with, but had not thought about in many years. He remembered a quote from Jesus. "He that is without sin among you, let him first cast a stone at her."

Should he consider forgiving them the affair? They did try to hide it from him, so they were not out to harm him. Maybe Young Nae got in over his head and felt he needed to lie to protect Randy. He could certainly see the situation more objectively if he forgave them.

That was a huge stretch. It was all still too soon and too raw. He wasn't anywhere near ready to take that high a road.

Jesus's Sermon on the Mount came back him. "If someone strikes you on the right cheek, turn to him the other also."

Yeah. Way too soon.

As he lay there wrestling with his emotions, another song bubbled up from his subconscious. Paul McCartney's sweet, pure voice made a strong case. Waking up to the sound of music, Mother Mary spoke words of wisdom. Yeah, maybe he should try to just accept what had happened, and let it be.

•   •   •

Sanantha was walking back to Randy's room after getting a cup of coffee when she heard what sounded like a nurse having a conversation in the room.

She peeked around the door and he was holding his head up and tentatively turning it side to side. "Well, you must be feeling better!"

"Yeah," he grunted. "Hurts a lot."

"Most excellent!" Sanantha congratulated him, and then caught herself. "Not about the hurting part. We'll have you up and about in no time."

He tried to raise a hand off the bed. His voice was a hoarse whisper. "So stiff. Feels like splinters in my muscles."

The nurse finished her notes to his chart and left.

Sanantha picked up the chart and looked at it. "Yes, and that's on some pretty powerful pain meds. The poison upsets the sodium balance in the nerves. Your nerves and muscle fibers need to all reload. Go slow, but do try to keep moving. You'll only get those kinks out by moving the muscles."

He shot her a disappointed glare. "Feel like the Tin Man."

She frowned. "I'm afraid I don't get the reference."

"Oz."

"Oh, right. Well, I'm afraid there is no oil can to loosen you up. Just detox and PT. On the other hand, I imagine it feels good to be able to move again."

He nodded, and winced. "Weird. My thoughts have been clear all day."

"It's three o'clock in the afternoon. You've had some quiet time to think. Anything you want to talk about?"

"Went to Jakarta to visit where Cheri worked. She and Young Nae were having an affair."

She blinked involuntarily. "Someone told you that?"

"Figured it out. Wasn't too hard."

She frowned and blew out a breath. "That must have been hard to take."

He averted his gaze. "Yeah."

"You found this out, what, the day before yesterday?"

"I spent that night sitting in a strip club staring at a scotch, torn between how badly I felt and how much more scared I was of falling back into the drunken haze that started all this craziness. It was a horrible, sleepless night. Then I flew back yesterday."

"Right, because you were still in Jakarta when I called you at 7 in the morning. Sorry about that." She was trying to make small talk as she gathered her thoughts. Having his wife cheat on him with his best friend was exactly the same scenario that drove Randolph's father to suicide. Randolph could easily be at that same brink. "How has this discovery left you feeling about Cheri?"

"Betrayed, of course. Although I'm still confused enough about how she died that I'm not ready to write her epitaph yet."

"How she died? Have you discovered something else?"

"Yes. Her coworkers thought she had died of the snakebite in January. They never heard of the car crash in February. I have recovered one image from my blank period. It was the image that tripped the heart attack trap. It didn't make sense at the time, but now it fits. It was Cheri lying unconscious on a hospital bed, but with no car crash injuries."

Sanantha's eyebrows climbed up her forehead as she considered his words. "Does that mean the whole car crash death is suspect? With it, Young Nae too?"

"Yeah. Ask me how I feel about Young Nae right now." He grimaced as menacingly as he could, given the partial paralysis in his face muscles.

"Fighting mad is a healthy reaction. I'm glad to see it."

Randy blinked in surprise.

"What, you thought I was going to go all sweetness and light on you at a time like this? Someone is out to get you and your family. Me too, remember."

"True. I am having a hard time getting past the betrayal to focus on the crime. All day today, every time I tried to sort through the clues, I kept falling back to the affair. It's like I can't even force myself to think about anything else."

Sanantha nodded. "Not a surprise. That was a big shock, and it's going to take time to process. You know I'm here to help with that. I'm also here to make sure all of this bad news doesn't overwhelm you. I'm really glad to see you able to talk about the affair and the crimes. I wonder, though, if that's just you hiding behind the intellectual puzzle. How are you coping?"

He frowned with his stiff face as he thought. "Frankly, better than I would have thought. I've been playing a lot of music in my head."

"Pardon?"

"Classic rock-and-roll. It's kind of my movie soundtrack of life. Playing music has always helped me focus and put things in perspective."

"That's good that you have that anchor. We all need something we can draw strength from, a safe place we can go. I don't mind telling you I am greatly relieved."

"Yeah, the 70s and 80s were good to me that way."

"Good, because we have work to do. Someone mutilated and poisoned you to keep you quiet, and they tried to kill me. That someone is still out there and they will be back. They will not wait for you to learn to cope with the affair before they strike again. Whether it's a high roller criminal like Lo Cheung, or your cheating partner Young Nae, we've got to figure this out. It can be figured out." She added with some venom, "We are going to get your memories back. We are going to put an end to this."

•   •   •

Sanantha let herself into the dark beach house with Randy's keys. She flipped on the light switch and was taken with the odd mix of smells: sea salt, coffee, beer, and sweat. This was where Randolph had spent four months strung out on nerve toxins and alcohol. The scene of the crime, as it were. Well, at least one of the crimes.

She was looking forward to sleeping in a real bed. She had eaten at the hospital before she headed out, so she only paused in the open kitchen long enough to see where the coffee making supplies were for the morning.

Sanantha was pleased with how efficient Young Nae's housekeeping staff was. She felt funny about sleeping in Randy's bed, but the sheets were fresh, as were the towels in the bathroom.

She sat down on the tan leather couch and pulled her PDA out of her purse. The hospital had made her turn it off while she sat with Randy, since its radio could interfere with the medical equipment. It had been hours since she had checked her email, and she was sure her inbox was overflowing.

While she was deleting newsgroup updates and ads, she heard a buzzing coming from inside her purse. She snatched it up off the floor and fished through too many unnecessary things in the large bucket-like handbag until she found her phone, but it was too late. The voice mail message surprised her.

"This is Lo Cheung. My spies have seen a woman who fits Desiree Macklin's description at Young Nae's vacation house in the mountains near Ipoh. I'm investigating further. Thought you should know. Later!"

She frowned at the phone for a long moment, trying to decide what to make of this. Lo was apparently out of jail. He was clearly continuing his cover story of being victimized by Young Nae. Now he was adding things to the story that made no sense. A third woman? Who was she supposed to be? How was that supposed to convince her that Cheung wasn't behind Randy's poisoning?

She decided not to reply. If Lo did find something useful, he would call again. She closed the phone.

22

YOUNG NAE OPENED HIS EYES JUST ENOUGH to see the light of dawn glinting in through the wall of glass windows. He closed his eyes and rolled under the satin sheets toward the middle of the king-sized bed. He could smell the warmth of Cheri's sleeping body next to him. He breathed deep of her sweat, her perfume, her breath, and her sex. She smelled like life. He opened his eyes and marveled at the curves of her tussled short black hair, the curves of her very tanned bare shoulders, the curves of her waist and legs that showed through the silky blue fabric. His hands wanted to trace all those curves and he had to stop himself and let her sleep.

He slid out of the bed and stood up. As physically fit as he was, he was amused to find his groin muscles tired from their marathon lovemaking. He leaned over and chuckled at how his testicles ached and were clearly smaller than usual. He looked back lovingly at Cheri. She was absolutely everything he had ever dreamed of.

Not just dreamed of, but made — brought back from the grave by his ingenuity and courage. She wasn't just the lover he saved from death — she was his crowning achievement. Anything was possible with enough ingenuity and courage. The thought warmed his heart.

He walked nude out onto the veranda that circled the back of the house. The jungle below him was just unfurling into color with the light of the rising sun. Usually June mornings were full of rain and darkness. Not today. Today was a special day. The mists crept back under broad leaves. The insects and birds revved up their chirping din. Life erupted before him.

Things really were coming together for him. He had seized a company away from his rival. There was no doubt Lo Cheung would try to fight him for it, but it was now his to defend.

It had taken him four months, but he had successfully woven a complex enough web that Randy would never figure out what he had done with Cheri's body, let alone Desiree. Even with Sanantha helping him, the furthest they were going to get was Lo Cheung insisting he wasn't to blame. He wasn't happy with the pacemaker removing his failsafe, but he was sure it would never come to that. At some point Randy was going to have to realize his only option was to go home and try to pick up the remaining pieces of his life.

He felt sorry for Randy, but not sorry for what he had done. Randy lacked ambition. Randy could find the answer to any scientific riddle, but he would never act on it by himself. It was only a matter of time before someone took unfair advantage of his genius. It might as well be his best friend. He didn't deserve a woman like Cheri.

Young Nae deserved all that he had won. In fact, he had won everything he had set out to gain. He looked out over the jungle and took a deep breath of the rising earthy smells. He wondered what the future held for him. What else could he aspire to?

The Heavenly Way taught of an upward path with no end, that all things are possible because God lives in each person. Just as he thought about God, his Haneulnim, the sun peeked up over the horizon and shone a warm, golden light on his hairless chest. Yes, God was in man.

Maybe that was where he should go next. Maybe he had come as far as he could on his own. He had mastered his outward world. Maybe he should nurture the godliness within himself. For that, he would need additional training and guidance.

He thought about his old temple in Korea. He recalled the quaint, dark wood hall on a hilltop in a peaceful suburban neighborhood of Seoul. It had been fifteen years since he'd set foot in that hall. Long enough, he thought. How pleased his old master would be to see how far he had come, and how eager he was to advance to the next level.

23

RANDOLPH GOT OUT OF THE CAB and hesitated for a moment, standing in the driveway, too distracted in his thoughts to be bothered by the early morning drizzle. Should he wake Sanantha in the beach house, or check on Desiree first? Sanantha had stayed up watching over him for most of the two days he spent in the hospital. Let her sleep.

He had given his key to Sanantha, so he had to knock on the front door. Maria the housekeeper answered, clearly already up and into her daily routines.

"Ah, Doctor Macklin. Good morning. Welcome home from hospital."

"Thank you, Maria." He was about to step past her and head up to Desiree's bedroom, when he had an unpleasant thought. "Maria, can I have a word with you?"

"Of course, Sir. What can I do for you?"

He assessed her generous and subservient manner and struggled with how forcefully he wanted to confront her. He took a breath but didn't succeed in calming himself. "I have recently learned that Mr. Young was having inappropriate relations with my wife last year. I would very much like to know why you have not told me about this on your own."

Maria stood there staring at him with her mouth slack in an expression that under other circumstances would have been comical. "Dios mio! I assure you, Sir, I had no idea."

"How is that possible?" He could barely contain himself. "You're the housekeeper, for Christsakes!"

She lowered her head. "Only since March of this year, Sir."

"Oh." He blinked a couple of times. "Well, shit, I'm sorry. I had no idea. I didn't mean to take it out on you."

She smiled sheepishly. "That's all right, Sir."

"Wait. Young Nae hired you after my wife died and after my daughter was already here in a coma?"

"Yes sir."

"Did you know the previous housekeeper?"

"No sir. I never met her."

"Do you know what became of her? Was she fired, did she leave on her own?"

"No, I'm sorry, but I have no idea. I never thought it right for me to ask."

"Yeah, I guess you're probably right about that." He started thinking out loud to himself. "So there are no witnesses. Except for Desiree and me." He turned back to Maria. "Thank you. Again, I'm sorry about the accusation."

She bowed as he turned and hustled up the stairs.

When Randolph entered the bedroom, the night nurse was just gathering up her things. "Good morning. I take it Vera will be here soon?"

"Good morning, Doctor. Yes, she starts at seven."

He stepped to the bed. "How is she doing? I haven't been here in four days."

164

"She is responding well to the anti-viral sequence. Dr. Kwon was here yesterday and he was very encouraged by her progress."

"That's great. I see her skin tone is back to normal, so the jaundice is gone." He noticed the nurse had her purse and other belongings stacked neatly on a chair. He looked at his watch. "If you want to leave now, you can. I'll stay here until Vera arrives in fifteen."

"Thank you, Sir. I think I will. Have a pleasant day."

"You too."

As was his habit, he pulled up a chair and sat at Desiree's bedside. He picked up her limp hand and held it. "You gave us a bit of a scare. It looks like you're pulling through just fine."

He stood up and opened one of her eyes to check the color of her whites. What he saw stunned him like freezing water down his back. The whites were clear, but her iris was brown. He opened the other one and found it the same. "What the fuck?"

As he held her face in his hands, his mind did a somersault, and he recognized who he was looking at. The shiver magnified to frozen shock. This was Cheri. He tried to take a breath, but his lungs were already full and he couldn't take in any more air. He gasped, staring at her face in his hands, unable to comprehend what was happening. Finally, he let go and pulled back, as if taking a step back would give him more perspective. Now he saw that she wasn't just lying limply as before, but her face was less taut, older, like the woman in her forties that she was. His hands began to shake, his legs went weak and he had to sit down.

He wrapped his arms around his chest and stuck his hands in his armpits to stop them from trembling. "But you're dead." He started shaking his head side to side. "But you're dead." He pressed his eyes tight shut and finally took a deep breath. "But you're dead."

He got up and started pacing the room. "How in the hell could this be? What the fuck is going on? How? How could this happen? You've been on anti-viral ..." he trailed off. He looked back at her. "Virus." He grabbed his hair and his breathing became ragged again. "Virus. The fucking virus. No, no, no. My fucking virus!"

He took a step toward the bed and his torso locked up a spasm so tight he felt like someone had impaled him from behind with a sword.

He clutched at his chest, but found his left arm didn't respond. Then his legs went numb and he collapsed in a heap. The pain swept over him like he was on fire, exploding from within. He couldn't move, he couldn't breathe, he couldn't think.

In that moment of excruciating agony, he had a flash, a vision, a memory. He saw himself drawing blood from Desiree, and breaking it down to extract the DNA. He heard Young Nae say in a desperate, heated argument, "We've got to do something. With all this knowledge, we can't just let this pass."

Another spasm crashed through the memory. He heard himself telling Young Nae, "I'll use a slow virus, like HIV, to make sure it sticks around in the cells long enough to swap out the entire genome."

He realized the pacemaker was not stopping the heart attack. He wondered if he was going to die. Even with these memories, it still didn't make sense. Was he really going to die not knowing what had happened?

He flashed on one last bit of conversation. He asked Young Nae, "So how do I convince my daughter to donate an egg so we can clone her mother?"

While he was struggling to recall details and trying to make sense of it all, he didn't notice that the pain in his chest was subsiding. His body was shaking rhythmically, like his heart was being forced into lockstep. He first noticed that he felt warmer, as his blood started pumping again. He chuckled and began to cry in relief. He laid there exhausted, overwhelmed. He felt delivered. Technology had saved him.

What had technology done to his wife? What had Young Nae done to her?

When the pain let him move again, he twisted his arm under himself and had to push hard against the floor to sit up. He was so weak. He looked up at Cheri in the bed. If they were trying to clone a Desiree egg into a new Cheri, why did Young Nae turn Cheri into a copy of Desiree? Why would he want to do that? What was he trying to accomplish?

He struggled, and after a couple of attempts, managed to pull himself up into the chair. He looked at her lying there quietly. "You didn't die in a fiery car crash in February. You really did succumb to that snakebite in January, just like everybody keeps telling me."

He lowered his head and sighed. "I want to be mad at you for cheating on me. That seems kind of pointless now. When I thought you were dead, I could just put you in the past. Now here you are! Five months in a coma from a snake bite. Who the hell am I kidding? Young Nae only kept you alive to disguise you and throw me off the trail. I still don't know what the fuck he is up to!

"You're not coming back. Jesus, it was easier when you were dead. You were gone, and I could focus on Desiree, and getting my memory back and figuring out what happened. Now you're back. My memory is back. Now it's worse. Because my memory doesn't have any answers.

"Now I miss you more than ever." He stared at her, still trying to grasp her sudden reappearance.

"How could I have let us drift apart? Was I just so staid and boring? Could I just not hold your interest in your globetrotting, exciting lifestyle? Fate has brought you back to me, just so I can sit here and realize there is nothing I can do about it. Just salt in the wound. You'll be with me for years to come. Years of being reminded how the best thing I ever had in life was an illusion."

He ran out of words and just stared at her face. His eyes welled up and tears flowed down his cheeks.

24

S ANANTHA SAW RANDOLPH FROM THE DOOR, with his back toward her as he sat by the bed. The strong scent of antiseptic made it easy to see the bedroom suite as a private hospital. "Good morning. Maria said you took a cab from the hospital. I could have come and gotten you if I'd known you were ready." She stepped up on the other side of the bed. "How are you doing?"

He looked up at her and she gasped. "Randy, you look awful. You're so pale, and sweating. They released you from the hospital like this?"

He chuckled weakly. "No, I was fine when I left. I just had a heart attack ten minutes ago. The pacemaker saved me."

"*Merde!* We've got to get you into a bed, and get you some aspirin." She rushed around to him to help him up.

He held up his hand. "It wasn't that kind of heart attack. It was the chi trap. Now that it's sprung, it seems to have stopped trying actively to kill me. I guess it just snapped once."

"The chi trap?" She brightened. "You remembered! You remembered what happened to you four months ago?"

He lowered his head again. "Yeah, I remember."

She hesitated and raised an eyebrow. "I take it, it's not good."

"See for yourself," he said gesturing to the comatose woman.

She frowned at her, wondering what she was supposed to be seeing. The woman had brown hair, but her roots were growing in black. "I don't get it. You remember what happened to Desiree?"

He took a deep breath and straightened up in his chair. "Remember that weird conversation we had with that Malaysian shopkeeper and his odd wife, about what eye color the snake bite victim had?"

"Yeah," she said cautiously.

"My daughter Desiree inherited my blue eyes. Her mother has dark brown eyes. No mistaking the difference."

"Okay."

"Well, a week ago she came down with jaundice, and I spotted it from the yellow sclera of her eyes. Her doctor put her on an anti-viral sequence, and it cleared up. So did something else." He reached over and opened one of her eyes to reveal a dark brown iris.

"What? What does that mean?"

"Take a good hard look. You never met my wife or my daughter, but does that look like a nineteen-year-old girl to you?"

Sanantha snapped her head around at Randy and blinked several times. "This is your wife? What, she was disguised to look like your daughter? She was disguised by a … a virus? Oh, wait a minute." Her eyebrows shot up. "A gene therapy virus … that replaced Cheri's DNA with Desiree's." She stepped back involuntarily. "You said you had discovered how to use viruses to swap out huge sets of DNA, to cure entire syndromes of genetic diseases." She looked again at the woman. "Let me guess, Cheri has black hair and Desiree's hair is brown?" She turned her frown on him. "You didn't do this, did you?"

"No. It's my technology, but I did not do this. I believed Young Nae when he told me Cheri died in a car crash and her body was lost in a fire. Obviously, that never happened. He used my techniques to hide Cheri's body in plain sight, disguised as Desiree."

Sanantha shook her head and tried to line up the facts. It made no sense, and she was having a really hard time with the implications. "Why would he do that? What could this accomplish? Think of what he has done! Papa Legba, this is identity theft, kidnapping, murder, all wrapped into one. Injecting a disease into someone to turn them into somebody else? Against their will! Thank God she was comatose at the time."

Randy spoke up, but avoided eye contact. "Yeah, it's pretty bad. Unfortunately, I'm not ... entirely ... blameless in this whole affair."

"You said you didn't do this to your wife's body."

"Oh no, that's correct. Young Nae built this virus library by copying my technique. My original recollection was drawing blood from Desiree to make a virus of her DNA. He used it to convert Cheri's body into a copy of Desiree. I made the virus to clone a new Cheri."

"A clone?"

"That's the memory that triggered the heart attack. That's the memory Young Nae was willing to kill me for if I remembered it. I built a virus to clone a new Cheri."

"Go on."

"I was so grief stricken, and Young Nae was so adamant that we shouldn't just let her pass away. After all, we were the Masters of the Secrets of Life. Why should we let death stand in our way? So we were going to take one of Desiree's eggs, and inoculate it with a virus that would find any DNA that Desiree had inherited from me, and replace it with equivalent copies of the DNA she had inherited from Cheri. I don't remember the details, and frankly now that I think about it with a clear head, it doesn't work."

Sanantha saw he was retreating behind the clinical explanation, but she needed to keep him on topic. "The details don't matter at this point. I'm sure you made it work. Do you remember what happened to this clone? Did you inject the egg?"

"No, I don't think so. At least I don't remember doing it. Young Nae and I had huge arguments about what we were doing. I recall wondering why he always won those arguments. Here I was building cutting edge genetics, but I couldn't argue simple morals and logic. At some point, my memories just fade to sitting on the beach watching the waves for days on end. I really don't know what happened after that."

Sanantha nodded. "Once he got what he wanted from you, he started drugging you with the zombie poison. In fact, he may have started drugging you earlier, which would explain why you just ended up going along with whatever he told you."

"Wait. What?"

"The tetrodotoxin, the fugu fish poison he used on you, it saps willpower without impeding higher brain function. You can still think but you can't resist. It's really evil stuff. Once he finished with you, he let the drug build a state dependency barrier to block your memories. Then at some point he set the chi trap, so if you ever did remember, it would kill you before you could tell anyone. It was this cloning that he has been working so hard to hide."

Randy rolled his eyes as he put it together for himself. "That makes sense. Finally."

Sanantha blinked and shook her head with a terrible realization. "If this is Cheri, then where is Desiree?"

"Oh my Lord," he breathed.

"Oh now, wait a minute," she interrupted herself. "I know exactly where she is. Also why this whole camouflage effort was made." She looked Randy in the eye. "Young Nae's got her. This whole thing was a kidnapping."

"How can you be sure?"

"I got a phone message from Lo Cheung last night that his spies spotted a woman who looks like Desiree at a vacation house Young Nae has up in the mountains. At the time, I thought Cheung was just blowing smoke. Now I see he's been telling the truth all along. It was Young Nae, and not him behind all of this. If his spies are right, then that woman up in the mountains is Desiree."

Randy pressed his eyes tight shut and shook his head. "Why? What the hell?"

"Is it beyond reason with all the other things Young Nae has done, that he could also kidnap your daughter and hold her in some secluded spot? You would never go looking for her if you thought she was lying right here."

He bit down hard and clenched his fists. "My baby! Jesus, he's probably drugged her and brainwashed her. He couldn't have Cheri so he took Desiree instead. What a fucking mad man. God knows what he's been doing to her."

Sanantha had a chilling thought. "I need to warn you about something. After four months in captivity, she may not want to be rescued."

"What?"

"Sometimes when someone has been tortured for a long time, they start to make excuses for their captors as a way of coping with the despair. Sometimes these excuses go all the way to sympathy. It's called Stockholm Syndrome."

"Right, like Patty Hearst."

"Exactly. Be prepared for a fight when we rescue her."

"This brainwashing can be reversed though, right?"

"Yes. It takes a lot of therapy, but it is reversible."

"Okay. Thank you for the warning."

"I'll call the police."

"Wait a minute," he said holding up his hand. "I am really mad right now, and I know bad decisions get made when you're this mad. Is there any way we could be pinning this on the wrong man? Is there any way we have piled too much on Young Nae?"

She shook her head. "I'm afraid not. There is only the one explanation."

He looked around at the floor in desperation. "It just seems impossible. How could my best friend, my lifelong friend, fall so far? I mean, I still have some doubts about the affair. There's a lot of evidence, but how can you be sure? The same thing here. We're going to have him arrested for kidnapping Desiree and torturing me. We had better be damned sure of ourselves."

She looked him earnestly. "We are. His greed and hubris have been building for years. He clearly thinks he can do anything he wants, take anything he wants. He is not the friend you went to college with. He changed. He was seduced by the power your work gave him."

"Can we at least try to talk to him first, before we call in the police?"

She didn't want to be cruel, but she didn't want him to cling to false hope. "Call him up."

He fished his cell phone out of his pocket and took several deep breaths, blowing them out noisily to let go of tension. "Let's see if he is at his downtown office." He rolled his head around to clear it. "No hesitation. Young Nae is really good at reading people. Can't let him know anything is wrong."

"This is Young Nae Yoon. I am in the office today, but I can't take your call. Please leave a message, including your phone number, and I will call you back. Thank you." Beep.

"Hey, Young Nae! It's Randy! Pick up. Oh all right, I guess you're busy. Look, I'm gonna be in K-L this afternoon, and I was wondering if we could meet up? Give me a call when you get this message. It's about 10:30. You've got the number. We'll talk then. Thanks."

He turned to Sanantha. "Did I sound as nervous as I am?"

"No, you sounded quite natural. He's not there?"

"Actually, his message said he is in the office today."

"Well, that's good. Do you want to drive across the peninsula and see him face to face?"

"Yes. I'd feel a lot better about having him hauled away if I could just look him in the eye first."

"I understand."

25

WHEN MASTER HAN DAE PARK EMERGED from his Rectory apartment just after dawn, the dew was already gone in the warm June sunshine. He missed the morning fog of spring. The way it coolly clung in corners gave him tranquility, a reminder to slow down. Summer was surely coming. He looked out over the rooftops of suburban Seoul and up at the clear blue sky. He breathed deep, but smelled only dry. It was going to be a hot day.

As he walked across the temple courtyard to begin his morning chores in the sanctuary, he noticed the daffodils had died in the side yard garden. He would have to remember to pull the bulbs. In their place, the daisy bushes were in full bloom. Although they too were God's creatures, he never liked the messy riot of little blossoms, or the bees the daisies drew.

He unlocked the side door and immediately noticed the incense. Of course, the hall always smelled of the daily burning of incense. This wasn't a lingering odor, but the smell of actively burning embers. He hastened his step and swept his gaze around the spacious chamber to find the source. There in the center of the room, a man in white robes sat in lotus position on a grass mat, with an incense burner lit in front of him. The man did not move at Master Han's approach. His eyes were closed and his back was straight, clearly in deep meditation. He thought he recognized the man. "May I help you? The temple is not open for another hour."

Young Nae Yoon opened his eyes, blinked a couple of times, and smiled up at him. "Master Han. I was hoping you were still in charge here."

"I thought you looked familiar. Were you a member in the past?"

Young Nae smiled patiently. "I am Young Nae Yoon."

Master Han's eyes went wide and he smiled in return. "Young Nae! Please forgive an old man his failing eyesight. I am as pleased to see you as I am surprised." He thought to shake his hand, but then noticed Young Nae kept his hands resting in his lap. "Have you been sitting here long?"

"All night, actually. I have been taking in the joy of the old familiar surroundings."

"Such devotion. You surprise me again."

"I wouldn't blame you if you had assumed that I had abandoned the Heavenly Way. I have, in fact, remained devout."

"I am glad to hear that. I hope the Way has kept you well. I recall you were quite troubled when you left us. I prayed for you to find peace."

"Thank you. The Way has done me well. I have never doubted the presence of Haneulnim within me, or anyone else. I have attributed and dedicated all of my worldly accomplishments to the God who is within. He has given me great confidence to strive for greatness."

"Have you made the world a more godly place?"

He paused before answering. "Well, I haven't thought about it in those terms. I have employed a lot of people. I have helped people by putting a lot of good products on the market. Now I'm looking to get back to my spiritual self. I want to get more in touch with the spiritual God within me."

"A commendable goal," Master Han said with a small bow.

"How do I continue on the Heavenly Way? What do I need to learn to commune with Haneulnim at a higher, deeper level?"

The priest was slightly taken aback. "I think you may be confused. Seeking to be like God is not the same kind of process as seeking Enlightenment. You don't work your way up to a higher level of consciousness. Emulating God means working to include His principles in everything you do."

"Then why do you teach that the Way leads upward and has no end? Why are the heroes of our faith held out as gaining greater understanding of the Universe after communing with God? I have spent my life mastering how the Universe works. Now I am ready to learn more."

Master Han wasn't sure what to make of this. How could a pupil of Cheondogyo have so completely missed the central tenet of godliness? "Dare I ask what forms of mastery you speak of?"

"I live in Malaysia, and I have accepted their native ways as a truth to embrace. I have used the confidence the God Within gives me to master Silat Seni Gayong, and achieved a oneness with the Universe I never thought was possible. At times, fate itself seems to bend to my advantage."

The priest could barely contain his horror, and struggled to maintain a calm, constructive tone. "Silat is a form of mastery over men, and is a step in the wrong direction. Haneulinim lives within us so we may know Innaecheon, that God is the source of all dignity. Exercising mastery over men usurps their dignity. The Heavenly Way teaches us how to promote dignity in our fellow man. While the godliness in each of us is an incentive to strive for better, we must always respect the godliness in our fellow man. Remember the credo, 'Every man is God, and must be treated accordingly.' Do you not see that exerting your will over others is the opposite of the Way?"

Young Nae sat still and stared at him for a long moment. "I am not ignorant, or misguided. I know the truth of what you say. What you deny is the connection I have found between the God Within and the flow of fate, the Tao itself. If my path were evil and contrary to God's will as you say, then why have I been so successful? I know you are going to label me arrogant for using this example, but Dangon found this connection, and used it to defeat the enemies of our faith. I came here to learn how to see the path of righteousness, and how to avoid the path of self-indulgence and evil."

The priest was relieved to hear this. He had to make sure Young Nae understood. "It is not arrogant to want to follow in the footsteps of the hero of our people. Dangon faced the temptation of personal power and brought to us the lesson of respect. He made that journey so we don't have to."

"I am already on that journey. I can do things far more in tune with the Universe than my Silat master could teach me."

Master Han put his hand up and implored, "I do not want to hear what you can do."

Young Nae pressed anyway. "I can bend men's will with my voice. I can even kill with touch."

"Killing does not bring you closer to God."

"I brought my lover back from the dead."

The priest couldn't control the shiver that ran up his spine. He forced his feet still when he felt himself start to take an involuntary step back. "I don't know what you have become, but it is not closer to Haneulnim."

Young Nae remained sitting impassively. That he did not react emotionally to Master Han's insult unnerved the priest even more. "Are you telling me there is no higher communion? Is it just a myth? Or is it a closely guarded secret. Is there an initiation? Is it like the Jews keeping their Kabala hidden until a follower gets to age fifty? If the secret exists anywhere, it would be here."

"If you want to follow one of our heroes, then follow Hwanin, who begged God for the chance to redeem himself and mankind after falling from grace, by becoming more pure, more virtuous, more in touch with nature. When our founder and Great Master Choe Jeu discovered that God is in everyone, he also saw that anyone can live divinely. '*Sicheonju*, I serve God within me.' You get there by living purely."

"That's what I've been telling you. I am totally in touch with nature. How else could I do these things?" Young Nae sighed and shook his head. "If you will not tell me what I need to know, then I will arrange to see the temple Mudang shaman."

"Absolutely not. You will not sully the shaman's presence with your quest for power. This mastery you are so proud of is from evil. You must see that first, and turn away from it. You say you want to commune with God. Then look to the God within you and see that your path is corrupt. Maybe you can do amazing things, and maybe this means you are destined for greatness." He brightened with a thought. "Maybe this has been a test. What if Haneulnim has brought you to this precipice so you can see what real purity looks like? You said you brought someone back from the dead. Maybe you are destined to be a great healer. You could fulfill one of our principal ministries of removing suffering from the world. You could even help lead mankind into the coming age of selfless godliness, the Hucheon Gaebyeok."

A long silence hung in the air. Neither man breathed. The cavernous hall itself seemed to hold its breath.

Young Nae regarded him coolly. Such a transparent attempt to lead him by his ego was further proof the old priest was hiding something. "Plying me with promises of greatness will not dissuade me from getting an answer to my question. Do you know how I can refine this connection between my God Within and the Tao?" He took a breath, not through his lungs, but through his pores — a breath of the energy around him. Then he unleashed it at the priest. "Tell me!"

The force of his words wracked Master Han's body and flung him back. Still, the old man did not cave as Young Nae had hoped. When he turned back, Young Nae saw a tear run down his cheek. It was a tear of pity.

Young Nae sprang to his feet. "How dare you pity me? This is your chance to guide me, to be part of what I will become." He stepped up to the priest and loomed over him. "Yet the best you can do is feel sorry for me, because you think I have been seduced by evil?" He crowded him more, intimidating him. "This is your last chance."

Master Han looked up at him and Young Nae was pleased to see he had put real fear in those eyes. Yet, the priest's voice was still steady.

"If you strike down a servant of God, God will abandon you once and for all."

"God won't abandon me. God is the one who showed me the Way."

"Did you kill your Silat master as well?"

"No. He taught me all that he knew, and I thanked him, very generously. I am making you the same offer now."

"I don't know the power you seek. Your redemption lies in turning away from this evil that has taken hold of your soul. It was just this kind of selfishness that our Great Master Choe was trying to eradicate by founding this church."

Young Nae laughed at him. "Do you think you can eradicate me?"

"I am still in touch with your family. I will do everything in my power to stop you."

Young Nae reached down into the pit of his anger and frustration and found a place colder and darker than he had ever felt before. "Too bad." He thrust his fist out across the priest's neck and down past his chest. It was as if his hand knew where to go, seeking out the right path instinctively. He felt his hand take hold of something and rip it out of his body. He didn't physically touch the man. The man fell limp, instantly dead.

Young Nae stopped and looked, and realized what he had done. Had he really needed to kill his old priest? Yes, Master Han was the old path that had to be severed to find the new. He looked at his hand and felt it warm up again. He was surprised, and smiled a bit nervously. He looked down at the priest's body, lying sprawled where it had dropped. "It seems I don't need your secrets after all."

26

S ANANTHA DROVE AS FAST as her Fiat coupe would go west on Highway 99 across the Malaysian peninsula to Kuala Lumpur. Randolph next to her was taking lots of deep breaths and looking out at the jungle countryside. He glanced over and seemed to notice her driving for the first time. "Do you want me to drive?"

"Um ... no, I'm good. Thanks." She wanted answers, and needed to change the subject. Maybe getting him to talk shop would calm him down. "Disguising Cheri by making her into a copy of Desiree was creepy. I know you said you had discovered how to put as much genetic material into patches as you want to fix problems. I think you called the patches 'libraries.' That still doesn't get you to a whole person. How can a virus turn somebody into someone else?"

He smiled and cocked his head. "It really doesn't. That's why we haven't gone public with it, and why we can't get it to reproduce. The virus doesn't eliminate the old DNA. It sets it aside. I use a slow virus, a variant on Hanta, that sticks around and forms a symbiosis with the host cell. The virus goes dormant after it finishes the initial swap. The cell doesn't recognize the displaced fragments of the original DNA as trash, so the pieces aren't metabolized. They stick around, and find their way back into the master sequence that drives RNA creation. The virally encoded genetic material has to stay alive to maintain the equilibrium, to keep the new right stuff in place and the old wrong stuff silent."

Sanantha was glad she had another cup of coffee before they left. Listening to Randolph explain his work was like watching a billiards hustler run a table. "If you are curing something like hemophilia, the patient has to stay infected with the slow virus?"

"Yes. It's a symbiosis, which is not really a cure. It's more of a mask, which is what Young Nae decided to use it for."

Sanantha took a deep breath as she tried to digest his explanation. "Okay, Dr. Kwon gave Cheri interferon that killed the virus, and her old DNA moved back into position and she turned back into herself?"

"Yes, exactly, but interferon only helps the body fight a virus once the body has identified the virus as foreign. Slow viruses hide and go dormant, which is why interferon doesn't cure AIDS. Something in the hepatic infection must have triggered some kind of immune response. Something shocked the symbiosis equilibrium and unmasked the virus as foreign which brought it out into the open where the drugs could kill it."

"An immune response? Like an allergic reaction?"

"I'm guessing. She was in a coma, which masks lots of symptoms. I didn't notice the jaundice until it was pretty far advanced."

"How could an allergic response mess with a virus?"

"Allergies are the body attacking foreign matter, usually proteins. Your symptoms are the sudden breakout of war on a cellular level. The antibodies attack the foreign proteins, thus labeling them. Something must have labeled the Desiree DNA, and that allowed the interferon and her antibodies to find it."

Sanantha went silent and just drove, staring intently ahead.

"You look like something is still bugging you," Randy observed.

She grinned sheepishly at having been caught. "It is. I'm not sure how I can explain this. You've been having nightmares that showed us how you have wrestled with all of this. Well, I had a dream too. It was a vision sent to me by my goddess of mercy, Madame Erzulie. I've never had a vision like this before, and it's been preying on me for two days now. Even with what we just learned, it still does not make much sense." She looked at him to gauge his reaction before continuing.

He smiled. "Go on. Yes, I am amused that my shrink gets religious visions. Frankly, with everything else, that's hardly the strangest thing to happen."

"Okay." She smiled and nodded. "Thanks. In the dream, Erzulie, who is kind of like Mary to the Catholics, took me to Legba, who is kind of like Jesus. He showed me a nesting doll. You know, the hollow ones that fit one inside the next? There was a daughter inside a mother. Seems pretty apropos. Then inside the daughter was a snake. It was the snake that Legba wanted me to find. Everyone was panicked looking for it, but I was the only one who could find it."

He shook his head. "Every time I have told you about one of my dreams, you have cautioned me that dreams only show that your subconscious is working on something, and that the actual content of the dream is unlikely to mean anything."

"You're right, normally content doesn't matter. This is not normal. Hidden in your dreams have been bits and clues that have turned out to be useful. This dream was more like a vision than a dream. I mean there was a distinct message. I'm supposed to find a snake."

"Well, we found the mother, hidden inside the daughter, and the mother was still alive because she was comatose from a snake bite and not dead from a car crash. Your sequence is a little screwed up, but you've got all the facts."

"I guess. I still feel like we might have missed something really important."

"Welcome to the club. Some of my dreams have left me convinced we're on the wrong path. That one with the bread and the knife, that one still freaks me out. It still makes no sense."

"That was rather shocking," she agreed. "Are you sure you're okay with me listening to advice from gods? I mean, frankly, I'm not comfortable with it."

"Not a problem for me. I tried to make sense of my nightmares despite your guidance. Whether it's my subconscious or if there are gods involved doesn't matter. I don't see much point in arguing ecumenical sources. Remember, I'm an Episcopalian. We make a point of trying to reconcile the scientific with the supernatural. Otherwise, you end up denying one or the other, which is both bad science and bad religion.

"If you think we've missed something, then I'll keep an open mind," he continued. "I've looked to religion, and all I have been able to conjure up is old Sunday School axioms that say I need to let go of my anger and trust God. My rock and roll has been a greater comfort than religion. My dreams are my tortured brain trying in vain to cope. I could use a good, productive vision. I mean, we're dealing with someone who believes in *his* visions."

"Young Nae has visions?"

"Yes, from his god Haneulnim. He used to tell me about them when we were just starting out together. He was sure he had divine providence on our side."

"He follows Cheondogyo, the shamanistic Korean Heavenly Way?"

"Yeah. Our company symbol is derived from the Cheondogyo flag."

"Well that's just bizarre," she thought out loud. "Followers of the Heavenly Way believe God is in all of us, and our godly nature is to love one another. He must have abandoned that faith to be acting like this."

"I think it's more like he's twisted it around. He told me the Heavenly Way was the path to the divine through personal perfection. At the time that sounded like a really nice, egalitarian concept. That anyone can succeed because each of us has God within us."

"That is what that faith teaches," she confirmed.

"Young Nae has taken it to mean he can justify anything by citing his own development as fulfilling his divine destiny."

"Madmen often use their religion to excuse their abuses. History has shown us that. I have seen it with my own eyes."

"Great. So he's doing all of this, feeling justified by God?"

"From what you've said, that's what it sounds like."

•   •   •

She knew she was dreaming, but it was so delicious, she didn't care. She knew she could only expect spotty sunshine through the windows of the solarium porch, but here in her dream she was on a white sand beach with the sun roaring down, massaging her muscles with glorious heat right through her naked skin. She rolled over onto her back and marveled at the tingle that spread across her stomach and chest as sweat broke out from her pores. She could feel the heat fill up a depth of her body. She giggled when a droplet of sweat crawled under her breast and down her ribs.

Without opening her eyes, she wiped the sweat away and felt an odd ridge on her sternum. She propped herself up on one elbow, took off her sunglasses and examined what her free hand had found. A line of bumps on her skin stretched from the base of her neck all the way down to her navel. They weren't sores or blemishes. They were soft, and felt like skin. Were they scars? She couldn't recall having open chest surgery, but that was certainly what it looked like.

She picked at it and teased up an edge. It didn't hurt, so she gave into curiosity, however adolescent, and pulled on it. To her horror, the wound opened up. She quickly pushed it shut and smoothed it down.

She sat up fully and felt along the length of the ridge with all her fingertips. The whole opening was closed, but just sitting closed, with no healing holding it shut. She realized she had better not lean forward, lest all her guts fall out.

Trapped between fear and fascination, she tried an edge again. It came right open, ribs too, revealing all her internal organs, pumping and churning away. There was no blood, no pain, everything was healed, so this had clearly been done some time ago. What kind of surgeon leaves a person like this?

As she sat and marveled, the sun overhead shone in on her organs, and it felt warm. In fact, it felt really, really good. She leaned her head back to let the sun shine directly in, and it felt like someone pouring warm milk in to fill up her body cavity. The warmth radiated out into her limbs. It was as if she had been freezing but hadn't known it, and now she was being bathed with healing heat, inside and out, thawed out, imbued with life. No, brought back to life.

As weird as it was, she was swept up in the sensation, and laid back flat on the sand, holding her chest cavity open to the sun with her fingers. All thoughts about what was happening were washed away, and she let her mind swim free in the all-encompassing warmth.

The first thought she could put together was that she was chilly. Chilly didn't make sense. She opened her eyes, and it made perfect sense. She was lying naked on a chaise lounge in a room made of glass, but it was dark and raining outside. She took a good hard look at her chest to make sure it was not dissected with an open surgical wound.

She blinked several times to reassess where she was. Not only had the dream seemed very real, but she wasn't sure where she was now. She got up, grabbed the plush white robe that was draped over the chaise next to her, and put it on. She stood there for a moment trying to remember this room. The disquieting dream was the least of her problems. How could she be sunbathing naked during a rainstorm in a strange house and not remember how she got there?

She had gotten drunk at a party a couple of years ago and woke up not knowing how she had gotten home. This had that drunken episode beat hands down.

Her surroundings were quite benign, posh in fact, so she didn't feel threatened. She felt her forehead, thinking maybe she had a fever, but she was fine. Standing there wasn't going to get her more answers, so she went exploring.

· · ·

Randolph waved at Sanantha to slow her down as she started to race across the wide, tiled plaza in front of Young Nae's office building. He had to raise his voice over the stiff wind that blew through the skyscraper-lined downtown. "My pacemaker only pumps at a certain speed. If I take off running, I'll pass out from insufficient blood supply."

"Oh. So the pacemaker is the only thing …?"

"Yep. I'm pretty sure the chi trap has completely interrupted my heart's ability to beat on its own."

"All right, then."

As they mounted the stairs, the wind buffeted them, and Randolph felt the warmth drain from his body. He saw a stocky, expensively dressed Chinese businessman and his entourage bursting out of the entrance, clearly furious about something. He started to step aside to let them pass, when, much to Randolph's surprise, Sanantha stepped up to the man.

"Doctor Mauwad! What a pleasant surprise." The anger on the man's face was a complete mismatch to his greeting.

"Mister Lo. This can't be a coincidence."

Randolph was shocked.

"If you are here to see Young Nae Yoon, then you are out of luck." He bristled when he said Young Nae's name. "The dog's testicle is not here."

"His answering machine says he is."

"It always does," he dismissed.

"You came here to confront him? We did too."

Lo stopped and pulled himself up straight. "Really? What have you figured out, Doctor?"

"We know he kidnapped Desiree Macklin, used genetics to disguise the comatose Cheri Macklin to look like her daughter, and then poisoned Doctor Macklin here to make him forget."

Lo stepped up to Randy and extended his hand. Randy shot Sanantha a hesitant glance, then shook it.

Lo caught his doubt and grinned from behind his gaudy, gold-framed yellow sunglasses. "Didn't think we would meet face to face, eh? Well, I am very glad to meet you." When Randy said nothing back, he continued. "Why did he do this to you?"

"He couldn't have my wife anymore, so he took my daughter instead."

Lo blinked his surprise.

Randy pressed. "Something must have changed for you too, for you to confront Young Nae openly like this."

Lo bit down so hard, Randy could see his jaw muscles bulge. "Yes. The *hun dan gou* put my niece's husband in the hospital and tried to strong-arm his partner into taking over one of my companies. Business is one thing, but he's gone too far attacking my family."

The wind howled again, and Randy had to raise his voice. "If he's not here, how do we find him?"

Of the six men in black suits who accompanied Cheung, one of them was not hugely muscled. The thin man stepped up and handed Lo an open laptop computer that had a box attached to one side with an antenna sticking up. "He has fled to Korea, with the four million dollars he just liquidated a few days ago, and your daughter, no doubt."

Sanantha spoke up. "We don't know that for sure. You called me last night to say your spies had spotted a young woman at Young Nae's mountain retreat. Can you call them and see if she is still there?"

"I can leave him a message, but I'll have to wait for him to call me back. Such is the spy biz." He nodded to his assistant, who whipped out a phone and started dialing.

He turned back to Randolph. "I thought your daughter was in a coma at the beach house."

"That's my wife."

Lo raised his eyebrows too high. "Ah, yes. The famous car crash that made no sense." The assistant handed him the phone.

"Hello? Yes? Right now?" He gave Randy a thumbs up. "Okay, you stay there and keep an eye on things. I'll be there in an hour." He handed the phone back. "My spy says not only is your daughter still there, she has created quite the ruckus, with police cars, an ambulance, and what looks to be search parties." He started walking away. He turned when Randy and Sanantha didn't follow. "Are you coming?"

"Where?" she asked.

"To the enemy's lair in the mountains. I have a helicopter on top of my building ten blocks from here."

Randy and Sanantha fell in behind him. "How far is this place?"

"It's near the village of Landang Pandrak, which is sixty kilometers east of the city of Ipoh, which is 250 kilometers north from here."

Sanantha asked Lo, "You know how the police here work. Do you agree we now have enough evidence on Young Nae that we can tell the police? Because I for one would really welcome some official help."

As they arrived at his limo, Lo smiled at her. "Yes, Doctor, you can call in the police now."

27

THE ONLY THING KEEPING DESIREE FROM COMPLETE PANIC was how her body seemed to know its way around the house. Her hands knew where light switches were around corners. Her feet knew how many steps it was down the main staircase. The pang in her stomach led her directly to the kitchen. She still had no recollection of where this was, or how she had gotten there, but she couldn't help but conclude she had been here before. She clung to that assurance and kept walking in hopes of something looking familiar. The longer she explored with no recognition, though, the harder it became to keep hoping, and the easier it was to let doubt turn to fear.

The house was enormous and empty. The only sound was the rain outside. She fleetingly considered if this might be a nightmare, and this rambling house of frustration was somehow her psyche breaking down. That she was padding around the unbroken hardwood floors in bare feet, naked under a Turkish robe, only added to the otherworldly experience.

She found the main living room, which was more of a great hall. An enormous metal sculpture, at least ten feet high, of half a man's face protruding into the room, dominated one wall. It was very simplistic and stylized, clearly Asian, and had a stern, unforgiving expression. It made what was already a mysterious house seem positively oppressive.

She went back upstairs and found a bedroom with closets full of clothes that fit her, even though they did not look familiar. She went through the closets and was somewhat alarmed to see how many of the dresses were flimsy and rather tawdry. She found some Capri pants, a sweater, and some sneakers, and started to get dressed. The underwear she found in the drawers was expensive and very sexy. What really disturbed her was finding her privates shaved bare. Fear crept back up her spine.

Putting the clothes on felt surreal. Clearly, they were her clothes. There was no way they would fit so comfortably if they were not. Yet she knew she had never worn them before.

She went into the bathroom and her appearance in the mirror threw her again. Her hair was cut way shorter than she wore it, and it was black. She ran her fingers through it in disbelief. "Geez, looks like my mother," she said flippantly. There was also something odd about how it laid on her head. She leaned in close and felt it. The length of it was overdyed black, but still her usual soft texture. Except at her scalp. She fingered her hair away from the part and found the inch of hair closest to her scalp was jet black, thick, and smooth with no curl at all.

Had she been sick? Can an illness make your hair grow thick and straight and black?

While she was up close to the mirror, she caught a good look at her eyes. There were strange flecks of brown at the center around the pupil of her blue eyes. She remembered a friend of hers who was into reflexology had once tried to convince her you could gauge a person's health by the patterns of color in their irises. Maybe she had been sick.

She continued exploring the house. Six bedrooms, four baths, a library, the sun room, a veranda off the master suite, a workout studio, and a movie theater. That was before the maid's quarters. The fact that

190

the maid was not there added to the feeling that this situation was not real.

At last, she found the office. It didn't take very much rifling to turn up the owner's name, Young Nae Yoon. What in the world was she doing living in Uncle Young Nae's house? In Malaysia? Now the jungle outside made sense. At least she finally knew she was in a safe place.

Then she saw the date on the bill she found was June. June? The last thing she remembered was her mother's funeral in February. A lot can happen in four months. She felt better about having ended up in friendly territory. God knows what might have happened to her in four months. Now she needed to figure out what did happen.

She found a phone but had no idea what number to call. She recalled that her father was with her at the funeral. She dialed his cell phone. "Finally, a way to make sense of all this."

"We're sorry. Your call cannot be completed as dialed. Please check the number and try your call again."

"Well, at least the message was in English. Crap, of course, I'm in Malaysia." She dialed the U.S. code 1-110 and then the number.

"The number you have reached is no longer in service. Please check the number and try your call again."

"Damnit, Dad. Oh, wait. If I've been in Malaysia for four months, maybe Dad is too." She looked dubiously at the phone in her hand. "Don't know if this is going to work here." She dialed 411.

The automated voice asked her a question in an Asian language she didn't even recognize. She pushed zero.

The phone clicked a few times and a woman came on the line, again speaking what Desiree took to be Malay.

"Do you speak English?"

"Yes, ma'am. What city and listing please?"

"I don't know what city. Can you search the whole country?"

"Yes, ma'am."

"Oh good. I'm looking for Doctor Randolph Macklin."

"One moment please. I'm sorry ma'am. I show no listing for a Doctor Randolph Macklin."

"Can you try Young Nae Yoon?"

"One moment please. Ma'am, that is an unlisted number. Oh, wait. Excuse me, ma'am, but you are calling me from that number."

"Yes, I am at his house. Do you have any other numbers, like a business number for him?"

"One moment please. Yes, ma'am, I do, but that number is also unlisted."

"Okay. Now we're getting somewhere. How can I get that number? This is an emergency, and I really need that number."

"I'm sorry, ma'am, but we are not allowed to give out unlisted numbers."

"Look, this really is an emergency. I woke up at Young Nae's house, and I think I have been kidnapped, or drugged or something. He's my father's best friend. I've known him all my life. Look, can you call him and tell him to call me at his house here? Tell him Desiree Macklin needs to talk to him right away. Can you do that for me?"

"This is highly irregular, ma'am. We are the phone directory, not a message service."

"I wasn't kidding about this being an emergency. It's either you make the call, or I will have to get the police involved. I really need some help here. Can you please help me out, just this once?"

"Hold the line, please."

The line was silent for a long minute. She didn't know if the operator was asking her supervisor about making the call or what. She reminded herself not to get her hopes up too high.

"Ma'am, I placed the call for you, but voice mail picked up. I left the message you gave me."

"Thank you! Thank you very much!"

"Do you want me to contact the police for you, ma'am?"

"No, as long as Young Nae calls me, I think I'll be okay."

"Well, ma'am, the outgoing message said he is in the office today."

"That's great."

"Is there anything else I can do for you today?" the operator asked in her practiced, perfunctory fashion.

"No, you have been a huge help. Thank you again."

"You're welcome ma'am. Thank you for calling Malaysian Bell."

She put the phone down on the kitchen counter. Then she realized she was really hungry. Her stomach had steered her to the kitchen earlier, but she had been too freaked out to think about eating. Now that she had made contact with the outside real world, she was feeling a lot less like Alice, trapped in some unbalanced, other-self world.

She made herself a sandwich and sat down in the breakfast nook to eat it. The rain outside had stopped, and the clouds were parting to show patches of blue sky. She looked around through the windows that formed most of the outside wall of the house and realized it wasn't a jungle she was seeing, but extensive gardens of tropical plants. She finished her snack, put the phone in her pocket, and went outside.

The smells of wet earth and decay were intoxicating from the moment she stepped out. She was disappointed that even such strong smells still did not jog any memories. As beautiful and as sensual as this place was, she felt completely sure she had never seen it or smelled it before.

Walking among the tall ferns and fan palms, she realized how peaceful this place must be, would be for her, if not for the storm of confusion within her. She paused to watch a tiny beetle crawling up a frond, only to be hit head on by a large water droplet running down. The bug lost its footing and was swept off the leaf onto the ground.

"You and me both, buddy."

She looked up into the jungle canopy and listened to the buzz of insects busying themselves now that the rain had stopped. Life, the universe, was going about its business, regardless of whether she was in tune with it or not.

"Young Nae will call," she steadied herself. "It will all make sense once he calls."

She walked further from the house and came upon a trail that led out into hilly open land. She felt a compulsion to start running. She realized her body was trying to tell her something, so she went with the feeling and started to jog.

It was mild but humid, and within ten minutes, she was sweating. She was pleased to notice she wasn't at all out of breath. Whatever she had been doing for the last four months, she had at least kept herself in shape.

She stopped running, scooped her short black damp hair off her forehead with both hands, and took a deep breath to collect herself. How can a person just lose four months of memory? To just wake up one day, with no injuries or anything? Set up in the lap of luxury, no less? It was like she was living somebody else's life.

She took a step and her foot slipped on something round and smooth, but before she could look down a sharp pain seized her in the back of the knee. She cried out and clutched her leg only to find two large holes above two rows of smaller pinpricks. She ran back a few steps until she spotted a slow sinuous movement among the litter of fallen leaves headed away from her.

Trying as hard as she could to remain calm, she whipped off her sweater and tied it tight around her thigh. Frantically searching the ground for a stick to twist the tourniquet tight, she found nothing. She took a step and numbing, stunning pain sent her toppling to the ground. Screaming at the top of her lungs for help, her confidence broke and she began to cry. The stabbing, stinging pain was now all the way into her hip. She pulled as hard as she could on the knotted fabric. Still the pain crept upward.

She pulled out the phone and dialed 911. Nothing connected. She tried it again, and again got nothing. "Stupid backward country!" She dialed "0."

"Pengendali."

"Do you speak English? This is an emergency. I've been bitten by a snake and I need an ambulance right away!"

"Let me connect you to Emergency Services."

She pulled the sweater tighter. Her leg above the tourniquet was swelling and turning red. "This is Emergency Services," the young man's voice came on the line. "What is your name and your location?"

"Desiree Macklin. Shit! I don't know! I'm at Young Nae Yoon's house out in the country."

"Do you know what city?"

"I have no idea! Oh my god! You can't get to me 'cause I don't know where the hell I am! Can't you look it up? Directory Assistance found this number a few minutes ago. Can you see this phone number?"

"Yes, I see the number."

"Can you see the address that goes with that number?"

"I'm afraid we don't have that kind of system."

"You're kidding! Can't you work with the phone company and figure out this address? I've been bitten by a poisonous snake! I'm lying here squeezing my leg and it feels like it's on fire. I think I'm gonna die if you can't get someone out here."

"Hold on. I will see what I can do."

She realized she was going to have to deal with this herself. She fought back panic as best she could and looked around for something sharp.

"Ms. Macklin? I've found the address."

"Thank you. I am on a trail about a half a mile in back of the house. Just come through the garden and you can't miss the trail. How long do you think it's going to be?"

"Realistically, it could be a half an hour or more before we can get to you. You are at a rather remote location."

"Jesus Christ, a half an hour? All right. I can try to get back to the house."

"Walking on it will spread the poison faster. You should stay still. What kind of snake bit you?"

"I didn't see it. It was in the leaves."

"What does the bite look like?"

"Two big holes and line of little holes below each big one."

"You said your leg feels hot? Is that heat spreading?"

"Yes, it's trying to push up my leg. I've got a tourniquet above the knee. I found a sharp rock. Should I make a cut to let the poison out?"

"I'm afraid that doesn't really work. The venom is in veins deep within your leg and a surface cut isn't going to drain it effectively."

"What do I do? I can't walk, I can't cut, and you can't get someone here for half an hour or more." Tears started streaming down her cheeks. "I'm going to be dead by the time you get here."

"Probably not. The most common snake in Malaysia that fits your description is a cobra, and cobra bites are not necessarily lethal. Stay still, hold the tourniquet, and just try to keep the venom in your leg. Even if it spreads, you will just pass out. We can revive you once we get to you."

"The poison isn't just going to stop my heart?"

"No, cobra venom shuts down voluntary muscles. The worst that can happen is it will shut down your breathing. That takes a long time, and we'll be to you before that happens."

"What's your name?" she asked quietly.

"My name? I'm Adamo."

"Adamo? Can I tell you how glad I am you speak English?"

"Okay."

"Can you stay on the line with me until they get here? I know that's asking a lot, but ..."

"Yes, of course. We've got other dispatchers who can handle the incoming calls."

"Oh shit."

"What is it?"

"My stomach muscles are tightening, by themselves. Painfully. Man, that hurts."

"Keep holding the tourniquet. You can't stop the spread, but you can buy time by slowing it down."

She took a deep breath and tried to focus on his words, trying not to panic. "Thank you for staying with me."

"I'm glad to."

"You sound really nice. Heckuva way to meet someone."

"Life can be funny that way."

The pain surged, she gritted her teeth and groaned.

"I know it's hard, but try to breathe through it."

"Don't know ... how much more ... I can take." The pain blotted out all other sensation. She couldn't feel her hands on the sweater anymore. The fire shooting up into her body crushed whatever hope she had of stopping the poison.

She noticed she couldn't take a full breath. Renewed panic seized her. She pushed as hard as she could, but with no effect.

"I don't want to die," she sobbed. "Adamo, tell me I'm not going to die!"

She didn't hear his answer. The insects and birds never missed a beat as delirium gave way to unconsciousness. Her hands let go the sweater, the phone fell from her shoulder, and her blue eyes closed.

28

THE FIRST AND ONLY THING SHE FELT when she awoke lying on the jungle floor was a hunger so great all she could do was double up in a ball around the hollow, wrenching ache in her stomach. After a moment, she lifted her head and searched the jungle around her for something, anything, to eat.

A shiny yellow carambola fruit, segmented into a star shape, hung seductively from a bush a few yards away. She tightened her gut against the pain and staggered to it with complete single mindedness. Her legs felt like lead, and every movement was a painful struggle. It felt good to sink her teeth into its pulpy flesh, and taste its perfumy juices. It felt even better to swallow as she devoured it — skin, seeds, and all.

Her stomach audibly growled as it pounced on the food and in a moment, the pain lessened. It wasn't until then that she noticed her sweater was tied in a knot around her leg. Still too dazed to cope with how it had gotten there, she unwrapped it and put it on. This distraction only lasted a few seconds before she was back scanning the surrounding greenery for edibles. A few unripe plantain bananas she could jump up and reach were good while they lasted, but still the hunger persisted.

The more active she became, the warmer she came to feel. She discarded the sweater. Soon the cool morning mist in the air did nothing to comfort her growing fever. Eventually she had to deny her insatiable hunger and sit down to try to cool off. Then the hunger returned redoubled and she had to move on. Soon she was reduced to a foraging machine, unable to think of anything but food.

$$\bullet \qquad \bullet \qquad \bullet$$

The pig obviously trusted humans. It didn't even shy away from her. With a strength she didn't know she possessed, she killed the scrawny but still luscious looking beast with a single crushing blow to the back of the neck. She ripped its throat out with her bare hands, and gorged herself on huge gulps of its hot blood, burying her face in the wound. For the first time since she awoke, she felt like she might finally satisfy her hunger.

She was so consumed by her need, she didn't even notice the farmer who found her until he cried out and charged up to her. She did not know the Malay curse words he yelled, but his anger and the rifle he leveled at her made his meaning clear. The look of horror on the face of the little boy who ran up alongside the man made her shame complete. She looked at what she'd done and then back at the animal's owners, not even sure if she wanted their forgiveness.

"I'm so sorry," she offered genuinely in perfect Malay. "I'll make it up to you. I didn't mean to kill your pig, I'm just so hungry." She held up her bloody hands in supplication, but it was obvious she wasn't getting through to this man. What she had done was just too inhuman for him to grasp.

She hurriedly wiped her hands on the grass and stood up to move away from the carcass, hoping she could reason with him better if she distanced herself from her deed.

As she stepped back he hollered in Malay, "Hold it right there!" and shot her in the shoulder.

The pain totally obliterated all thought. Hot, searing pain piled on top of unbelievable pressure. It seemed an eternity before she even became aware of her surroundings. Whether she was standing or lying down, whether the deafening ring in her ears was real or not, there was no way of telling, no way of getting past the pain.

Finally, she managed to focus on other sensations and found she was somehow still standing, facing her attacker. She realized what had happened and started to examine her arm. She was so revolted when she saw the crater of flesh the impact had caused, she had to look away.

When the ringing in her ears subsided, she could hear the little boy screaming and the man yelling at him to go away. Reason gave way to fear and anger. She saw the end of the gun waver and she leapt on the man, knocking him to the ground and sending the gun flying out of his hands. All she had wanted to do was equalize things. Mounting delirium from the gunshot compounded with her already fevered state and suddenly her plans were lost in the frenzy. She hauled back with her good fist and struck him with every ounce of animal hatred she had. There was a familiar sickening crack and the man stopped moving, much like his livestock before him.

She rolled off of him and sat there aghast at what she had done. The little boy stood paralyzed in wide-eyed terror. She looked up at him and he ran off screaming into the jungle. Kneeling next to the man, she grabbed him by his shirt and shook him gently, trying to revive him. "Please, please wake up!" she pleaded. "I couldn't have hit you that hard!" She held his head in her hands and examined the side of his head. There was a visible indentation the size of her fist.

Then she noticed that both he and she were covered in blood, both hers and his. The sight was just too much. Her brown-edged blue eyes went wide and her breathing accelerated as panic set in. She stood up and stepped back shaking, staring at her bloody hands. She ran.

•　　　•　　　•

Lo Cheung pointed out the helicopter's window at the village below them. "That's Landang Pandrak. Young Nae's villa is up behind that mountain in its own little valley."

Randy couldn't see any clearing around the buildings of the town. He thought it looked like the homes and businesses were sinking into the endless miles of dark green jungle like animals dying in quicksand. "It's so remote," he said to himself. His microphone picked it up and both Lo and Sanantha, under their own oversized earphones, nodded in reply.

He pondered his mental image of the buildings sinking. Then he imagined the jungle green as a sea, rising and swamping them. Either way they were doomed.

He caught himself. The homes would still be there, just flooded, buried, hidden, masked. His blood ran cold. "Mr. Lo? Your spy said the woman he spotted at Young Nae's ranch looked like my daughter. How would he know what my daughter looks like? My wife was a public figure. Your man could easily look her up, and probably did when he researched me after you gave him the job, but Desiree isn't all over the Internet."

"I'm not sure what you're driving at, Dr. Macklin."

"My daughter is nineteen. My wife is forty-five. Your man saw a nineteen-year-old. Yet he recognized her from pictures he had seen of my wife."

Lo turned to his assistant who handed him the laptop. It was an awkward move with everyone in headgear and strapped into their seats, but he managed to turn the screen around and hand it to Randy. "This is what he saw. It took bloody five minutes to download that picture even on my DSL. Must be at least three megabytes, maybe four. It does give you pretty good detail. Must have used a telephoto lens."

Lo's prattle about the picture fell on deaf ears. Randy was dumbstruck looking at the image. It wasn't Desiree. It was Cheri, her brown eyes clearly visible, at nineteen years old.

Randy turned to Sanantha. "I know why Young Nae kidnapped Desiree, and what he was doing with the viruses." He had to stop and catch his breath, the shock of it was so overwhelming. Then anger kicked in and he teared up in rage.

"Holy Legba, Randy, what is it?"

He turned the screen around to show her. "My recollection about who got injected wasn't wrong after all. Yes, he injected Cheri's comatose body to disguise it to look like Dez. He also injected Dez with a set of viruses made from Cheri's DNA — to turn her into a copy of Cheri."

"Can you do that?" Lo Cheung blurted out.

"Oh my God," Sanantha breathed. "What would that do to Desiree? Wouldn't a complete cloning like that erase her memories and personality, since those are all encoded using her DNA?"

He continued her thought in awestruck terror. "That's just too horrible to believe. It's like my state dependent memory, but a thousand times worse. I couldn't get to my memories because they were encoded with the poison in my system. With her DNA pushed aside and replaced by Cheri's, Desiree's memories would no longer be available. In fact, the new woman would have no memories at all, a blank slate." He clenched down and shook his head. "He wiped out my daughter to get a plaything blank version of my wife."

Lo commented, "She looks so young."

"She's such a mash up of genetic material, somehow having a body full of nineteen-year-old telomeres has held her age while she was turned into a copy of Cheri."

"A ready-made sex slave," Lo Cheung let slip as he thought out loud. "Oh shit, sorry."

Randy nodded. "We were all thinking it anyway."

"That's absolutely diabolical," Sanantha added. "This must have been what you and Young Nae argued about so vehemently before he decided to take you out of the picture. To sacrifice Desiree to bring Cheri back from the dead."

"He made her to have for himself," Randy concluded through gritted teeth. As he seethed, it occurred to him that Cheri had been nineteen when he first met her, when he and Young Nae had just graduated from college. Had he always loved her?

Sanantha had a look of sympathy that told him she wanted to help, but couldn't find the words. She just blinked and slowly shook her head from side to side.

He began sobbing. "How could I have not seen this? How could I have participated? I built the goddamn thing. I mean, we were used to taking matters into our own hands, but what kind of insanity justifies making a weapon like this?"

Sanantha finally found her voice. "You were insanely sad, and laid open, vulnerable, and he took complete advantage of you. Remember, he drugged you with tetrodotoxin. Your will was not your own. He could have made you do anything under that influence. You cannot blame yourself. You thought he was going to do this to one of Desiree's eggs. That's what you agreed to. You argued against this. Even in your darkest hour, you saw the moral implications, and you fought for what was right." She grasped his hand. "Please do not blame yourself for this. Your friend has descended into evil. He is capable of anything."

"How could he have descended so far without my even seeing it?"

"If I might quote the Buddha," Lo started, "Do not think lightly of evil that not the least consequence will come of it. A whole waterpot will fill up from dripping drops of water. A fool fills himself with evil, just a little at a time."

Sanantha looked Randy deeply in the eye. "I have seen evil. This is evil. This is not you."

He bit down hard. "It's going to take a lot of soul searching before I can accept that."

"That's okay. That's what I'm here for. Now we can move ahead."

Lo was shaking his head and glancing around inside the helicopter, clearly trying to grasp what Young Nae had done. "That's kidnapping, identity theft, enslavement, rape, murder, all at once. He has forever exiled himself from the Pure Land."

Randy frowned, but Sanantha knew what he meant. "I agree, with a crime like this, he has poisoned his karma for all time."

Randy couldn't unclench his jaw as hot tears brimmed over and his voice shook. "Then he can burn in hell forever."

Lo brightened. "These are your viruses, right? Can you kill them and get your daughter back?"

Randy sighed and looked heavenward. "I wish it was that simple."

"Wait a minute," Sanantha interjected. "You said the old DNA is still present, just held down by the virus."

"That's true."

"You also said the reason the disguising virus failed on Cheri was the symbiosis was upset, and somehow the Desiree DNA was labeled as foreign, so it could be attacked. I think you called it a shock."

"Yes. We would have to mark the Cheri DNA in this clone so it could be routed out."

"It's your dream about the bread mold! Good grief, Randy! Penicillin! You said you couldn't figure out why you would dream about sending your wife into anaphylaxis. It's not your wife you need to shock, it's the clone. If the clone is exhibiting Cheri's features, then wouldn't she currently be allergic to penicillin?"

"Yes." He thought about this for a moment, then walked through it out loud. "Interesting. Dez is not allergic to penicillin. Anaphylaxis would be a systemic stressor the same way the hepatic infection was a stressor for Cheri. That would trigger her immune system. If her white cells started killing cells that were using the Cheri DNA fragments, then they would switch to using the Desiree fragments to survive. That would leave her exhibiting Desiree traits and it would leave the Cheri fragments exposed as viral, and susceptible to attack by anti-viral meds." He blinked a couple of times as he mentally double-checked his calculation. "Who would have thought you could use an allergic reaction to jumpstart a genetic change?"

"You did, apparently. Even if subconsciously."

He chuckled.

Sanantha seemed glad to see it.

"Jesus, we're going to have to be really careful. You're talking about a juggling act with her life in the balance."

"Is it possible?" she asked bluntly.

"Yes, it is. I want to be really clear here. If we do this and it starts to go badly, I will pull back and let her stay the clone. I'd rather deal with the clone than kill her completely."

Sanantha and Lo both nodded. "Agreed."

As the helicopter rose over the next mountain, the green carpet continued, but this time it was speckled with white police cars and red ambulances and fire trucks lining the road that led to the large house that overlooked the canyon.

"This does not look good," Lo commented. Then to his pilot, he said, "Put us down on the road as close as you can to the house without hitting any of those cars."

The police in the street started to wave off the chopper, but when they saw it was going to land anyway, they moved back.

Lo unbuckled himself and popped open the door the moment the skids touched blacktop. His large silent bodyguard shadowed him. He hurried straight to the waiting cops and started talking with them loudly over the rotor noise. Randy could see he was smiling broadly and pointing at the house, the jungle, and then the helicopter. Randy turned to Sanantha. "Quite the character you've found."

She took the headphones off and unbuckled herself. "He certainly adds to the adventure."

As they approached, Lo turned to Randy and Sanantha. "They say they are looking for a mad woman who is running through the jungle. She killed a farmer and some livestock. She matches your daughter's description."

Randy was shocked. "That doesn't make any sense. She should be fine and healthy." He paused in thought. "Unless Young Nae did something awful to her."

Sanantha suggested, "Is there any way to use the helicopter to find her?"

"There's no place to land it out in the trees once we spot her. I can have my pilot hunt her down and call me. Then we'll all converge to intercept her."

Randy walked over to one of the ambulances.

•   •   •

The cool water startled her when she stooped by the stream's edge and splashed her face. It felt colder than it should have. It cleared her head long enough to notice the blood that completely covered her arms. She washed it off and tried to comprehend what she had just done.

She still couldn't believe she had slain the man so easily. True, he had tried to kill her. Was that all just a misunderstanding? She struggled to remember exactly what had happened. She looked at her shoulder and was amazed to see it had stopped bleeding already. He had shot her, hadn't he? Something had happened, the clotted blood and ripped tissues proved that. Confusion led to frustration as she found she couldn't remember past the fever to piece all the details together.

How did she get here? What was she doing dressed only in shorts and a t-shirt in the middle of a jungle she could only assume was on Malaysia. She needed answers.

The sound of children's laughter drifting on the morning air caught her attention. Maybe they could help.

A little boy and girl of perhaps four and six were playing in a puddle with an old tin can under the watchful eye of a girl who was about nine years old. Cheri was amused by their play, and stayed back in her hidden vantage of bushes and watched for a moment.

The innocence of their play seemed to belong here. It was a simple pleasure in a simple place. As tired as she was, Cheri wanted to be a part of it, to escape the confusion and ugliness of the hunger. She purposely stepped on a dry twig to get their attention as she moved forward out of the bushes.

"Hello," she greeted in Malay with a warm smile. "How are you?"

She anticipated any number of possible responses, but not the one they gave her. As one, they stopped what they were doing and stood up straight, as if caught doing something prohibited, their big dark eyes staring innocently at her from their expressionless, slightly downturned, little faces.

Cheri laughed a nervous, surprised chuckle and insisted, "No, please, go ahead and play."

When they didn't move, she considered that their reaction might not be fear, but a trained behavior. Children just didn't play in front of adults. Or maybe it was white adults.

"It's okay," she tried again, stooping down by the pool and pointing at the can. "Don't mind me. Continue as you were." She picked up the can and handed it to the little boy with a big friendly smile. "Here, take it."

His gaze on her faltered as his eyes flitted to the outstretched can and back to her face. After a couple more quick glances at the toy, he turned to look up at the older girl for permission.

She looked down at him, over to the can, then straight onto Cheri's eyes. The suspicion melted and a tiny grin curled the corner of her mouth. She nodded and the boy snatched the can greedily with both hands.

The little girl reacted instantly and, ignoring Cheri, latched onto the can and tried to wrestle it from the boy.

The nine-year-old introduced herself as Anitelle.

"My name's Cheri," she offered, shaking the girl's formally extended hand.

Anitelle started to tell her the other children's names, but had to stop and break up the fight that had erupted between them.

A wave of lightheadedness took Cheri by surprise and she staggered to a large nearby rock to sit down. Her first suspicion was she had been squatting too long or had gotten up too fast. This thought was crushed by fear as nausea and racking cold chills thundered in behind the dizziness. She clamped her eyes shut and clenched her fists, refusing to let delirium take control again.

She was glad the children had busied themselves and she hoped she could regain her composure before they noticed her distress. Clasping her arms around her body, trying to get warm and stop shivering, she felt the sweat that had erupted from her every pore.

She took a deep breath and resolved to leave quietly. She knew she was fast losing ground to the fever, but she would not let panic get the better of her.

Cheri opened her eyes just as the boy yanked the can from the little girl's grasp, cutting her finger on a sharp edge. The girl cried out, the sitter slapped the boy, and Cheri's hunger gripped her gut with the speed and strength of a hangman's noose. She wanted to look away, to get up and leave, but her body wouldn't respond. Saliva filled her mouth as her eyes fixed on the little red droplets. She was horrified that she could even consider blood as food. She tried in vain to turn away but her legs, as if driven by their own power, lifted her and walked toward the girl. As the world spun and blurred to her rational mind, she tried to cry out to the children to flee for safety but, to her horror, her voice came out soothing despite its menacing tightness. "Oh, you've been hurt. Let me look at that."

She made it as far as sitting beside the girl and reaching for her injured hand when the sharp, jolting sound of a gun shot in the jungle behind them made all four flinch and cower together. Over the children's quiet whimpering, Cheri heard men yelling and footsteps thrashing about in the brush nearby.

The fever had already strained her hold on sanity. The sudden roar of a swooping helicopter sent her right into panic. Completely lost to her most basic animal reactions, she grabbed up the little girl and bolted into the jungle.

"Don't cry, Desiree. Mommy's got you now."

29

RANDY'S HEAD WAS SPINNING, and he couldn't calm his breathing. He wanted to blame the mismatched artificial heartbeat, but he knew that wasn't the problem. This was it. After all the lies, all the dangers, all the loss, just when he might have finally cut through it all and found her, now this. A manhunt in this remote wet jungle for his last chance at getting his life back. More unknowns, more obstacles. He scrambled to hold onto hope like a wet rope that held him over the abyss. He watched the helicopter take off and looked out at the police fanning through the brush. What had he set in motion?

Sanantha put her hand on his shoulder. "You gonna make it? We're going to find her and it's all going to finally end."

He sniffed wetly. "Yeah. Let's do this."

He took three steps into the jungle when a gunshot rang out from what sounded like just a few yards away. He and Sanantha dropped to the ground. "Jesus, don't shoot her!" he blurted out. He heard the police yell commands amongst themselves, and he got the impression it wasn't a cop who fired the shot.

He and Sanantha exchanged a frown. "Angry villagers?" she guessed.

He got up and pressed on. "Great, now we're dodging stray bullets."

He got another three paces when the brush in front of him ripped open and Cheri came hurtling out, almost colliding with him. She was tightly clutching a young Malay girl who was bawling in fright. Cheri stopped abruptly and blinked at him.

As much as he had thought about this moment, seeing her like this caught him flatfooted. She was covered in dirt and sweat, and was that blood? She wasn't Desiree. She was clearly Cheri, but young. He just hadn't prepared himself to see her as his wife, and nineteen again.

He caught himself, and realized she was just staring at him too. Didn't she recognize him?

"She doesn't know if you're her husband or her father," Sanantha deduced.

That snapped him around. "You think she's in mid-transition?"

"That's my best guess."

"Desiree," he tried.

The woman turned the child in her arms away from him. "Why are you talking to her?"

Randy blinked, then tried again. "Cheri, it's me, Randy. We're here to help you."

When she turned, he could see the enormous crater-shaped wound in her shoulder, with flesh peeled wide. Remarkably, it wasn't bleeding.

"You've been hurt. Let me help you."

"You tried to kill me," she spat. Then she seemed to waver. "Didn't you?"

"No, honey, I've never done any such thing. Take a second and think. Do you actually remember me hurting you?"

She looked around furtively before staring back at him.

"Of course not. Everything is all mixed up, isn't it? You look ill. We're here to make sense of all this craziness. Now, that isn't really Desiree, is it? Our little girl is all grown up, isn't she?"

Cheri looked at the girl and frowned.

"She seems really frightened. Maybe we should let her go back to her family. Let my friend here take the girl back to her home."

A couple of policemen saw what was happening and came over to help. One of them spoke into his radio, telling his comrades they had found her.

"Look, the police will take the little girl home. Won't that be the right thing to do?"

She double took on the police and then looked back at Randolph. "Aren't you a fugitive?"

"No, I'm not."

Cheri set the little girl down, and she ran to the police. "I'm so confused. Nothing makes sense."

Having had a moment to compose herself, Cheri didn't look so much like a hunted animal anymore. In fact, she was looking more and more like, well, his wife. "I am sick. I'm really hot, and I'm starving no matter what I eat."

"What the hell happened to your arm?" He pushed his luck and stepped closer to her. "It looks like you were shot."

"I was. A farmer shot me when he caught me eating his pig."

"That was just today?"

"Yeah. Couple of hours ago, maybe."

"Can I take a look?"

She hesitated a moment. "Sure."

He was amazed to find the wound looking like it was at least a couple days old. The bleeding had stopped, and the tissues were visibly beginning to knit back together. He couldn't fathom how this was happening. Could this be the virus?

"If you didn't beat me, why did Young Nae say you had?"

He looked her in the eye. Those dark brown eyes he had thought he would never see look back at him again. Despite his artificially calm heartbeat, he felt his blood pressure kick up a notch. "He'd say anything to keep us apart."

He heard Sanantha clear her throat purposefully behind him, but it didn't seem to matter. It was as if he had stepped into a dream. All the fear and danger and pressure were gone. Here she was. The Cheri he had fallen in love with so many years ago. Back right in front of him. Ready for him to take her back.

Sanantha stepped up and put her hand on his arm. "Randolph, remember who this really is."

He started to object, but then bit down hard. He took a breath and looked at Cheri again. This time he saw the touches of blue clinging near the pupil of her irises. Blue. His daughter's blue. He blinked. Then he sighed his resignation and looked back at Sanantha. "You're right. We have work to do."

"What does she mean, 'Remember who she really is?' Who is she?" Turning to Sanantha, Cheri asked with some venom, "Who are you?"

"No one of consequence," interrupted the voice of Young Nae Yoon.

The policeman nearest to him turned and started to raise the shotgun he had, but Young Nae dropped to the ground in a fluid motion that ended with his kicking through the cop's knee with a sickening crack. The other cop hollered, "Berhenti!" but of course, Young Nae did not stop. The cop shot at him with his pistol, but he twisted away and sprung up at the cop like some jungle cat. The man was not ready for the move, and Young Nae caught him in the throat with a flashing fist.

As the cop fell back, another cop jumped out from behind a bush and fired a Tazer at him. Young Nae's hand moved so fast, Randy wasn't sure he saw what Young Nae did. The Tazer cartridge bounced back and hit the officer in the chest as it went off.

Lo Cheung and his bodyguard came running up. The bodyguard pulled his gun and drew a bead on the Korean. Young Nae struck a ready stance, but then barked a single word, "Freeze!"

When the man did not fire, Lo yelled at him, "What are you waiting for? Shoot him!"

Young Nae sprung on the man, who started to defend himself, but too late. The gun went off, but only after Young Nae had stepped around the upheld pistol. He struck the big man in the groin, the stomach, and the throat in one rapid-fire sequence of punches.

Lo Cheung didn't wait, but sprung on Young Nae while he was still dismantling the stunned bodyguard. Young Nae rolled out from under the one blow Cheung managed to land, and as he ducked, he poked Cheung's forearm and neck. The Chinese man buckled under the chi attack. As he doubled over, Young Nae finished him off with one more poke in the middle of his back. Cheung fell flat on the ground and stopped moving.

Randolph had picked up the pistol from the downed policeman and held it up at Young Nae. "Why would you sacrifice Desiree so callously, when you weren't really going to get Cheri back? The most you were going to get was a copy of her body."

Young Nae grinned condescendingly. "No, no. Don't underestimate the proportion of personality that comes from genetics. Over the last four months, I have seen she is the same."

Randy noticed Cheri wasn't taking any of this well, and had cowered back. She looked like she was getting ready to bolt into the jungle.

"You have twisted everything around to suit your own selfish desires. Is nothing sacred to you? My science, our friendship, our business, even your own religion. You told me God is within each of us. That means we're supposed to respect one another. All you see is an excuse to call your greed divine justification."

"You don't know what the fuck you're talking about."

Sanantha added, "There is no way Haneulnim approves of genetic identity theft."

Young Nae regarded her coolly. "The last person who told me that, I killed with a thought."

He turned to Cheri. "Come with me."

Randy felt the power of the words and realized he wasn't just asking Cheri. He thought about shooting him, but was pretty sure that would just get himself killed.

Randy expected Cheri to step up, but she didn't.

"Cheri, you have to come with me, now," he commanded again. She just stood there looking frightened.

As Young Nae stepped closer, Randolph spotted Lo Cheung slowly moving his arm out to retrieve the shotgun the first policeman had dropped. Randy taunted Young Nae, "Have you lost your touch with the ladies?"

Young Nae flashed him a threatening look, and Randy stepped back. He didn't step back from the threat. Sanantha had stepped back too, for the same reason. Randy considered if there was any way to bring his friend back from the edge. Young Nae wasn't at the edge. He was long gone down the slippery slope. He could forgive him the affair, but what he had done to Desiree was unforgivable. The blast was deafening.

Cheri screamed and jumped back in horror.

Randy knelt down over Young Nae's blood-soaked body. He rolled him over onto his back and held up his head. "You let it take you over. That kind of power is too seductive."

"It was a gift," he whispered. "I couldn't … not use it." He stopped breathing.

"Ordinary men, like you and I, can't handle such power."

30

SANANTHA KNELT DOWN NEXT TO HIM and interjected, "Speaking of control, why couldn't he control her?"

"What does that matter?"

"No seriously. He stopped that bodyguard dead in his tracks. You felt the power in his voice. That's chi energy. That's the soul. Yet it had no effect on her. You said you don't know why she is so sick. Something has messed with her soul." She got up and put her arm around Cheri's waist. "Your virus has done something, and we need to figure out what."

Cheri asked her, "Are you a doctor too?"

"Yes, and I'm here to help you."

Cheri looked back at Young Nae's body.

"I'm sorry you had to see that," Sanantha added.

"My poor Young Nae. Did he have to die? Why was he being so mean?"

"Randy, she's burning up. I'm really afraid we've missed something."

Cheri wavered and staggered. Sanantha tried to steady her, but her legs went limp and Sanantha had to set her down on the ground.

"Oh, Papa Legba!" All she could think of was the last time she held someone like this. Back in Washington, D.C., she had held Charles Redmond as his life slipped away. Events had spun out of her control back then, and there was nothing she could do to save Charles. Charles had chosen to sacrifice his life. Desiree Macklin had not made such a choice.

Randy took her pulse and felt her forehead. "I don't know what could kick the virus into such a feeding frenzy like this. It's like the virus has turned on her and is consuming her."

Then Sanantha looked into her eyes and saw the blue near the pupils of her otherwise brown irises. "The blood flow to the iris is from the outside. Her eyes are changing from blue to brown. If Young Nae changed her from blue-eyed Desiree into brown-eyed Cheri four months ago, why is she showing signs of changing from Desiree into Cheri now?"

Randy clenched his fists and his voice cracked in desperation. "I don't know."

Sanantha flashed on a memory and took a sudden shocked breath. "This was my vision. Everyone was frantic, looking for something. Papa Legba trusted me to find it, and I did. It was a snake."

Randy quickly examined her arms for marks. Then he moved to her legs. "Got it. Here on the back of her knee. It's healed now, but this is clearly a snake bite."

"There's no hemorrhage, so it's a neurotoxin type, probably a cobra," Sanantha deduced. "That should have stopped her breathing hours ago. What would the virus do if the body was dying of a neurotoxin?"

Randy grabbed his hair. "Her cells would shift from a structure that was failing under the attack to a structure that wasn't under attack. The venom would trigger a shift into the other woman."

"That means she was Desiree, with blue eyes, when she was bitten. How could that be?" Cheri passed out and went limp in Sanantha's lap.

Randy's eyes went wide. "The Billy Lights."

"What?"

"I erroneously set up bilirubin UV lights to help with the jaundice the other clone had. If Kwon hadn't given her the Interferon, the lights would have started killing the virus. Look at her bronze skin. She's been tanning in the tropical sun for months. The sunlight was slowly killing the resting virus in her tissues. At some point, she tipped and turned back into Desiree. Then this snake bite flipped her back."

Sanantha pulled her snakebite kit out of her bag, and took out the vial of neurotoxic snake venom antidote.

Randy looked at the kit in amazement.

"I carry anti-venom with me ever since the snake attack in my apartment. We've got to give her this to stop the venom first. If we don't clear the venom from her system, when we shift her back to being Desiree, the venom will kill her for sure."

"You're right, the virus is keeping the venom from finishing the job. Wait a minute." He blinked several times. "With the Desiree proteins rejected, the virus is just running amok with nothing to keep it in check. The virus really is the only thing still alive."

"You mean Desiree is already dead?"

"You said something was wrong with her soul."

"Oh my god. The virus doesn't have a soul for Young Nae to manipulate. That's why he couldn't control her." Sanantha was stunned, but she refused to give up. "Then we've got to move now to get her back before we lose her for good. We need to give her the anti-venom and the penicillin. Stop the poison and the virus. The virus may be keeping the venom in check, but look at what the virus is doing to her running free like this. It's going to kill her too."

"You're right." He pulled a vial of penicillin and a syringe out of his pocket.

She frowned at it.

"Got it from the ambulance just in case." He thought for a moment. "Hold on. The virus running free isn't killing her. Look what it's doing to heal the gunshot wound in her shoulder. It's just acting like a disease now, but we can bring it back under control with drugs."

Sanantha double took on him. "You mean, inject her with nothing now, let the poison kill Desiree, and let the virus finish cloning out the body?"

"Well, it would be less traumatic on the body. We don't know if Desiree is still alive in there."

"Randy, we're here to save your daughter. All you would get is the monstrous clone Young Nae was trying to build."

She waited for him to react, but he didn't. "It wouldn't be Cheri. You know that."

He looked at the unconscious woman, and Sanantha saw that he was still in the thrall of seeing his wife.

"We haven't come this far to give up on Desiree. Your daughter is counting on you to save her. You've got to try. Inject her with both needles. Do it now before it's too late." She grabbed his arm and looked him in the eyes. "Cheri is gone. Young Nae already took your wife from you. Don't let him take your daughter too." She held up one of the needles at the ready.

He looked down at the woman and blinked. A tear rolled down his cheek. He picked up the other needle, and together they injected her with both solutions.

31

"HOW LONG DO WE LEAVE THE PENICILLIN in there unrestrained?" Sanantha asked as the paramedics ran onto the scene.

"As long as her body can take it. Epinephrine will keep her breathing until her liver metabolizes the penicillin. Hopefully that will be enough time to label the Cheri proteins as foreign and turn her immune system on the virus."

He turned to the paramedics. "I'm this woman's physician. She is about to go into anaphylactic shock from an allergic reaction to penicillin. I need you to monitor her vitals and only administer epinephrine when the reaction starts to impede her breathing. Until then, do not give her anything to prevent the allergic reaction. She is on experimental medications and we need to let this reaction run its course. Do you understand?"

The two medics nodded, and set about taking her vital signs.

Sanantha looked over and saw another medic helping Lo Cheung. She got up and went to him. He was sitting up and being his usual talkative, charming self. "You look pretty good for a man who should be dead. How did you survive Young Nae's chi attack?"

"Ah, remember, I know a thing or two about chi myself, being a lifelong practitioner of Kung Fu. When I saw how fast he was, I realized there was no way I was going to survive our first round. I forced my chi down into my legs, away from the kill points he was sure to aim for."

"It worked." She was genuinely impressed.

"When I regained consciousness, I had enough life in me to finish the job."

She looked back at the corpse. "Yes, you did."

"How is the girl? Did you figure it out?"

"I think we got it. She's only hanging on by a thread."

"Well, after all this, I certainly hope she makes it."

A flurry of activity from the paramedics interrupted them. She overheard the lead medic explaining to Randolph. "We're still waiting for the labored breathing you warned us about, but her heart rate, blood pressure, and body temperature just dropped. We're giving her the epinephrine to keep her heart going until we can get her to hospital."

Sanantha turned back to Lo Cheung. "Can we use your helicopter to transport her?"

"Of course. There will be just enough room for the three of you and the two paramedics. Go on without me. I'll call for a car."

"Thank you!" she called back as she ran.

By now, the helicopter had landed back on the street in front of the house. They rushed her on board, and as soon as they figured out how to secure the gurney board in the cockpit, they took off.

The medics checked her again. "All her vitals are failing. You said she is on experimental medications. What can we safely give her to keep her going?"

"Give her anything you would normally," Randolph said. He checked her eyes, and turned to Sanantha. "The change is working, but now she's dying."

"From the bite? We stopped the poison," she insisted.

"No, Sanantha, it's what I feared. She's changing back into a person who is already dead."

"The poison killed her before the virus turned her? That's outrageous! She had to be alive for the virus to have anything to work with."

Randolph seemed resigned, defeated. "The only thing keeping her alive was the virus, which we are now killing. Young Nae couldn't find her chi, because it was already gone."

Sanantha could barely contain her frustration. "I refuse to believe that we've come all this way, figured out this Gordian Knot of a problem that Young Nae created, only to have arrived too late to save her. The irony stinks. If this is how it's supposed to turn out, then why did Erzulie and Legba bother to show me the solution?" By now, she was ranting and waving her hands, nearly knocking her headset off. "I had a divine visitation! A vision! I've never had visions before. Why bother? She's dead before we got to her!"

"Sanantha, you're getting hysterical. You're distracting the medics from their job."

"I am not hysterical. I am mad as Hell. I am sick and tired of trying to fix problems and save people who are only in trouble because mad men can't control their egos! I am ..." She felt a pressure on her chest. "Oh, *merde*, I'm having an anxiety attack." The pressure increased and she felt a distinct warmth. She put her hands over her heart and took a breath to try to calm herself.

One of the medics saw this and shifted around to face her. He took her pulse, then, taking his headset off, listened to her heart with his stethoscope. "You're not having palpitations."

"No, it's not fast. It's hot."

He put his hand where she indicated. "I don't feel any heat."

"I definitely do. Wait a minute. Put your hand back." He put his hand flat against the center of her chest, and she pressed it tight with her hands. "That's it. That's what I feel."

"I still don't feel anything."

"Really? It's so hot, it's really uncomfortable. At the same time, I feel suddenly calm, and strong." She released the medic's hand, sat up straight in her chair, and started taking deep breaths. "I can't explain it, but I feel like it's … all going to be fine, that it's all been taken care of."

"You're not making any sense," Randy said. "If fact, you're starting to freak me out."

She put both hands over her heart and smiled hugely. "No, really. We're in good hands. I'm in good hands. Oh wait!" She looked at Randolph with amazement in her eyes. "Can it be? Oh my lord. That's it. I wasn't led astray. I wasn't abandoned. I'm being mounted!"

"You're what?"

"This is Madame Erzulie!" Tears welled up in her eyes. In her whole life of being a Voodoun, and as many mountings as she had witnessed, she had never been graced with a personal intervention. The tears streamed down her cheeks. "Randy, I've been touched. My gods really have shown me the way."

Her hands picked up the heat from her heart. She reached over and put her hands on Desiree's chest.

"Now we're reduced to faith healing?"

She didn't answer him. She couldn't hear him, and it had nothing to do with her headphones or the helicopter noise. She was oblivious, ecstatic, bathed in the love of her patron, and she let it flow out through her hands.

She lost track of time, but at some point, the warmth faded, and she became aware of the helicopter cabin again. She opened her eyes. Randolph was staring at her with clear disbelief. "Did I pass out?"

"You were gone for a minute. It looked like you were attempting some kind of chi transfusion."

"I guess so." She withdrew her hands and looked at them. They were no longer hot. Neither was the handprint spot on her chest. "I guess you can move this stuff around. Lo Cheung survived Young Nae's attack by hiding his chi in his legs. How is she doing?"

The medic smiled at her and shook his head in disbelief. "She's stabilized."

Sanantha lit up with her broadest, deepest-dimpled grin of hope.

Although it was nearly masked in disbelief, the smile Randy gave her back showed a glimmer of hope as well.

32

RANDY SAT DOWN IN THE CHAIR FACING SANANTHA'S and chuckled to himself. "This seems so pedestrian compared to what we've been through together."

She pursed her lips and nodded. "It is. That's a good thing. It's about time the adventuring ended and the healing resumed. It's been three weeks since we retrieved Desiree. That was a day filled with changes, many of which neither you nor I was ready for. How do you feel about the decisions we made and where those decisions have left you?"

"Obviously I am thrilled to have Desiree back. She has responded very well to the antiviral drugs to clean out her system, and to the steroids to rebuild her body chemistry."

"That's wonderful news. Has she said anything about her experience of what happened three weeks ago?"

"No, we haven't talked about it. We have talked about how we're going to piece our lives back together. I need to stay here for a while to figure out how to run CytoCorp. By the way, I am looking into starting FDA testing on the products we have on the shelves."

"Good!"

"I think Dez just wants to take the time off from college to get her feet back under her. She can take as long as she likes as far as I'm concerned."

"Would you mind if I talked to her, to make sure there is no lasting psychological damage from having been two people within a short time frame?"

"Oh, no, that sounds like a good idea. You'll have to ask her if she's ready to talk about it."

"I promise I will give her the option of not talking if she isn't up for it. Now, aside from the obvious business side, losing Young Nae has to have affected you. I'd like to help you sort that out. You came into this grief stricken from Cheri's death. Along the way, you discovered she and your best friend were having an affair, and that he had kidnapped your daughter and thrown you under the bus. Are you going to be able to blame him for all of it?"

Randy took a deep breath and let it out slowly. "What you're really asking, of course, is how much of this am I going to blame on myself. Okay. I have thought about this. Young Nae was seduced by power and descended into evil. At the same time, I had started down that same path. I had been cutting corners on research and testing for years. I had run my life by what I think Robin Williams once called the Jesuit School of Management — that it's easier to get forgiveness than permission. When life stole Cheri from me, it didn't take much convincing to get me to go along with a plan to clone her. I knew how, and I felt that I needed to do something. Young Nae's last words were, 'It was a gift. I couldn't not use it.' I felt the same way, and it nearly cost me my daughter."

"Let me interrupt you. It is good to reflect on your mistakes and learn from them, but I think the devil is in the details. That you would consider using your knowledge to correct an injustice is not a moral flaw. Young Nae had been having an affair with Cheri. He had his own reasons for getting her back, so he pushed you into it. You told me you recalled having heated arguments with him about how to proceed. You said you found yourself unable to resist him. That was probably the poison he gave you. You thought the virus was going to be used on an embryo, not Desiree. Isn't it more fair to yourself to recognize that you did look down that slippery slope on your own, and hesitated, and that it was Young Nae who dragged you over the edge?"

"That makes a lot of sense. Intellectually, I can live with that."

"Emotionally you still feel like you bear some of the blame?"

"I think I said this before. What parent isn't going to blame themselves for letting harm befall their child?"

"Did you let harm come? Once you had made the virus for him, Young Nae drugged you to get you out of the way. You played no role whatsoever in exposing Desiree to the virus. You can't compare what Young Nae did to say, the Manhattan Project. Those scientists lived with a lot of guilt for developing the atomic bomb, because although they wanted to figure out how fission worked, they knew all along that it was going to be used to make a bomb. You never knew that, and you didn't condone or contribute to it."

Randolph blinked and frowned, but said nothing.

"I know that's a big pill to swallow. I don't expect you to jump up out of that chair feeling suddenly free from guilt or remorse. As you chew on this, though, please include this perspective. This whole episode began with an injustice, Cheri's death. You owe it to yourself to be fair to yourself."

"She's not really dead."

"That is going to make it harder on you, having her around in a coma."

"I've already been there. At one point I told her it was easier when I thought she was dead. I hope she didn't hear me."

"Whether she heard it or not, you said it, and it is true. Not only is she not physically gone, but you saw what looked like her up and alive and nineteen years old. I saw how that affected you. I know you're happy to have Desiree back. The question is, are you convinced Cheri has been gone since January when she was bitten by that cobra out in that factory town?"

Again, he thought hard, but didn't answer.

"Yes, I used the word 'gone'. You should start using it too. The woman you loved left this world in January, before Young Nae called you to Malaysia. Everything else that has happened since has been smoke and mirrors. She's still gone. The sooner you accept that, the better."

"Is this what's prescribed for loved ones of people who end up in irretrievable comas, normally?"

"Yes. Whether you know the secrets of the universe or not. Whether your wife had an affair or not. Whether your best friend kidnapped your daughter or not. Even if he disguised the coma victim as your daughter, so you wouldn't go looking for her. At some point, you have to move on with your life and accept the coma victim as gone. Again, hard pill to swallow. I don't expect you to buy into it all at once."

"I'll have to work on that. I'm still going to miss her, especially when I see her body. I will work on it, along with whether I'm going to forgive her."

Sanantha brightened. "I am so glad to hear you say that word. I've been waiting to see when the hurt had subsided enough to let that word back in."

"I first considered it back when I was lying paralyzed in the hospital. That was way too soon."

"Three weeks is pretty soon too. I'm proud of you."

"Having Young Nae to blame makes it easier."

"That's true. I want to make sure you face the facts honestly. You're the one who has to live with how you feel about this. Making excuses for her might feel good in the short term, but you will at some point need to decide if you really forgive her or not."

He frowned in thought. "Sounds like we will be talking about this again."

"Oh, yes. How you feel about their affair will have a more lasting effect on you than everything else that happened. It will be well worth the time to sort it out properly."

"You know, it's interesting you mentioned how Young Nae cloned Cheri so I wouldn't realize Desiree was gone. He wove such a complex web of lies, I really feel lucky that we ever figured it out. Lo Cheung reopened the police file, and we're pretty sure the woman who burned to death in the car crash in February was Young Nae's housekeeper. I mean, I still wonder why he just didn't kill me once he had the virus."

"Maybe he kept you around in case the clone needed help," she suggested.

"True. He mentioned something to me when he was trying to convince me that Lo Cheung was the bad guy behind all of this. He said that karma dictated that you can only get away with being as bold as you really need to be, and beyond that, your soul gets weighed down, and fate, I guess, won't let you succeed."

"That's not just karma. That concept shows up in magic and ritual all over the world. I once knew a magician who was fighting a demon, and the demon acted more boldly than it needed to, and the magician took advantage of the slip."

Randy cocked an eyebrow at her. "Doctor Mauwad, are you pulling my leg?"

"I guess that did sound a little strange, didn't it? No, I'm afraid I'm not making up that story. I think I mentioned at our first meeting that I have seen some strange things in my life. It would seem our adventure together has added to that list."

•   •   •

"How did you get him to accept that the clone wasn't his wife?" Simon handed Sanantha a dinner plate he had just washed for her to dry as they stood in his kitchen.

She took the plate, toweled it off, and stacked it at the end of the counter. "She never was his wife. She was always just his daughter in disguise."

"No, seriously, consider where his head was at that point. His best friend had just sacrificed himself in complete belief that this was an acceptable substitute for Cheri. Everything he knew about genetics said that letting the virus run its course would give you as near a copy as could be obtained." He handed her another plate. "Getting her back, even just getting a bad copy of her back, would mean not having to face the grief of losing her. Whereas your option would mean suffering all that grief a second time. I'd say, on a purely emotional level, your option was lacking."

"Well, good thing I wasn't being controlled by my emotions," Sanantha countered. "If I had let him be guided by his, he would have committed murder. We have to report crimes we hear about in sessions to the police. Don't we also have the right, the obligation, to stop a crime when we see one happening?"

"Sure. I just was wondering how you got him over that hump."

"I didn't let him have the option of doing the wrong thing. I told him: this is the right course of action. Then I appealed to his intellect and asked him if he agreed. Thankfully he did."

"You just pressured him into it?"

"She was dying simultaneously of a cobra bite and a virus run rampant. I didn't have time to break out Freud."

"Okay, true."

"Do you think you would have handled it differently?"

"Hindsight is always twenty-twenty. It's not fair for me to armchair quarterback the play after the fact. It just seems there should have been some other way to get there without becoming a player in the drama yourself. Maybe comparing outcomes."

"Well, let's do that now. The clone had been created with all her memories wiped clean by the transformation. All of her previous memories had been encoded to only be read by a brain built with Desiree's DNA. Starting with a blank slate, Young Nae brainwashed her for four months into thinking Randolph was an abusive husband that Young Nae had rescued her from. If Randolph ended up with the clone, she wouldn't trust him.

"Then there's the matter of Randolph's resentment that the real Cheri had an affair with Young Nae. Even the clone had been Young Nae's love slave. He would have to get over the affair and the fact that the clone was sullied. Both women were Young Nae's. Randolph's love for Cheri had bordered on the obsessive, so I really think it will be healthier for him to let her go instead of trying to retool how he feels about her.

"You're saying getting the clone back might have saved him some grieving over losing her, but it would have created a whole mess of problems that would prevent either of them from ever living happy lives together.

"On the flip side, now that Desiree is back, she should only think of Randolph as her loving father."

"How so?"

"All the memories she built while she was the clone were encoded using the virus Cheri DNA. When she changed back, all those memories should have been wiped out, just like her original Desiree memories were wiped out when she was changed into the clone. I need to test her to make sure her Desiree memories are intact and the clone memories are gone."

"If the science holds correct," Simon concluded, "then she should fit right back into being the daughter."

"Yes, that's what I am hoping."

He was quiet in thought for a moment. "Wow. That's still a tough choice for him at that point in time. He's lucky he had you there to guide him. I guess anytime you start messing with people's identity, you jump straight into a moral tangle."

"Thank you. Why do you think it was so tough?"

"Well, what better way to get over the resentment of your wife cheating on you with your best friend than to make an innocent clone of her, who happens to also be only nineteen?"

"That's a remarkably Neanderthal view."

He smiled playfully. "I guess it is."

"This, coming from a man who shies away from making tough moral decisions?"

He handed her the last of the dishes and pulled the plug on the sink full of suds. "*Moi?*"

"*Oui, vu.* You still haven't filed your divorce papers."

"I guess we aren't talking about professional ethics anymore." He grabbed another dishtowel and dried his hands.

"It's not a matter of professional ethics to condemn murdering your daughter to make a blow-up doll version of your comatose wife."

He laughed out loud. "I guess it becomes pretty clear when you reduce it down to that level."

"You do know, or you certainly should know, that I do not hold your divorce status against you. I fell in love with you knowing full well the circumstances."

"Glad to hear it."

"On the other hand, you need to watch what you put out there, even just for argument's sake. Someone who doesn't love you as much as I do might question your ethics after a comment like that, and that could include your divorce status. I don't need to tell you, we are held to a higher moral standard, since folks trust us with their mental health."

"I stand corrected." He smiled genuinely. "Thank you for looking out for me."

Sanantha accepted his peck on her cheek with a smile, but as she watched him turn and leave, her smile faded.

33

V ERA GREETED DOCTOR MAUWAD CHEERFULLY as the black woman came into Cheri's suite. She had seen the psychiatrist in the house before, talking to Doctor Macklin, but had not had the chance to meet her. "Hello. I'm Vera Shin, the day nurse."

She stepped across the room and shook Vera's hand. "It's so nice to meet you. I'm afraid I haven't actually introduced myself. I'm Sanantha Mauwad."

She had never heard an accent like the psychiatrist's before, but she tried to hide any surprise. "It is very nice to finally meet you. I have heard of the wonderful things you have done for this family."

She smiled a deeply dimpled grin. "Well, I can tell you it has been quite an adventure. One that I am glad to say is finally winding down." She nodded at the comatose woman in the bed. "How is she doing?"

"She ..." she hesitated. "Mrs. Macklin, is stable again."

Dr. Mauwad chuckled. "Yes, this is Mrs. Macklin now. I guess that took some getting used to. You said 'stable.' Was she not stable?"

"She had some difficulties when she was changing with the death of the virus." Her temperature was hard to maintain, and she didn't digest her food properly. She's doing much better this week."

"That's good. I have a treatment I would like to give her that should help her get over any lingering side effects of the virus."

"Have you told either Doctor Kwon or Doctor Macklin about this treatment?"

"I told Doctor Macklin. It is homeopathic. It's a mud wrap. I'm hoping to draw any remaining toxins from her with this mud I brought," she said, holding up a white plastic tub.

Vera considered calling Dr. Kwon, but a mud wrap did seem pretty benign. It actually sounded very kind. "What kind of sheets will you need? I've got a rubber sheet under the bed pad. I can put another rubber sheet on top."

"I'm not going to cover her whole body, just her abdomen. Yes, a rubber sheet to catch any spills would be good."

With both of them rolling Cheri's body and pulling the sheet into place, they made quick work of the preparations. Vera undressed her and laid a blanket across her legs.

The mud Dr. Mauwad spread on her body was smooth and black. She spread it with her fingertips from below her breasts all the way down to her pubis. She pulled the blanket up to cover her. "Now we let it dry. Should take a half an hour."

"It will draw toxins out?" Vera asked.

"Yes. It's an old home remedy."

Vera grinned shyly. "Sometimes those work the best."

"I have some calls to make. I'll be back when it's ready."

Once the psychiatrist was gone, Vera opened the jar and sniffed. In addition to the obvious earthen smells, it also had hints of camphor and peppermint. As long as it worked. This poor woman had been through enough, and certainly deserved some pampering.

•   •   •

After checking her voice mail, Sanantha logged onto her PDA and found an email from what looked like a government office. She half expected it to be a phishing message from Nigeria. Instead it was from the Malaysian Office of Customs and Immigration.

> Mr./Ms. Mauwad, please be advised that our status review of your Alien Work Permit has been terminated. All hearings and other actions related to this status review have been cancelled. Your Alien Work Permit status is restored to Active. The government of Malaysia thanks you for your cooperation.

Sanantha blinked at the screen a few times, and saved the message so she could print it out for safekeeping. Young Nae's machinations unwinding? Random bureaucratic bumbling? She resigned herself that she would probably never know. It was one less thing to worry about.

She headed back upstairs.

When she entered the bedroom suite, Vera wasn't there. She checked her watch, and it had been twenty-five minutes. She peeled the blanket back and saw exactly what she had expected. As the mud had dried, it had cracked and discolored, and formed a distinctive pattern all down the length of her body of a cobra. "Old home remedies do indeed work," she commented to herself.

She looked around and was glad the nurse wasn't there to see this. She found a tongue depressor and began scraping the mud off, starting with the telltale pattern.

Vera walked back in. "Did it work?"

"I think so. As you can see, it dried and clumped up, just like it's supposed to. Sadly, we can't ask her how it feels."

"I had a mud bath once. It felt wonderful."

"Good for you."

As they washed Cheri off, Sanantha mentally ran down the list of extraordinary things she had faced, starting with Randolph dropping dead during hypnosis and ending with finally seeing the cause of Cheri's coma. She promised herself some day she would go back to Haiti and share the whole story with Father Gorvil.

●　　　●　　　●

The tropical warm water rushing past his body was soothing and invigorating at the same time. Randy found himself kicking his flippers harder just to feel the joy it brought. The crystal-clear waters and the stunning array of colors on the coral below him heightened the bliss of the moment.

The muffled sounds and the rhythmic hollow breathing in his ears seemed to close him off from the world inside his scuba gear. It gave him space and time to think. He decided to think about nothing.

A swirl of blue caught his eye out of the side of his face mask. A school of parrot fish turned as a single unfurling carpet of color around the end of a rock outcropping. He started to follow, but saw that on the other side of those rocks the bottom fell away dramatically. No need to become a target for something big and hungry down there.

He rolled over onto his back and watched his bubbles float up into the sun glinting across the surface. He spotted the outline of his rowboat, and it reminded him to keep track of his time. He checked his watch. Indeed, it had been half an hour and his tank was going to run out soon. He kicked lazily up towards the vessel.

Cheri was waiting for him in the boat. He was surprised to see her there, and glad too. She looked enticing with her short black hair wetly framing her face and clinging to her neck above her shoulders shining over her strapless one-piece suit. "Hi. I thought you were staying ashore."

"I got bored of the beach. I wanted to swim. Actually, I really need to talk to you. Let me help you with that tank." She reached over him and lifted the steel canister up off his shoulders, and set it down in the boat.

He pulled himself up and in. He knew he wanted to talk to her, but he hadn't thought that she would want to talk to him.

She blinked a lot and couldn't make eye contact while she gathered her thoughts. "I have a confession to make. I know you know that I had an affair with Young Nae. I need to tell you myself. Yes, I cheated on you. All I can say in my defense is that I never meant to hurt you. It was halfway around the world, and I thought there was no way you could ever find out. I knew finding out would hurt you. The last thing I would ever want to do is hurt you."

He kept his tone as calm as he could manage. "How can having an affair not be a reflection on me? On how you feel about me? How can I not be hurt by that?"

"It was never about you. I never stopped loving you. You have always been the best thing in my life. Young Nae was exciting. Letting him fall in love with me was so easy and so outside of my normal experience, I thought I could try it out. I never wanted it to be anything more than a dalliance."

"It lasted for a couple of years. It's not like it was a one-night stand."

"I know. He just became part of my other life on the road."

"Your life on the road was an escape from our home life?"

"I never felt my road life was better than our home life. I have thought about this a lot, but I really have no excuse. The best I can come up with is I'm sorry."

"I am glad to hear you say that."

"I can't even bring myself to ask for your forgiveness. I do want you to know how sorry I am."

"You know, we found out how dangerous Young Nae was."

"Yes, I saw that. Thank God Desiree survived the ordeal. Who could have known?"

"He led me away from ethics, got me used to cutting corners, got me used to not asking the tough questions about wrong and right. He had his own selfish agendas. He nearly killed Desiree to get a copy of you. I'm pretty sure you are not completely to blame for the affair. You said it was easy to let him fall in love with you. I'm pretty sure Young Nae never did anything in his life that wasn't planned and purposeful."

"That's ... that's really very understanding of you."

"Well, he suckered me too. How can I lay all the blame on you? It still hurts. I don't know at what point I will be able to forgive you. I do not see forgiveness as an impossible goal."

"I feel like I didn't tell you enough how much I love you."

"Even when I found out, I didn't stop loving you."

She slid off her bench, knelt down in the small boat, and hugged him around the waist. He wrapped his arms around her.

"I still love you, even though you're gone."

"I am here now."

"I know I'm dreaming. I needed to hear you say you're sorry, so my mind is playing out the scenario."

"No, Randy, it's me. I needed to tell you I'm sorry."

"My only wish is this could have been a happy dream, with us making love, and all this pain was behind us, forgiven and forgotten in a dream reality."

She squeezed him tighter. "There will be plenty of time for dreams like that once I'm gone." She looked up at him with those dark brown eyes, so deep he could lose himself there in an instant. Tears ran down her cheeks. He felt his own well up. She reached up and kissed him more tenderly, more sincerely than he could ever remember. He swore he would remember this kiss after he awoke.

She pressed her head against his chest. "I wish we had done this kind of thing more often when we had the chance."

"Make out in a dinghy?"

She grinned up at him. "Take the time to be honest and open."

"I'm sure most couples should heed that advice. Life gets in the way. Things always work more smoothly in dreams. Dreams are unencumbered with the details of reality. I mean, when did you become a strong enough swimmer to cover the half a mile from shore?"

"That's all right. You've never learned to scuba dive either!" she said playfully, and pushed him hard in the chest. As he fell back overboard, the last thing he heard her say was, "Goodbye, my love!"

Instead of hitting the water, his back landed on the floor next to his bed. Waking up didn't surprise him. Suddenly being dry felt weird. He sat there for a long moment, reveling in how she had felt in his arms and how true she had sounded. He was glad the dream had been so vivid. He was happy to remember the kiss.

He thought about how persuasive Young Nae could be, and how much slack he should give Cheri for having fallen into his thrall. He had never been able to stay mad at her for very long. He loved her too much.

He started to get up and had to untangle himself from the sheet his fall had dragged off the bed. He heard a faint strain of music from the living room and went to investigate. It was coming from his laptop on the desk on the far side of the room. It was his usual WBIG feed. He must have been so tired he forgot to turn it off last night. He turned up the volume of Blue Oyster Cult's "Don't Fear the Reaper."

The words hung on him like a mist. "She had taken his hand; she had become like they are."

His mobile phone on the kitchen counter rang. "Hello?"

"Doctor Macklin, this is Vera, upstairs. Can you come up right away?"

He looked at his shorts and t-shirt. "Sure. What's going on?"

"We need you right away. It's your wife. We're losing her."

He hung up and ran.

As he came in the door of the bedroom suite, the heart monitor started its long high wail. "Everything just shut down. I can't even tell what's wrong. She was fine just a few minutes ago." Vera started to climb up onto the bed to get a better reach for CPR.

He walked over and put his hand on her arm. "There's no need to do that."

"But Doctor, I have your written instructions to use extreme measures if necessary to keep her alive."

He grabbed up the clipboard that she had left on the foot of the bed. "This was from when we thought this was my daughter. I rescind these instructions. Cheri has been through enough. This is the brain damage from the original asphyxiation catching up to her. She won't be coming back."

Vera climbed off the bed.

He stepped up and caressed Cheri's face with his hand. His concerned frown melted away into a caring smile. "Goodbye, my love."

34

"THANK YOU FOR AGREEING TO CHAT WITH ME."

Desiree sat on the couch facing Sanantha who sat in the armchair in the living room of the main beach house. "Not a problem. I've been wanting a chance to get to know you better."

"Really? How nice."

"You got us through the whole episode. I'm pretty sure I wouldn't be sitting here today if you hadn't stepped in."

Sanantha nodded politely, but ducked the spotlight. "You and your father have been through a lot, and I've spent a lot of time with him making sure he's handling it well. Now I wanted to check in with you too. It's been nearly two months since your trauma. Your father says you're making great progress medically, and he is confident you will make a complete recovery. Can we talk about how this has affected you?"

"I think my biggest reaction is relief that it's over. I mean, it was bad enough waking up to being sick as a dog for two weeks straight. Then realizing how awful everything had gotten. My mom died after being in a coma for five months, my dad lost his mind, the whole cloning thing with Uncle Young Nae kidnapping me, and then he got killed in a firefight with the police. It's all way too Hollywood for me. I'm just a sophomore History major at Georgetown. That really is exciting enough for me."

"I see you changed your hair. Auburn suits you."

She ran her hand through the new angular, swept back cut. "Yeah, I didn't want to go too red all at once."

"Are you putting the black behind you?"

Desiree grinned her crooked dimpled smile. "Very true. Besides, it was a hodgepodge, what with four months of Mom's jet black roots. So, yes, it's part of my new start. By the way, I really like your turban. You're lucky you can wear that gorgeous yellow. I love how high you wind it. Very regal."

Again, Sanantha sidestepped the attention. "Thank you. You said you realized all these things had gone wrong. How much of it do you remember, and how much of it have you pieced together from what people have told you?"

"That's hard to say. I know all the gory details because I've been over it multiple times with the lawyers."

"Yes, I heard about the trial for the farmer's death. It all turned out well, didn't it?"

"Yes, Lo Cheung's lawyers did a good job of getting me acquitted. I never had to appear in court, since I was bedridden. My dad also offered reparations from Young Nae's life insurance money, which pleased the judge. Of course, your friend Simon helped a lot too."

"Simon Herrera?"

"Yes, didn't you know? He got himself appointed the Medical Examiner for the State. He backed up everything you said in your report. With both sides saying the same thing, the judge had to let me off."

"He hadn't told me anything about this."

"Well, he actually told me not to tell you until it was all over. I guess you two had a spat about ethics or something. I guess he wanted to make up for it."

Sanantha was surprised enough that she lowered her guard. "Well, well, well. The judge found you temporarily incompetent when the farmer was killed?"

"He commented that there was reason to believe I was not in my 'right mind' at the time"

"You do understand that is accurate? You were literally someone else."

"Yeah, I get that. My dad explained that the virus put my mind on hold while it changed my body to look like Mom. You know, that's what bugs me through all of this. I am so frustrated that everyone keeps talking about all the stuff I'm supposed to have done, but I can't remember doing any of it."

"What do you remember?"

"Just enough that I can tell where the gaps are. I remember coming to Malaysia after Young Nae told us Mom died. I remember the funeral. I remember Dad and Young Nae having a series of big fights about their business and Dad's discoveries. Then there's this huge blank. Four months. Then I remember waking up in Young Nae's house out in the jungle, and wandering around totally lost, not knowing where I was or anything. That was very strange. All the clothes there fit me, but I swore I had never set foot in the place before.

"Then I got bit, and I called for help, and I passed out. Then I woke up in the hospital. Initially I thought, okay, this makes sense, I'm in the hospital recovering from the snakebite. Then I found out about the whole farmer killing thing, and the gunfight with Young Nae, and I'm thinking, what else did I miss? I get that the blanks are when the virus was in control. It's still very frustrating."

"Do you find the blanks frightening?"

"No, because I've learned what happened. Just aggravating that so much happened outside of my control."

"Are your memories intact from before you came to Malaysia?"

"You mean, are there blanks in my memory of my childhood? Like my memory is failing?"

"No, I don't suspect that you have any memory disorders. I just want to know if this scrambling of your memories has affected your ability to retrieve things from before all this happened."

"No, I don't think so. Just the other day I was sitting in bed daydreaming. They make me rest a lot, so I do a lot of daydreaming. One of my favorite childhood memories came floating back to me."

"What was that?"

"I'm riding my bicycle home from school. We lived at the top of a long hill. I'm tired by the time I get to the house. I go inside, and my mom comes out of the kitchen and greets me with a plate of fresh-baked cookies. My mom travelled a lot on business, so I was used to her not being home for weeks at a time. It's just a really special memory."

"It's a lovely memory."

"I think everything else is still intact up here," she said tapping her temple.

"That's good. How do you feel about losing your mom?"

"I thought she was dead back in January. Then when I found out she had been in a coma all this time, it was a bit of a shock. It wasn't like she was back. I mean, she was still gone. I'm sad that she finally died. I think my dad was hoping she might pull out of it."

"Does her passing leave you with any open questions?"

"I'm not sure what you mean."

"You and your dad are going to be grieving her passing in different ways. At the same time, you two will have to be there for each other as you move ahead to remake your family without her. If you have outstanding issues with your mother, then you and I can talk about them without it spilling over on your relations with your dad."

"Well, you've kind of opened a Pandora's Box with that question. I have always lived in my mother's shadow. She was always this superwoman charging off to save the world. My dad adored her, and could forgive her anything."

"Did he neglect you in his adoration of her?"

"Oh, we have always been great friends. He's been my buddy dad my whole life, but I've always known I was a distant second to his affections. I feel bad talking about her like this, especially now that she's dead."

"Respect for the dead shouldn't have to include denying your true feelings."

"I loved her too. She really was a kind, loving mother. She just wasn't around that much."

"Your father was?"

"Yes, I never wanted for anything. It was also clear that his love for her was the most important thing in his life. I imagine he will be grieving for her for a long time."

"He and I are working on that. Did you grow up feeling his love for you was lacking?"

"Lacking is probably too strong a word, although you've got the idea. It'll be interesting to see if that changes now that she's gone." Desiree frowned as if she were struggling with how to say something. "You know, I have noticed something, about me. When I thought Mom was dead in January, I was really worried about Dad sinking into despair and completely forgetting about me. I remember that being a very real worry of mine."

"Has that changed?"

"Yes, and I don't understand why. It just doesn't bother me as much this time, now that she really is gone. It's like I have a whole new outlook on where I fit into the picture. I feel so much more confident about how Dad and I are going to move forward."

"That's a good thing. This bothers you?"

"It is a good thing, but it's a big change, big enough that I noticed it."

"You had a brush with death. People often come away from those with a fresh perspective on life."

"I guess."

"While we're talking about how you feel about yourself after all these changes, I want to talk with you about how you feel about what happened to you while you were cloned."

"I actually have thought about that a lot. I remember seeing the sexy clothes and the expensive lingerie in Young Nae's jungle hideaway, so I know what he was doing to me. On the other hand, I have so little connection to that time, I just don't feel like he was raping me. It really feels like it was somebody else. Which I guess biologically, it was."

"You don't feel violated?"

"Well, I do feel violated. I was kidnapped and my identity was wiped out. That's not the same thing as if he slipped me a ruffie and date raped me. As far as I can tell, the clone actually loved him."

"We'll never know. You know how you feel."

"I am grossed out thinking about my body having sex with Young Nae. On the other hand, I don't think I'm scarred like a rape victim."

"How do you feel about your body?"

"I don't feel dirty or wounded. When I first thought about this, I thought I should feel like something had been stolen from me. I don't. I feel in my bones like that happened to somebody else."

"Do you think you will be able to have sexual relations and not be reminded of what happened?"

"That's a good point. Probably not. I can only hope I can learn to deal with that when the time comes."

"I want to stay in touch with you. If anything comes up, please call me. Even years from now. I'm pretty sure no one has ever gone through what you've been through, so there is no history we can look up. Trust and intimacy could potentially be difficult. There are also fragments of memories still floating around in your brain that were encoded with the virus DNA. It is possible you will recall things that do not make any sense. I expect you will be having déjà vu moments because of the mismatches. You may also have nightmares caused by conflicting bits of memory. Please keep note of these, if they happen, and let me know about them."

"I can do that." Desiree paused and chewed her lip. "Now I have a question for you. Did that snake bite kill me?"

"Apparently not. Here you are."

"I'm here because you brought me back. My dad dodged the question. He said the two of you didn't know if I was alive or if it was just the virus keeping the clone alive. I have to wonder, how big a gamble was it to kill the virus?"

"It was the only way to get you back."

"Wasn't it something like two hours between the snake bite and when you gave me the antidote?"

"Yes, but cobra venom kills by stopping your breathing. The virus stepped in and kept you breathing throughout. Mind you, it did that by rearranging you genetically. At no point did your breathing stop."

"Until you got me to the helicopter."

"How so?"

"Going over the evidence for the trial, I saw the record of my vital signs on the helicopter. Just before you revived me, everything went flat. It would seem the only thing alive at the time was the virus. What did you do to bring me back?"

Sanantha wasn't prepared to talk about this, and hesitated.

Desiree pressed. "Lo Cheung says it was a transfer of chi energy. My dad called it a spiritual defibrillation. Figures he'd give it some mashed up medical name. I recall from my Medieval Studies that Dark Age healers did something called a 'laying of the hands.' What did you do?"

"I asked God for mercy. It worked. How it worked, I have no idea."

"Dad told me specifically not to bring this up, but you want to talk about what's bothering me. He said I was going to sound insensitive or ignorant of other cultures. Which god did you ask to intervene?"

"Yes, I believe in Voodou. Yes, it was the Voodou goddess of mercy whom I asked for help. If it was She who saved you, and I can't say that it was, then you should know her name is Erzulie. She has helped me through difficult times my whole life. There is nothing dark or sinister about Her. I would be happy to get you some good books if you want to read up on Her, and the religion as well."

"I will probably take you up on that." She paused in reflection. "Hold on, that name is familiar. I read about Erzulie in Caribbean art history. She and her counterpart, Legga?"

"Legba."

"Right, Legba, they're usually depicted as snakes. I think he's usually black and she's usually white. Is that right?"

Sanantha sat stunned. She blinked and failed to hide how amazed she was.

"Did I say something offensive?" Desiree asked worried.

"No, oh no. Not offensive. Just genius," she sighed to herself. "The white snake inside the daughter is Erzulie." She blinked and met the girl's concerned gaze. "Erzulie tried to tell me how this would all turn out and I, of course, did not see it until now. She always knew she would be the one to save you."

Desiree frowned deeply but then smiled. "That's pretty awesome. If your goddess drops hints that work in spite of all the craziness that was going down, then maybe I should start listening to her too. I mean, seriously, I was dragged halfway around the world to Malaysia by a mad man who wanted to kidnap me and make my body into a clone of his lover, my mom. Then I was saved by my dad's psychiatrist who summoned divine intervention from a Voodou goddess."

"Oh, you forgot the part about how the mad man, your father's best friend, had also mastered ancient arts so he could kill people with a thought. I'm just glad the only supernatural entity on the field was on our side this time."

"This time?"

Sanantha realized she should not have let that slip. "Yeah, I haven't told you much of my other adventures. Young Nae was taken by evil. At least it wasn't a demon.

"This has indeed been a tour de force of the weird and mysterious. I want to point out though, through it all, your dad has been very focused on your well-being. We originally thought you were the one in a coma upstairs. He was there every day for you. You said you have always suspected his love for Cheri overshadowed his love for you. He showed me no signs of that when he thought you were helpless in that bed. I have no doubt he will be there for you going forward. When you say you want to return to a normal, peaceful life, I think the two of you can start building that right away with each other's help."

"Are you suggesting I move forward and not be too worried about how it all went down?"

"Of course you can ask questions and settle any doubts you have. You just don't want to linger on the past. There is a lot of ugliness there that you don't want to let take over your thoughts. Yes, life moves on. So should we."

•　　　•　　　•

On the way into Kuala Lumpur International Airport, Desiree noticed that her father missed the turn into the terminal drop off lanes. "Dad, I think that was our left turn."

"Oh, I'm going to park and walk you in. Did you think I was just going to drop you off?"

"It'd be a lot easier."

"No, I'll walk you in. Pretty girl in a crowded airport full of pick pockets. Besides, Security is always a hassle."

She rolled her eyes. "Thanks, Dad."

He picked up a CD to put into the dashboard player.

She intercepted him and slipped it from his fingers. "Deep Purple? Seriously?"

"Hey, my geezer rock gave me the comfort to stay sane throughout this whole mess."

She pursed her lips and nodded. "Okay. I can believe that. Just please, don't make me listen to it."

He smiled broadly. "All right, all right. Did I remember to give you a company credit card? What about the house keys for when you get home?"

"Yes, I've got both right here in my purse. Are you sure you're okay with me heading back home without you?"

"Oh, yeah. I have every confidence you will fit right back into your life at home."

"Actually, I meant are you going to be okay alone here in Malaysia?"

"Don't worry about me. I've got more work than I can keep up with, figuring out how to run CytoCorp. I won't have time to be lonely."

"Good. Are you going to stay and run the company yourself?"

"I haven't decided whether to take up Lo Cheung's offer to manage things for me. It is tempting, but I'll wait and see if I can do it first."

Her dad pulled into a parking garage and three young men approached, offering to park the car for him. "No thanks," he called out through the open window. "I'll park it myself." Then to his daughter he added, "Every time they touch a door handle or a piece of luggage it'll cost you." He circled around and found a spot. It was a tight fit with the Land Rover between all the tiny commuter cars crowded into the lot.

"What's the first thing you're going to do when you get home?"

"Finish telling my friends I'm not brain dead."

"Really? Didn't you spend a bunch of time online getting your friends up to speed?"

"I'm still in the middle of sorting that out. Young Nae hacked into my accounts and mass emailed all my friends that I was in a coma. Most of my friends sent condolences, and a few thought it was a joke. Now I have to figure out how to tell people that I'm fine. I mean, does anyone need to know I was kidnapped?"

"I'd only share that with my best friends who are going to hear the whole story."

"That's my point. What can I say to the majority of people who I am not going to tell the whole story to? 'Hi, I'm fine. That message you got four months ago that I was brain dead was just a misunderstanding.' That's going to raise more questions."

Her dad got out and opened the tailgate. "You could only tell your best friends anything at all, tell them the whole story, and let word spread that you are okay."

She considered the option. "That could work. Thanks."

He got her luggage out and organized it, with smaller bags stacked on bigger wheeled ones. Once he got it all out, he paused and took a big sighing breath.

Not a good sign, Desiree thought. "I remember that sigh when you first sent me off to college."

He smiled. "Actually, that was a different sigh. This is the 'I've got something to say but I don't know how to say it' sigh."

She shrugged and gave him her goofy, crooked smile. "I'm all ears. If it would make it easier, we can walk while we talk."

"Sure. We've talked about the horrific stuff that happened this year. Between those talks and the lawyers filling you in on everything, I think you have a pretty good picture of how it all went down. Now it's just down to the two of us. I want to make sure you and I are okay going forward."

"Why wouldn't we be okay?"

"I made some bad decisions along the way. I gave into fear and temptations and I made things a lot worse. In fact, despite plenty of evidence to the contrary, I still feel like I put you in harm's way."

"By making the virus in the first place?"

He looked relieved at not having to explain this point. "Yes."

"I'll grant you that if you hadn't made it, I wouldn't have ended up being kidnapped and cloned. Seriously, though, I don't think you had much say in the matter. After seeing all the people Young Nae manipulated or maimed or killed, I don't think you could have stopped him. The drugs he gave you took away your willpower. I assume you've talked to Doctor Mauwad about this. Did she tell you to talk to me?"

"No. I mean yes, we have talked about it. But no, she didn't tell me to come talk to you. Are you sure you don't blame me for the cloning?"

"I know you were devastated when we thought Mom had died. I also remember you arguing with Young Nae. Now I know those fights were over how to clone Mom. Don't ever let a mad scientist suffer a grievous loss. There's no telling what he'll do. To your credit, you refused to bring me into it, so he took you out with poison and booby trapped your body to self-destruct."

Randolph nodded. "Yes, he did all that."

"I can only imagine how hard it was for you to bring me back when it looked like you could get her instead. You did choose me over the clone. Yeah, I can see where you were tempted. I can also see where you stood up for me." She reached over and squeezed his hand. "I miss her too. Thank you for saving me."

His voice cracked. "I can't tell you what a relief that is for me. I am so proud of you for being able to see through to what matters. Goodness, you have matured so much. You've certainly got a clearer head on you than I do."

They had walked to the terminal and stopped in front of the large glass windows that formed the front of the building. She didn't want to compete with the noise inside the terminal.

"Since I have returned from the cloning, I have a whole new perspective. I get the whole brush with death, new lease on life thing. It's more than that. I just see things more clearly. It's easier to see the positive now. I think I surprised Doctor Mauwad with how intact I am after what could have been a really scarring experience."

Just then, a sparrow flew past them and right into the large window. It bounced off the glass with a ringing thud, and fell motionless on the ground next to them.

"Oh, no. Poor little guy probably broke his neck."

Her dad added, "It's so sad that animals have no idea what manmade structures are, especially glass."

Desiree bent down and picked up the bird. Its head dangled limply.

"You're going to want to wash your hands after that," her father advised.

"Come on, little fella," she said as she stroked its back. She gently felt around his neck to see if its head was still on straight.

"Do you feel it breathing? I think that's a dead bird."

The bird did not move for a long minute. Then it twitched its wing. Then it opened its eyes and looked around.

"Hey, there you are," she cooed.

It fluttered and stood up in her hand before flying away. "I guess it was just stunned."

Randy stood there and stared at her hands for a long moment. "I guess so. Nice work."

"You were saying how glad you are that I came through this okay, and I was saying I think I'm more than just okay. I think I've got a whole new outlook."

He looked her over with that proud look that she loved to get, the look that said he not only loved her, but he loved being her dad. "I can't say how happy I am that you came out of this on top. One of the big goals Sanantha set for me is to forgive myself for endangering you."

"You and I can't afford to be anything but absolutely honest with each other going forward. We're all we've got. Believe me when I say it's all in the past. I forgive you, Dad. Now you can forgive yourself."

MUSIC ACKNOWLEDGEMENTS

ABOUT THE AUTHOR

Jay Hartlove is the award-winning author of the urban fantasy "Goddess Rising" trilogy (*Goddess Chosen, Goddess Daughter,* and *Goddess Rising*) and the fantasy romance *Mermaid Steel*. He is also the playwright, director and producer of *The Mirror's Revenge*, the musical sequel to the "Snow White" fable, which had its theatrical run in the San Francisco Bay Area in August 2018 to rave reviews.

His stories are filled with conspiracies and the supernatural, gods, dreams, angels, and hidden connections. His creative motto is "Dark Secrets Revealed". He loves to take stories where the reader does not expect, with sympathetic villains, heroes with very dark pasts, and lots of plot twists. He was selected as one of the "50 Authors You Should Be Reading" by *The Authors Show*.

Jay is a former competitive costumer, having won Best in Show at both San Diego ComicCon and WorldCon. You can read more about Jay's creative adventures, including much of the research he put into his books, at *jaywrites.com*.

YOU MIGHT ALSO ENJOY

GODDESS CHOSEN

Book One of the *Goddess Rising* Series

by Jay Hartlove

The man who would beat the devil isn't a hero, but a ruthless madman.

MEMORY AND METAPHOR

by Andrea Monticue

Civilization fell. It rose. At some point, people built starships.

THE STORK

A Shelby McDougall Mystery

by Nancy Wood

Shelby McDougall's past is behind her. Almost.

Available from Paper Angel Press in
hardcover, trade paperback, digital, and audio editions
paperangelpress.com

www.ingramcontent.com/pod-product-compliance
Lightning Source LLC
Chambersburg PA
CBHW030248200626
46816CB00002BA/549